George O. Shields

Rustlings in the Rockies

hunting and fishing by mountain and stream

George O. Shields

Rustlings in the Rockies
hunting and fishing by mountain and stream

ISBN/EAN: 9783337287559

Printed in Europe, USA, Canada, Australia, Japan

Cover: Foto ©Andreas Hilbeck / pixelio.de

More available books at **www.hansebooks.com**

RUSTLINGS IN THE ROCKIES:

HUNTING AND FISHING

BY MOUNTAIN AND STREAM.

BY

G. O. SHIELDS.
(COQUINA.)

CHICAGO:
BELFORD, CLARKE & CO.
1883.

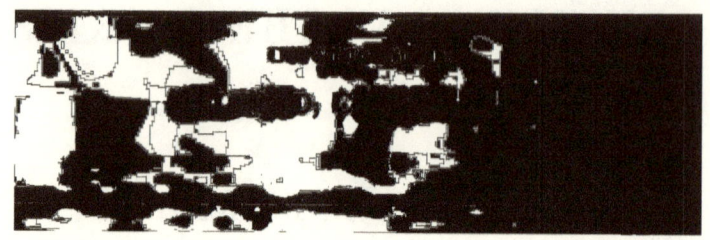

Printed and Bound by Donohue & Henneberry, Chicago.

INTRODUCTION.

As the author is so well known to American sportsmen through his contributions to the *American Field*, it is not necessary that I should commend the book to their consideration.

Being in favor of educating that portion of the public who are not sportsmen to the importance of healthy outdoor sports as the surest and best method of securing and maintaining good health, and believing that sketches such as this book contains contribute most forcibly to this end, by creating a desire to participate in such scenes and pleasures as they recount, it is, therefore, to the general reader that I commend this book.

Not physically only, but mentally also, are outdoor sports invigorating ; and rapidly are the people realizing what the greatest savans have long since realized : *mens sana in corpore sano*.

Satisfied that the protection and propagation of game birds, game animals and game fishes, apart from an economic point of view, demand the attention of the people as affording the facilities for the maintenance of health and repairing overworked bodies and brains, I look upon a book like this, which treats of the pleasures of the gun, rifle or rod in a most entertaining manner, as a missionary sent out to enlighten a people on the healthful recreation they know not of, and enlist them in the protection of game and fish which unwittingly they may have been aiding the destruction of.

The author has had the experience necessary to furnish material for interesting sketches; and being an ardent advocate of the protection of game and fish during the close season, and opposed to the wanton slaughter of them during the open season, I again commend this book.

N. ROWE,

EDITOR "AMERICAN FIELD."

CHICAGO, February 15, 1883.

CONTENTS.

CHAPTER V.

A PERILOUS EXPERIENCE.

CHAPTER VI.

IN THE BIG HORN MOUNTAINS.

CHAPTER VII.

IN THE YELLOWSTONE VALLEY.

CHAPTER VIII.

AT THE FORKS OF THE ROSEBUD.

CHAPTER IX.

THE HAPPY HUNTING GROUND.

CHAPTER X.

THROUGH THE CANYON OF THE LITTLE BIG HORN.

CHAPTER XI.

A GRAND DAY'S SPORT.

CHAPTER XII.

A BUSY DAY.

CHAPTER XIII.

FROM CUSTER TO KEOUGH.

CHAPTER XIV.

TEN DAYS IN MONTANA.

CHAPTER XV.
LIFE ON THE PLAINS.

CHAPTER XVI.
AFTER THE BUFFALOES.

CHAPTER XVII.
TWO HUNDRED THOUSAND BUFFALOES.

CHAPTER XVIII.
THROUGH AN EXTINCT HELL!

CHAPTER XIX.
THE GULF COAST OF FLORIDA.

CHAPTER XX.
THE GULF OF MEXICO.

C' ..PTER XXI.
SNEAD'S ISLAND.

CHAPTER XXII.
ON BOARD THE " SKY-LARK."

CHAPTER XXIII.
DEER-STALKING AND FIRE-FISHING.

CHAPTER XXIV.
FOUR DAYS ON THE MYAKKA RIVER.

CHAPTER XXXI.
AUTUMN RAMBLINGS IN NORTHERN MICHIGAN.

CHAPTER XXXII.
THE ISLAND OF MACKINAC.

CHAPTER XXXIII.
A NARROW ESCAPE.

ILLUSTRATIONS.

RUSTLINGS IN THE ROCKIES.

CHAPTER I.

RUSTLINGS IN THE ROCKIES.

CLARK'S FORK—MR. ALLEN—FRONTIER YARNS—ROGERS DIDN'T WANT
TO BE KILLED BY A BUFFALO—"WHY DIDN'T YOU CATCH THE BULL
BY THE TAIL?"—HIRAM STEWART'S NARROW ESCAPE—TWENTY
YEARS IN THE MOUNTAINS AND NEVER SO NEAR DEATH.

AFTER a pleasant journey of eighteen hours over the Chicago, Milwaukee & St. Paul railroad from Milwaukee to St. Paul, and another of forty-eight hours over the Northern Pacific from St. Paul, we arrived on the first day of September at the famous town of Billings, Montana, at that time the temporary terminus of the Northern Pacific road, I at once sought the quarters of my old friend Major Bell, of the 7th Cavalry, who was camped near the station, but was sadly disappointed to learn that he was under orders to go to Bozeman in a few days, and could not therefore join me in a hunt. He had given four of his men permission, however, to start the next morning for a five days' hunt in the Pryors Mountain country, thirty-five miles distant, and kindly offered me a mount if I desired to go with them ; but as this would not be as long a trip as I wanted to make, I decided to decline his offer and go with some friends who had gone out with me. On the following day, therefore, I met them in Coulson, two miles from Billings, and we arranged for a three weeks' trip into the mountains toward the head of Clark's Fork.

9

During the time of making preparations for our start we were entertained in a most enjoyable manner by Mr. William Allen and his accomplished wife.

Mr. Allen is a capital story teller and a fine actor. He is an old timer on the frontier, and in his varied experience has passed through some strange adventures. He gave us some choice selections from these the first evening we were there, which, if they could be reproduced here with all his actions, gestures and points, would furnish fun for the readers of this book for a year to come. I will repeat one or two of them as nearly in substance as possible, but they will lack the unction and action with which he delivered them.

Some years ago, when living on his ranch ten miles above Coulson, he was subpœnaed to serve on the grand jury which was to meet at Miles City. A neighbor named Wm. Rogers, hearing that he was going to Miles, called on him and requested permission to go with him. Mr. Allen gladly accepted his company, and it was arranged that they should start early the next morning, and go down the river in a skiff. When they got all their traps on board it was discovered that neither of them had provided a gun, Mr. A.'s gun being out of order and Mr. R. having lately sold his. They talked the matter over, and it looked like a risky piece of business to start on a voyage like this of a hundred and fifty miles down the Yellowstone river, through a country where they were liable to be jumped by hostile reds, without a gun in the boat. Besides, there was plenty of game along the river, and it would be extremely provoking not to be able to shoot any of it, even though it should walk over them. But what should be done? Neither of them had a firearm of any kind, not even a revolver, that was serviceable, and it would be difficult to borrow one for so long a time, so they decided to do the only thing to be done under the circumstances—go unarmed.

Now this Rogers is a great " blow," and is always boasting
what he would do and how valiantly he would fight if
corralled by Indians ; how he would stand his ground and
shoot any bear to death that ever roamed the mountains,
before he would run ; how he would not be afraid to ride
into a herd of buffaloes anywhere on the plains and 'slaughter
dozens of them, and would not be afraid of getting eaten up
by them either, and all that sort of stuff.

On their cruise down the river, Rogers regaled Allen with
accounts of how he would grapple with any Indian, or other
wild animal, that should dare to molest them, single handed,
and kill or put them to rout. Yes, he was a valiant son of
Mars ! Well, it happened on the second day of their voyage,
as they were floating quietly along, they saw several old
buffalo bulls moving down a trail that led down the side of a
steep bluff, and ordinarily between the bluff and the water's
edge, to a point farther up the stream where it led out again.
But at this time the water was high and the trail at the foot
of the bluff was submerged. The bulls didn't discover this
fact until they got to the water, and then they were on a part
of the trail that was so narrow, and the bluff, both above and
below them was so precipitous, that they could not turn
around, leaving them no alternative but to plunge into the
river and swim out.

By this time Allen and his valiant *co-voyageur* were alongside of the bulls. Allen had the oars. " Now," said Rogers, "when they jump into the water you run the boat right
in amongst them, and I'll catch one of them by the tail, pull
him down stream until we drown him, and we'll have some
fresh meat, and be darned to the guns."

" All right!" replied Allen; "they've jumped into the
water, and by the great Sault Ste Marie the water is over
their backs. They're swimming already. Look ! they are

making for the other shore, and are going to cross right in
front of us. " Well, here goes for a big bull.   Now Rogers,
grab a tail.''

And with two or three powerful strokes of the oars he
shot the skiff right in amongst the terrified beasts who were
making the angry flood boil all around them in their frantic
efforts to get away.   But when Rogers, this mighty hunter,
this stalwart slayer of grizzlies, this terror of Canyon Creek,
this red-handed Indian slayer, came to face the music, he
weakened; he turned pale, and his knees knocked together.

"Get out of here, quick!" he cried in terror; I don't
want to catch one of them old cusses, he'll jump right plum
into the boat if I do, and drownd us.''

"Oh, no, he won't!" shouted Allen.   "Grab one
quick.   What's the mater with you?''

"Get out of here, quick, I say," pleaded the terror-
stricken terror of Canyon Creek.

"Well here," replied Allen, "you take the oars then, and
I'll catch one.''

"No, I won't," answered Rogers.   "Pull out of here
quick, for God's sake.   I don't want to be killed by a cussed
old buffalo bull.''   And so there was no recourse for Allen
but to pull out, and leave the bulls to pursue their way in
peace.

"Well," remarked Rogers, after they had gone some distance down the river, and he had recovered his breath, "did
you ever see such frightful lookin' critters in your life as
them bulls was?   Why, they was just a puffen' and a snorten'
like an old steamboat, and their nostrils was jest as red inside
as two coals of fire, and their eyes was as big as a tin cup,
and they looked like they had just been varnished.   And
their tails stuck up and spread out till they looked just like
parasols.   As sure as you live, Allen, if we'd ever 'a ketched

HE DIDN'T WANT TO BE KILLED BY A BUFFALO!

one of them bulls by the tail, he'd 'a jumped right into the boat and killed us both.''

Allen has never got through laughing over that adventure yet, and to this day whenever Rogers goes to blowing about what he would do under certain circumstances, somebody asks him, '' Well, why didn't you catch the buffalo bulls· by the tail ? and then he collapses, and has nothing more to say to that crowd.

On another occasion Allen told us he was out hunting with old Hiram Stewart, a noted hunter and trapper, who had spent more than half his life in the mountains, and had killed more bears and· other large animals probably than he had hairs on his head. It was in May. As they were crossing a coulee one day, in which the brush grew thick, and in which there remained some patches of old snow, they saw where the ground had been disturbed. Passing along, they saw a hole in one of the ·snowdrifts, which looked as if some one had set down a coffee sack full of rocks. But there was a row of such holes, and on further examination they were forced to conclude that they had discovered a bear track, and the largest one, they both agreed, that they had ever seen. They followed the trail to where it led into a dense jungle of box elder, water beech, rose bushes, etc., at the head of the coulee.

They walked around this, and seeing no trail leading out of it, concluded the bear must be in there. They threw rocks and clubs into the ticket to start him out, but he would not start. Then Allen got down on his hands and knees, and pushing his gun ahead of him, crawled in. He could not see any bear, but after he got in about twenty feet he heard such an unearthly growl as convinced him at once that the outside air would be healthier for him, and slid out backward, much faster than he went in. Then old Hi. said

he would go in. Allen told him he had better not, but he
would not listen to caution and crawled in. He had not
gone far when he met the old leviathan coming out, and
raising his rifle, took a hasty aim and fired. This ball entered
the bear's breast and knocked him down, but Hi. saw at once
that he was not dead, and attempted to throw the shell out of
his rifle. But an accident to a gun almost invariably happens
just at the most critical moment. Or, if a fellow ever pulls
the wrong trigger, it is sure to be when the fine shot are
in that barrel, and the buckshot in the other, and the deer
gets away again. Joe's shell stuck in the chamber of his
rifle, and refused to budge. He knew he had no time to fool
away in swearing at his bad luck, so he slid out just as fast as
the nature of the ground would permit, but before he got out
the bear had recovered from the effects of the shot sufficiently
to get up and start after him. Hi. wore an old buckskin suit
that had been in the service for years, and that was so stiff
from having been daubed with blood, grease, molasses and
other animal and vegetable matter that he could take it off
and lean it up against a tree, and it would stand there until
he wanted it again, just the same as if he were in it. He was
sadly handicapped in this race by a game leg that was about
two inches shorter than the other, and when he got out of the
thicket there was not a tree in reach large enough to climb,
so he started up the hill side with the bear at his heels,
growling and roaring at every jump, and Hi. yelling
"Murder, save me, shoot him, kill him quick."

Allen said the spectacle was so ridiculous that had it been
his own funeral instead of Hi's, that was coming off so.soon,
he must have laughed all the same. Notwithstanding Hi's
old coat was as stiff as a shingle, it stood out behind until
you could have played billards on it, if the bear hadn't been
in your way. At every jump Hi. made he would careen over

SAVED BY A LUCKY SHOT.

toward the side his game leg was on, just as a chair goes over when one leg falls out of it. Finally Allen braced up so that he could shoot, and turned his Winchester loose on the grizzly. The first shot caught him behind the shoulder, and the second in the neck, but he paid no attention to them more than to stop and scratch the spot with his paw, and then go on after Hiram. But the third shot, fortunately, caught him at the butt of the ear, and dropped him in his tracks.

By this time Hi. had reached the ledge of rocks that he had started for at first, and which he thought would save him. He had just grasped a thin shelf that stuck out, to pull himself p by, but it broke off, and let him fall to the ground just as the bear dropped, and in his death struggle he caught Joe with one of his hind feet and threw him more than twenty eet down the hill. Joe gathered himself up, rubbed the mud off his face and hands, felt of arms and legs to see that they were all whole, looked at the great monster, which now lay dead, and as soon as he could recover his breath enough to speak, said, as he shook with terror from head to foot: "Great God, twenty-five years in the mountains, and I never cum as near gettin' killed as that."

He laid down on the ground, and it was more than an hour before he was able to walk. Allen said his face was as white as the snow in the coulee, excepting the space around his eyes, and that was yellow. Poor old Hiram never recovered from this terrible shock, and died a year afterward. Several who knew him claim that the scare was the direct cause of the sickness that ended his life. He was a mental and physical wreck from that time to the day of his death. Allen took from the bear one hundred and eighty-seven pounds of oil, and his skin when stretched and staked out on the ground measured over nine feet wide by ten and a half in length.

2

CHAPTER II.

THE PARTY ORGANIZED.

MIKE MASHED — SAWYER AND HIS PONY PLAY CIRCUS — SAWYER'S WANDERINGS IN MID-AIR — TERRA-FIRMA AT LAST — A CHASE AFTER SAWYER'S PONY — ALLEN WANTS HIM TO "BUCK SOME MORE" — THE CAYUSE SUBMITS TO THE ARGUMENT OF CLUBS — SAWYER DECLINES THE HURRICANE DECK FOR THE FUTURE — SUPPER ON MOUNTAIN TROUT.

WE completed our arrangements for the hunt, and starting from Billings on Sunday evening, September 3, rode to Ed Forest's ranch at Canyon creek, ten miles west of Billings, and camped for the night. Our party as now organized, consisted of Mr. Allen and his son Willie, of Coulson; R. J. Sawyer and M. Weise, of Menominee, Michigan; "Doctor" J. W. Trinler, of Coulson, our teamster, the most worthless, unmitigated vagabond that ever any hunting party was afflicted with, and "the undersigned." Mr. Allen was mounted on a bay complexioned cayuse that had blood in his eye, as we shall presently see. I had procured a tough, good-natured, ambitious little black pony, and the other members of the party were mounted on — the wagon.

After an hour's ride Allen offered to change seats with either of the boys in the wagon. Weise eagerly accepted the offer, and mounted the bay pony, which made no objection at the time, but a close observer might have seen by his eye that he was only awaiting an opportunity to take the conceit out of that pilgrim; and the opportunity came too soon. When we reached the little settlement of Canyon Creek it was dark, and a light burning in a tent at the roadside attracted the

A DECIDED MASH.

19

attention of the cayuse. He turned square across the road
and stopped to look at it. Before Mike could induce him to
move on the wagon came up, and the tongue struck him with
a solid shoot squarely amidships. At this he concluded to
break camp and move at once. Stiff-legged bucking set in.
He waltzed, polkaed, bucked and shook Mike's frame almost
to pieces. Finally he missed his footing and fell. He rolled
all over Mike, and when he had mashed and churned him to
his heart's content, got up, shook himself, and was ready to
be mounted again.

None of us were in love with our teamster or his team
from the first, but it was the only outfit we could get in town.
We hoped, however, that when we reached Ed Forest's
ranch we should be able to get him to furnish a team and
take us out, and turn "Doc" back; but, unfortunately,
Forest's horses were out on the range, and had strayed away
so far that he had been unable to find them after a hard day's
ride. So we were compelled, much against our wishes, to
take up our march the next day with the same three plugs
("Doc." and his two horses) that we had started with.

On Monday morning we drove up the Yellowstone five
miles, forded it, and proceeded up Clark's Fork river to the
mouth of Rock creek, where we had expected to find good
hunting, but we met an old Crow Indian, who told us that
several lodges of his tribe were camped on Rock creek, and
had been for many "sleeps"; so we knew we should find no
game there, and must keep on up Clark's Fork. We camped
on Rock creek that night, and in the morning held a council
of war. We had noticed all the previous afternoon that one
of "Doc's" plugs was very weak, and we had serious doubts .
about his being able to stand a long drive. If we had found
game on Rock creek, and he could have grazed there two or
three days while we were hunting, he would have gathered

strength from the good feed there—so much better than he
had been used to at home — so that he could have stood the
rest of the trip all right; but now that we must push on for
four or five days up to the mountains before finding game in
paying quantities, we felt sure that plug at least would never
be able to make it, and we decided to turn back to Forest's
ranch, hoping that by the time we should reach there Ed
would have found his horses and would be prepared to take
us out.

So we loaded up; "Doc" managed with our help to get
his team hooked up, and while we were putting the finishing
touches to the load, Sawyer having concluded to ride the
bay-complexioned cayuse that morning, climbed onto the
hurricane deck and put his feet in the stirrups just as if he
felt perfectly at home there. The pony was browsing on the
rose bushes which Sawyer thought entirely unnecessary, inas-
much as he had been in good grass all night. He pulled his
head up several times, and said "Ho" to him, but this
didn't last long. Presently the pony put his head down to
take another bite, and Sawyer kicked him on the nose and
said "Ho." Well. you should have seen the storm that
arose then ! That hurricane deck became the roughest place
that ever poor Sawyer was stranded on. The patient cayuse
reared up behind and plunged down before; then he reared
up before and plunged down behind; and all this time his
legs were as stiff as hop poles. Sawyer said he thought in his
soul that all his upper teeth would come out when the cayuse
came down. He said "Ho" again, but the pony wouldn't
" ho." He made one more leap into the air and humped his
back up. This time Sawyer concluded, like Sir Joseph Porter,
to go below, but he couldn't even have his own way about
that. At first he shot up into the air like a flaming meteor or
something of that sort. He clawed out in every direction

ON THE HOME-STRETCH.

like a man hunting for a match-box in a dark room.   His hat
flew east, and his gun flew west, and his field-glass flew over
the cuckoo's nest.   And when he had got as high as the pony
wanted him to go, he turned and went down into the weeds
head first just as a big green bull-frog goes down into the
water off of a high bank.

Sawyer picked himself up, we all got around him, deployed
and skirmished until we found his hat, gun and field-glass,
made an inventory of him and found he was all there; and
then the next thing was to catch the pony.

I mounted my black charger and started after him.   He
headed for a large herd of Indian ponies that were grazing in
the valley half a mile above us.   My pony could easily out-
run him, even although handicapped with my weight, and I
soon headed him off, but he was too smart to let me get
within reach of his bridle, and would shy off every time I
came alongside of him.   I didn't like to run my pony
unnecessarily, so I returned to the wagon and told Allen to
take a rope and lasso him.   He took one of the picket ropes,
got onto my pony and started.   By this time the bay was in
the midst of the Indian herd.   Allen soon singled him out,
but the rope was too wet and heavy to throw.   It would not
spread, and the only way of getting the fugitive was to run
him down.   Over the prairies, through brush, across the creek
and back again, out onto the prairie through a large dog
town, where we momentarily expected to see either horse
thrown three times his length by stepping into a dog hole.
The poor little black kept neck and neck with the bay, and
Allen laid the coils of that heavy rope across the little imp's
back, with such force at every jump that he carried the marks
of it for several days afterward.   The race lasted for half an
hour, and then the little rogue came shambling up to the

wagon, neighing piteously, and submitted gracefully to being taken in.

Then there was still another circus. Allen put on a big Mexican spur, picked up a cotton-wood club, mounted him and told him to " buck some more." The little devil tried to obey orders, but he was too tired. Allen hammered him with the club and roweled him with the steel until he so completely subdued him that from that time on, for the three weeks he remained a member of our outfit, that cayuse was as docile as a kitten. He never smiled again, at least not while we knew him. But Sawyer was quits too. He never climbed onto that hurricane deck again during that trip. We couldn't coax him to. He said once was enough for him, thank you, and it would be a cold day when we ever got him into that kind of a muss again.

We drove back to Forest's ranch, where we arrived that night at dark. Ed was still out hunting for his horses, and his man told us had been out all day; but at nine o'clock he rode up with them, and then there was great rejoicing in our camp. Before we went to bed everything was arranged. In the morning we paid " Doc." off, and were all heartily glad to be rid of him. By noon Ed had his traps in shape, and after dinner we pulled out. We drove to the Yellowstone again, and as we were going out at the other side of the ford we saw a horseman crossing behind us and signaling to us, so we halted on the bank until he came up. It proved to be a messenger from Mrs. Allen, requesting Mr. A. to return at once to attend to some important business. Allen mounted his pony and started for Coulson, and we went into camp on the bank of the river. It was arranged that we were to make a short drive the next day, and that Allen would go home and attend to the business that had called him back and overtake us at our camp the next night. We caught several handsome mountain trout in the Yellowstone, within a few yards of our camp, on which we feasted that night and at breakfast the next morning.

We moved up Clark's Fork the next day, crossed Rock creek and camped on the bank of the river five miles beyond. Clark's Fork is a beautiful stream ; clear, very swift, and runs over large boulders nearly its entire length. It is full of mountain trout, most of them of large size. We caught all we wanted at every camp we made on the river and its tributaries, and feasted on them nearly the entire time we were out. At sundown we were delighted to see Allen ride into camp. Once more our party was complete.

CHAPTER III.

ON THE WAY TO WYOMING.

INDIAN'S QUESTION, "SHOSTIDA?"—HUFFMAN IN CAMP—AGREES
TO JOIN US—A FINE DOE! BUT HUFFMAN HAS MY GUN—A DAY ON
BENNETT CREEK—ALLEN IN LUCK—HUFFMAN CURSES HIS KEN-
NEDY PEA-SLINGER—NOTHING BUT "WOODCHUCK"—UNIVERSAL
DAMPNESS—THE LUCK TURNS.

WE pulled out early the following morning and continued
our march up the river. We were in sight of large herds of
Indian ponies nearly all day, and in fact during the three
days that it took us to cross their reservation. Their tepees
were scattered all along the river, and we never passed one
without being challenged. A warrior would ride up to us,
shake hands with us and shout "shostida" (where are you
going?) in an authoritative, if not impudent tone, that gave
us to understand at once that they considered us intruders,
and would like to have us get off their ground as soon as
possible. Our answer that we were going across the line into
Wyoming, and that we were not going to hunt on their
reservation, was generally satisfactory. But if we had killed
any game or attempted to do so on their ground we would soon
have been served with a peremptory notice to quit the premises.

Two young warriors rode with us several miles this morning, and finally told us if we would give them some fish-hooks,
they would catch some trout and bring them to us for dinner.
We gave them the hooks gladly enough and hoped we should
not be bothered with them further, but sure enough, true to
their promise, they turned up at noon with a fine string of trout.

About eleven o'clock in the forenoon we met, away out

26

there on that lonely trail, my old friend L. A. Huffman, the Miles City photographer, who accompanied me to the Big Horn country last year and to whom I am indebted for most of the views with which this volume is embellished. He was just returning from the National Park, where he had been making stereoscopic views of the natural wonders of that great wonderland. We halted for dinner and plied him with the most earnest solicitations to turn back with us, to which he finally yielded.

Talk about the strange coincidences of life, but here is certainly one of the strangest. That we should both have happened to choose that same trail across a stretch of country hundred of miles in extent, where there were plenty of other game trails as plain and good as the one we were on — that, without any previous arrangement or knowledge of each other's whereabouts, he should have started from away off in the National Park and we from the Northern Pacific railroad and should both have timed our movements just so as to meet here (for he was going to leave this trail that evening and strike east to Pryor's Gap), was certainly one of the strangest freaks of fortune on record. He and his companion were almost the first white men we had seen since leaving the Yellowstone, and we were the first they had seen since leaving the Park. To say that we were all delighted is to draw it mildly, for we felt that Huffman was a man that, now we had found him, we could not possibly do without on this trip. The two Crows came up at this time with their fish, and we were also joined by an old medicine-man of the tribe. Altogether, we made quite a formidable if not respectable looking picnic party.

After dinner Huffman's companion took two of his horses and pursued his way toward the railroad, while Huffman took the other four and turned back with us.

On the morning of September 9th we moved early, and about ten o'clock in the forenoon crossed the boundary-line between Montana and Wyoming, which line is also the southern boundary of the Crow reservation. We heaved a unanimous sigh of relief when we got out of the jurisdiction of those pestiferous redskins. Huffman killed a deer while we halted for dinner, and so won the thanks of the outfit for our first venison. It was on the opposite side of the river from him when he killed it, and he was on foot, and some distance from camp. I happened along just then with my pony, and he asked me to go across and get it. ·He said I would have enough to do to handle the deer, and had better leave my gun with him. I obeyed his orders, and went after the deer while he went to camp. I dressed the animal, swung it into my saddle, and started to lead my pony up the river to get an easier crossing. Just as I got up the bank a fine doe jumped out of the grass, ran up onto a little ridge about forty yards away, and stopped and looked at me for several minutes. I didn't make any remarks then about a man that was fool enough to take another man's gun away from him, nor about a man that was fool enough to let another man carry his gun to camp. Oh, no! If I had pulled the wrong trigger on that doe, and the buckshot had been in the other barrel, my language would not have been more forcible nor less elegant.

We jumped a coyote that afternoon, and with four repeaters and one single shot we almost set the ground on fire around him, but as he started at about two hundred yards rise and ·ran away ahead of his ticket, we failed to make a score on him. I put out some poison for them that night and several nights following, but, although they howled around our camp a great deal, they didn't take the bait.

On the 10th we ran into a large herd of cattle, and

amongst them a herd of eight antelopes. They were a long distance from the trail, however, and we didn't go after them, but contented ourselves with giving them a few harmless shots at about four hundred yards rise.

We left the river that afternoon, and started up a creek that came down from the mountains on the west, hoping to

A DAY ON BENNETT CREEK.

find game near the head of it; but when we got to the foot-hills we found a cabin there occupied by the ranchman who owned the herd of cattle we had passed through, so we had to turn back again and go on up the river to the mouth of Bennett creek, another beautiful stream, also coming in from the west. We proceeded up this about two miles, and camped. The next day we explored it well up into the range toward its source, but it did not develop into a good game country, either. There were plenty of antelopes near our camp, however, and we put in a good portion of the day hunting them. Allen killed two, Sawyer two, and three of us collectively killed one, after putting six bullets through him.

On the 12th we pulled out up the river again, crossed it, and moved up Pat O'Hare creek, a tributary that comes in from the southwest and empties near the mouth of the Clark's Fork canyon. We followed this stream to the foot of the mountains and made our camp, determined to find game in this region or turn back. On the 15th Huffman and I scouted the foothills to the west thoroughly for a distance of ten miles. We found some bear signs, but none of elk or other game. Allen, Sawyer and Weise started up the side of the mountain. Allen jumped a white tail doe and killed her before he had gone a mile from camp. Thus the wolf was again (paradoxically) driven from our door by the presence of another supply of fresh meat. Ed Forest took a long tramp to the southeast, saw a black bear and nine elk, but did not succeed in getting a shot at any of them. However, the news that we had at last got into a country where there were elk and bear, revived our drooping spirits, and we were all on the war-path early the next morning, eager for the fray. I climbed the mountain clear to the top, and in a broad canyon where there were several springs and thickets of quaking asp, water beech, jack pine, etc., I discovered numerous fresh signs of both bear and elk, but failed to get sight of any of the game, although I hunted diligently all day.

Allen was the lucky man again, for he killed a half-grown black bear within a mile of camp. But all the hard words

were fired by and at Huffman, who returned to camp that
night with the news that he had rode up to the head of the
creek four or five miles from camp, and had there jumped
three separate jags of elk; one of about forty, another of
about twenty-five and another of about sixty; that he had
emptied his magazine and his belt into them at fifty to
seventy-five yards rise, that he had wounded several, but had
not killed any. He didn't swear. Oh no, of course not.
He wasn't mad enough. He just raved and danced like an
escaped lunatic; he tore his hair, slung his hat and tramped
our grub and cooking utensils into the ground with his big
boots as he waltzed around the camp-fire. He pronounced
all the maledictions he could think of on that condemned
little Kennedy pea slinger of his. He wished he had a car
load of them to dam the Yellowstone river with; and yet
he said he didn't know what the river had done to deserve
such punishment. On second consideration he rather
thought it was the guns that ought to be damned instead of
the river.

Sawyer said how he would like to have been there with
his Winchester Express; Mike and Allen would have liked
to have been there with their 45-75 Winchesters; and I
whispered in Huffman's ear that I might have wounded
another one or two if I had been there with my old 40-75
Sharps.

"Well, you sheep-eating idiots," he growled, "why in
thunder did'nt you come? I didn't tell you to stay away."
We finally all cooled off, and compromised with the few of
the elk that got away by promising them that we would be
with them bright and early on the morrow.

And sure enough, the next morning we moved on them *en
masse*. We went to the same quaking-asp thickets the same
coulees and springs where Huffman had been the day before;

we found trails, blood and hair, and smelt the sulphurous fumes of twenty-four-hour-old profanity, but there were no elk in that neck of woods.   And so we had to carry our several belts full of cartridges, and our several loads of disappointments, which were much heavier, back to camp.   The next day, Saturday, the 16th, we all returned and hunted the same section of country, but still the elk had not returned in any considerable numbers.   Sawyer, Allen and Mike saw three, and Sawyer got one shot, but missed.

We now began to get desperate.   It was beginning to be a case of woodchuck with us, for we were nearly out of meat again.   True, we had killed a good deal of meat, but when six able-bodied men and a boy sit down to eat in that country, meat vanishes before them like dry grass before a prairie fire. We determined to make a desperate effort the next day. When we crawled out of our tent the next morning the heavens looked gloomy.   The sky was hidden by a dense, dark mist, and heavy fog clouds were floating ominously about the mountain-sides.   Everything we touched felt damp excepting the whisky-bottle, and that was dry enough (inside) for a matchbox.   Our ardor was somewhat dampened by this outer dampness and absence of inner dampness, but we were not to be delayed by such trifles.

We started for the canyon where I had seen so many good surface indications on Friday.   But Huffman got stuck on the scenery—the fog clouds floating around the mountain tops, and returned to camp to make some views.

The rest of the party went up the trail about two miles and separated; three of us went directly up the mountain into the canyon, the other three ascended by another trail farther to the south.   When Forest, Sawyer and I got into the canyon we separated, Sawyer going up near the south wall, I near the north, and Forest through the center.   He

told us to be ready for business, for he meant to run game
over us if we didn't keep out of the way.   I had not gone
more than three or four hundred yards when, sure enough, I
heard a great commotion in the midst of a quaking-asp
thicket, and knew at once by the nature of the sound that it

"THIS IS HOW WE GOT 'EM."

was caused by a band of elk, and that Forest had jumped
them.   They came directly toward me, but the fog was so
dense and the brush so thick that I could not see them until
they were within a few feet of me.   As they approached me

3

they separated, about five or six going on each side of me,
and so close that had the weather been clear I could almost
have counted their eye-winkers.   Finally, I caught a glimpse
of a small patch of red hair through the fog and leaves, and
sent a bullet into it; then another and another.   Then all
was oblivion again, so far as sight was concerned, but I could
hear them thumping and crashing against trees and bushes,
their hoofs clattering over the rocks in their mad flight, and
Forest yelling at me to "Give it to 'em."   I went to where
they were when I fired, and found a fine large fat cow elk
dead, with two holes through her, one through the hips and
one through the lungs.   She had presented herself at two
openings as she ran and had got a double dose.   The third
shot was carried away by a young bull.   I saw him dash
through a rift in the fog within twenty feet of me with blood
running from a wound high up in his side, over the paunch.

While I was admiring my prize I heard Sawyer's Express
belching forth her compliments to thè wapiti, and making
the rock-ribbed hills echo with her musical voice; one, two,
in quick succession, followed by the three shouts that we had
agreed should call the party together.   On repairing to him,
I found he had a fine yearling heifer down within fifty yards
of my cow.   We scoured the woods awhile in search of the
others, but they had lit out for tall timber.   We tried to trail
the wounded bull, but the undergrowth was so thick and he
had left so little blood, that we were forced to give up the
task.

For the past two hours it had been raining; one of those
quiet, modest, unassuming rains that follow a damp, foggy
morning; one of those rains that does not make any unnecessary noise, but which means business, as the Dutchman
says "fon the verd git," and we were wet to the skin; yes,
almost to the bone.   We returned and took the entrails out

)f our two elk. The other boys thought we had better cut
them up and each pack in a load of meat, but I objected,
as Huffman wanted some views of them ; and in fact, we all
lid.

"But," said Allen, "it's raining so he can't make any
views to-day, and if we leave the carcasses here over night
the bears will eat them up."

"I don't think they will," I said, "for I'm going to come
out here and sleep with them, and if the aforesaid bears want
to eat any carcasses they can try mine."

They all thought I would have rather a damp atmosphere
to sleep in, but I was anxious to save the meat and skins, and
determined to make the best of it. So we all went back to
camp. I fired a few cold potatoes, beans, chunks of meat
and hard tack into my neck, took a small piece of canvas
and my rubber coat, and started for another climb up the
mountain.

CHAPTER IV.

MEDITATIONS IN A WICIUP.

PHILOSOPHY IN A TENT — "ME T-R-R-RUSTY RIFUL" — AWAY FROM THE ILLS OF LIFE — ELK-HEART AND HARD TACK FOR BREAKFAST — THE PERORATION OF A DONKEY'S BRAY — WAPITI WINDS HIS HORN — THE MONARCH OF THE ROCKIES DIES AS A KING SHOULD DIE.

I ARRIVED at the seat of war about five o'clock, stretched my canvas across a washout, cut boughs and stood them up around three sides of it, and threw down a lot for a bed, built a rousing fire against a big rock in front of it, got up a supply of wood sufficient to keep it burning all night, and then crawled into my wiciup to meditate.

Now, thought I, this isn't so bad after all. Some folks might think it was, but it isn't. The wood is wet, to be sure, but by keeping plenty of it on it burns tolerably well. These bushes under me are wet, but I have spread my rubber coat over them, and that keeps the dampness from coming through and wetting me. Besides, my clothes are so wet that they couldn't get any wetter if I were to sleep in Lake Michigan; so what does it matter if my other surroundings are wet? Besides they are drying rapidly under the influence of this rousing fire. It is still raining steadily, but my little pup tent keeps it off. The night is cold, but if my back gets cold while my face is toward the fire I can turn over and warm my back. Some people might feel lonely out here, four miles from camp, and in a neck of woods that is full of bears and other frisky varmints, but I have "me t-r-r-rusty riful" with me, as the dizzy actor would say; besides, wild varmints are not apt to approach a fire. The carcases lie within a few yards of me on opposite sides of my camp, and the varmints aforesaid are not likely to disturb them either, so long as the fire burns. If they do, I shall be very likely to find it out, and death will forthwith go abroad in the land.

And then it is so nice and quiet here. That outweighs all objections to the place and its surroundings. The conductor will not interrupt my snooze to-night by shaking my arm and calling for "teekets," nor the brakeman by shouting "clamzoo, change cars for 'troit," nor the train butcher by yelling "peanuts." The infernal milkman's bell won't toll the hour of four o'clock to-morrow morning. I won't have to put my vest under my head to save that thirty-five cents in my pocket-book from the burglars. They will give my room a wide berth to-night. The landlord can't harass me this evening with that little "arrears of rent bill" of his. The grocer and the butcher can whistle for what I owe them, that is, if they feel like whistling. I don't care if coal is booming. Let her boom. I don't want any now. Have plenty of fuel for the present, thank you. I think of the little black-eyed widow away back at home, and wonder how she is faring in the battle of life. That's the only care I have to-night. But surely no ill can befall her when a fellow is away off out here. It would be a mighty cowardly fate that would steal a march on a man and rob him of his treasures when he is not there to defend them, so I will consign her to the care of Him who watcheth over the little sparrows, dismiss that care also, and betake myself to sleep.

The weather grew intensely cold during the night; the rain turned to snow, and the water that hung on the leaves froze. Ice formed on the little ponds of water, and Jack Frost woke me up several times during the night to replenish my fire. At four o'clock in the morning I took the heart of one of the elk, spitted it on a forked stick before the fire, and roasted it to a turn. On this and some hard tack which I had hastily shoveled into the pockets of my hunting coat when leaving camp the previous evening, I made a hearty breakfast, and at dawn was ready for the fray again. Before it was fully light an electric thrill was sent through my inmost soul by the sound of a bull elk's whistle, which was borne to my eager ears on the fresh morning breeze. Could it be possible? Were some of those monsters still hanging about to give me another matinee? Truly, for while I listened the sonorous and to me sublimely beautiful sound, came again.

My friend, did you ever hear an elk whistle?

"Yes, plenty of them."

So? Well, then I won't try to describe it to you. But there's another good-looking young gentleman over in the northeast corner of the hall who says he never did, and to him I would remark that it sounds more like the closing paragraph, the last sad note, indefinitely prolonged, the *tremolo-staccato*, the peroration, as it were, of a donkey's bray. Sometimes it is preceded or followed by a kind of grunt, although not always. In fact, scarcely any two elk whistle just alike. The same one varies his tones, but they average about as suggested. The noise is a very shrill one, capable of being heard to a great distance, and to a sportsman's ears it is probably the most musical and fascinating sound to be heard in the mountains. To me on this occasion it was peculiarly interesting, for I wanted above all things on this trip to secure a good head for mounting, and the questions that ran through my brain were: Is this an old-timer? Has he a fine, well-developed head and broadspreading, perfect antlers? And shall I be able to get him? The chances were largely against me, for the leaves and grass

were frozen, and so noisy that it would be almost impossible
to get within range of him without alarming him. The snow
was not deep enough to even deaden the noise, and so was of
no assistance to me. But I set out in the direction from
whence the music came. It came from the top of one of the
high ridges to the south of the canyon, probably half a mile
from where I was. I had to exercise the greatest care in
climbing the canyon wall, and when I reached the spot
where I had heard the whistle I found the tracks, large as
those of a three-year-old steer, but the author of them was
not there. While I was pondering over them and sizing up
(in my mind) the animal that could make such tracks, I
heard the whistle again away to the north. I picked my way
cautiously through gulches, over "hog-backs" and hills, and
when I reached the desired locality I heard Mr. Wapiti
winding his horn from the top of another ridge half a mile
to the south.

Away I went again, trembling all the time lest he should
wind me or hear some of the noises I was compelled to make,
and bid adieu to his present stamping-ground. But he was so
intent on finding some of the coy maidens of his harem
among these hills that he didn't notice me, and this time as
I reached the brow of the hill I heard a movement in a
thicket ahead, caught a faint outline of the monster as he
passed through the brush, and when he stopped I could see a
patch of reddish brown hair as large as my hat. In an
instant the old pill-driver lay with her heel pressing firmly
against my shoulder, a cloud of smoke arose from her mouth,
and there was a mad charge across the top of the ridge that
showed too plainly that the pill had commenced to operate.

As the broadside was presented to me in crossing an
opening I sent in another dose, and then all was still. I ran
up a little farther, and saw him standing in another thicket.

He was too badly hurt to run far, but I gave him another broadsider, and he started to run directly away from me. Then I gave him two in the rump. He turned to right again, and another leaden bolt caught him in the shoulder, another through the lungs, and another through the lower jaw, making eight in all. Then he came to bay again, and I walked up to within twenty paces of him. It was useless to add to his already too great suffering; he could go no farther. He looked at me, shook his massive head, pawed the ground, and his eyes gleamed like balls of fire. He would have charged me, but his strength was too far gone.

Then was enacted the sublimest death-scene I ever witnessed. He trembled all over. He inhaled until his sides expanded far beyond their natural size, he blew this vast volume of air from his nostrils in clouds of steam, accompanied by a noise like the exhaust of a steam engine. He pawed up the earth again, shook his head, then placed his antlers to the ground, and threw his weight upon them as if giving the death thrust to some prostrate antagonist. In this effort he forced his body into the air until his feet cleared the ground, he poised a moment, fell with a heavy thud on his side, blew the steam and blood from his nostrils again,—and the great monster was dead! Talk about great acting. I have seen great actors in their greatest death scenes, but never saw so grand, so awe-inspiring a death as this real death of the Monarch of the Rockies.

I sat down and gazed for twenty minutes upon his lifeless form, and bitterly did I reproach myself for bringing to an untimely end so noble, so majestic an animal. What a strange passion it is that leads men to such slaughter of innocent creatures, and what a strange fancy it is that leads them to think such slaughter sport! It is too deep a problem for my untutored mind ; I leave it to the metaphysician, to the psychologist.

When I had recovered from this gloomy reverie I walked up and surveyed the fallen hero. He was indeed a giant, much larger than Huffman's sorrel horse, which we knew weighed at the time over eight hundred pounds. He had by far the

THE MONARCH OF THE ROCKIES.

finest pair of antlers I have ever seen. They have since been examined by the Hon. J. D. Caton, Gen. Strong and several other gentlemen of high authority, all of whom pronounce them the largest and handsomest pair they have ever seen. Judge Caton says it would be worth a trip across the conti-

nent to look at them.   Each beam measures four feet nine
inches long, and the spread is four feet six inches.   There are
six points on one beam and seven on the other.

I got the entire head home in good condition, had it
mounted, and it now occupies the most conspicuous place in
my "den."   As I pause in the midst of this recital, and look
up at it, it wears that same grand, majestic look it wore there
on top of the Rocky Mountains in that cold crisp September
morning, and I have but to give my imagination play, and I
find myself surrounded by those same old snow-capped peaks,
those tall, rocky crags peering out above the pine-trees, which
are hung with their crystal fringe of ice, glittering in the
bright morning sun.   I can feel that fresh, frosty, invigorating atmosphere; I can hear those frozen leaves crush under
my feet as I walk, and my blood dances through my veins as
I climb from hilltop to hilltop in pursuit of the noble quarry,
stimulated the while by his fascinating whistle.   Ah! soon
come the time when I may again visit that land of enchantment.

But how our airy castles do crumble under the touch of
reality.   Enter Mrs. Coquina with a towel around her head,
a broom in one hand, a dustpan in the other, and a smile on
her face, as she says:

" Old man, you'd better put in some coal, or this fire will
be out."

CHAPTER V.

A PERILOUS EXPERIENCE.

AND now to return to my narrative. Either one of the eight balls that entered the elk's carcass would have caused his death in time, but I was anxious to get him down as near my temporary camp as possible, and for that purpose I kept on shooting until I saw that he had more lead than he could carry away.

It is frequently stated that the wapiti is the easiest of all the cervidæ to kill, that he gives up sooner after being hit than any other member of the family. But my experience does not lead me to think so. Six of these eight bullets passed entirely through his body and yet he lived nearly half an hour after the last one was fired. His was an exceptional case of vitality, but all the others that I have killed or seen killed required very hard hitting and in vital parts to bring them down.

After admiring my prize to my entire satisfaction, I returned to my temporary camp to wait for Huffman and the others of the party. They put in an appearance about noon. Huffman made his views of the two elk; we cut them up and packed the best of the meat on one of his pack-horses, and he, Mike and I went up to the other carcass. When we arrived we were surprised to find that a bear nad been at it, and had torn it slightly and eaten a small portion of it, but not enough to interfere with our purpose. As soon as Huffman had completed his work, Mike and I proceeded to skin the carcass and take off the head. While thus engaged, and while Huffman was packing his outfit on his horse, we heard strange noises on the hillside above us, and looking up we saw three grizzly bears charging down upon us. For a moment we were horror-stricken. They were between us and our guns when we first saw them, and if we ran and left our horses they would break loose and we would probably never see them again. We dared not even leave them to tree ourselves, and could not possibly mount them to get away, for they were crazed with fright, and we were compelled to stay by them. The bears had been there and got a taste of the elk, just enough to make them ferocious, when they had heard us coming back, and had retreated into the woods. They had waited for us to get away as long as they cared to, and had then resolved to drive us away or eat us up, and they didn't seem to care which.

They had evidently sized us up from away back on top of the hill, and knew just what and who we were, and how many there were of us. They seemed to come for gore, and lots of it.

It was the most frightful assault that ever I looked at. They came like a band of redskins assaulting an emigrant train and trying to stampede the stock. They were fairly jumping over each other in their eagerness to be the first in the fight. They were roaring like infuriated bulls, growling and snarling like mad dogs, puffing and snorting like locomotive engines, and the brush was cracking under them as if they were great rocks rolling down from the top of some mountain peak. Huffman had a buckskin lariat on " old sorrel " with a hack-more around his nose, and at the first sight of the infuriated beasts had taken a turn around his hand with the lariat. The horse reared and charged until he threw Huffman into the branches of the tree to which he was tied, and lodged him in them six feet from the ground. We were all fearfully rattled for a moment, for the assault was so purely unnatural and unexpected.

We should not have been half so much surprised had the assaulting party been Indians, but we did not expect and were not prepared for either. But we pulled our knives and rushed at them, yelled like savages, swung our hats, and when they found we were not going to run they halted, looked at us a moment, turned and walked slowly and sulkily back up the hill into the thick underbrush, and were out of sight by the time they had gone twenty yards. Mike now got hold of his gun and started in pursuit, leaving Huffman and I still in charge of the horses. He walked cautiously up the hill a few paces looking for the game, when suddenly the old female bear sprang at him from a clump of bushes right at his side.

She was within six feet of him when he first saw her, and there was no time for shooting; at least he thought there wasn't, and he turned and came back down the hill bareheaded, his face as fair as a lily, his hair (what little he had) and his coat-tail standing straight out behind him,—clearing about twenty feet at each jump, and the bear lighting in his tracks as soon as he was out of them. Huffman and I left the horses, rushed at the bear again, whooped and yelled for life (that is, for Mike's life), and again succeeded in checking the savage brute. She walked sullenly back up the hill again. I now got hold of my rifle and reinforced Mike. We both moved on the enemy, this time more cautiously, Mike shaking like a leaf from the terrible rattling he had just gone through. We had gone but a few feet when he caught sight of the old lady again, and with a lucky shot landed a bullet in the butt of her ear, laying her dead within twenty feet of us. At the report of his rifle one of the others raised on its haunches and I sent a bullet through its

UNITED IN DEATH.

heart, making another funeral in that family. The third one concluded he wasn't hungry just then, and, skipping away through the jungle, made his escape without giving either of us a shot at him.

We dragged the corpses of the two down and laid them

tenderly alongside of the elk, and Huffman leveled his camera on them again amid the plaudits of the admiring multitude.

I have heard a great many stories of bears attacking persons without having first been attacked or hurt themselves, but never believed them. I have always considered them "bear stories," and have allowed them to pass in at one ear and out at the other. But the experience of that afternoon banished all skepticism from my mind on that topic. I am prepared to believe implicity hereafter that a grizzly will fight for fresh meat, and shall in the future govern myself accordingly.

Many of my friends have expressed surprise at our being able to check them by rushing at them and without coming into actual contact with them. We hardly expected to be able to do so ourselves, and could only account for it by calling to mind instances in which we have seen a ferocious, savage dog rush at a man with the intention of tearing him to pieces, and have seen him quell and turn away under the influence of a stern and defiant demeanor assumed by his intended victim.

Our assailants were not frightened, understand, any more than was the savage dog, but they walked slowly and reluctantly away, in each case frequently looking back over their shoulders and showing us their ugly teeth. If we had attempted flight instead of standing our ground we would undoubtedly have furnished the cold meat for a grizzly picnic.

Mike says he don't want to run any more grizzlies unless they are muzzled and hobbled. He says he likes to see a dog so well trained that he will come promptly to heel when bidden, but he don't care to find another she "bar" so blamed fresh that she will insist on coming to heel without his bidding. But he showed good leather in staying in the fight until it was over. He had as close a call for a funeral as any man ever had that escaped it, and the shaking up that he and even Huffman and I got would have scared any man that ever wore pants. The woods are full of hunters that had they been dealt the hand that Mike got, would have been running yet.

Nothing of importance was done the next forenoon. In the afternoon Weise, Sawyer and Allen returned and skinned the two bears, after which they hunted up the canyon some distance. They saw another large grizzly, and Sawyer got a shot at him at long range, through thick brush, and missed. The bear then ran across toward Allen who got in two running shots, but with no better success. As they were returning Weise killed a grizzly cub, and saw an old one go spinning off through the thicket near by, but didn't get a shot at her.

Wednesday the 20th we moved camp up to the mouth of the canyon, and spent the day in making a new camp. Thursday hunted up canyon to the top of the range, from which we had a fine view of the main range of the Rockies, away off to the southwest. We could also see steam issuing from the geysers in the National Park. Saw no game except blue grouse, and no signs of anything larger. Thursday was uneventful, but on Friday afternoon Sawyer and Weise went back to the elk carcasses, and each got another shot at a large grizzly, but again made "unaccountable" misses. About this time Allen was visited by a large carbuncle, which landed on his cheek, and almost confined him to camp for the next two or three days. Otherwise things were quiet; no one made any good scores during that time. Sawyer set his gun near the elk carcass, Sunday evening, with a piece of fresh meat at the muzzle, and a string leading from it to the trigger.

Early Monday morning all hands started for the front to see what it had killed. Sure enough on arriving there they found that the bate had been disturbed, and the gun discharged. There were a few tracks of a bear still visible, but owing to a heavy rain having fallen in the meantime, the trail could not be followed.

Allen took a seat in a tree near the elk carcass, and before he had been there half an hour, heard the familiar "oh-woh, oh-woh" of a black bear, and looking up the hill saw one coming directly toward him. He waited until it came within about twenty yards, when he fired, the ball striking just in the sticking place, ranging upward and breaking the spine. Bruin never smiled again. When returning in the afternoon the grizzly that had fallen a victim to Sawyer's set gun the night before, was found. He was a very large one, was shot through the paunch and lay within one hundred yards of where the gun was set.

Wednesday the 27th all hands went up the same canyon again and found plenty of fresh elk signs. Sawyer soon got sight of a cow about two hundred yards away, running across him. He fired when she turned, and ran the other way. He fired again and knocked her down, but she got up at once, ran again and was soon out of sight. We tried to trail her by the blood, but could not find her. In a few minutes we heard Mike put in seven shots in rapid succession, and then shout. We went to him and found he had killed a fine cow. We dressed her, hung the hide, tallow and most of the meat up in a tree, and went to camp.

The time had now arrived for us to close the present campaign, and on the morrow, after collecting the meat, hides, etc., and bringing them in, we broke camp and started home. And thus endeth the narrative of our three weeks of "Rustlings in the Rockies."

4

CHAPTER VI.

IN THE BIG HORN MOUNTAINS.

AWAY TO THE MOUNTAINS — THE RED RIVER VALLEY — A GARDEN IN
THE DESERT — FROM BISMARCK TO GLENDIVE — THE BAD LANDS
ON THE LITTLE MISSOURI — "HELL WITH THE FIRE OUT" — FOUR
HUNDRED AND SEVENTY-THREE BRIDGES IN TWO HUNDRED AND
TWENTY-ONE MILES — A DRIVE UP THE YELLOWSTONE — BUTCHERS
AND BUFFALOES — A WORD OF WARNING — OFF TO THE BIG HORN.

A year ago to-day I started on my first trip to Montana,
and to-day, August 27, 1881, I find myself at the Chicago,
Milwaukee & St. Paul depot, with my rifle, cartridges, hunting
suit, and camp equipage packed, preparatory to another journey
to the same mystic quarter of the world, only that I am bound
further into the territory this time than before, and also into
the northern portion of Wyoming, my main objective point
this time being the Big Horn mountains.

I told the baggage man to check my baggage to Glendive,
Montana.

"Glendive! Is that all the further you're going?"

No, but that is as far as I can ride—I shall have to walk
the rest of the way.

My ticket secured, I retired to rest in the elegant and lux-
urious sleeper attached to the train, and awoke next morning
at La Crosse. At one P.M. we landed in the new union depot
at St. Paul. Here I stopped to visit a friend until the next
evening at seven o'clock, when I boarded the train on the
Northern Pacific railroad, and we pulled out for Bismarck.
While in St. Paul, I had the pleasure of meeting that sterling
old soldier, Major Guido Ilges, who commanded the perilous

expedition to the Upper Missouri in the winter of 1879–80, in which the Sioux chief Gall and his band were captured. This was a movement of great value and importance to the country, for it virtually broke up the hostile element of the Sioux nation. It left them too weak to successfully hold out against the army longer, and the ultimate surrender of Crow King, Log Dog, Sitting Bull and the others, followed as a necessary consequence.

After a night's run from St. Paul, we entered the famous Red river valley, the greatest wheat growing country in the world. The crop this year is bountiful, and is now being threshed and shipped. Steam threshers can be seen at work in every direction, and the grain, in many instances, is being hauled directly to the stations, and loaded into cars. West of Fargo to Bismarck, there are still millions of acres of un-cultivated lands, as rich and as valuable for farming and graz-ing purposes as any of those that are already under cultivation. But they are settling up rapidly.

Years ago, when this road was first projected, there were those who pronounced its originators insane. It was said that if a road were built across the continent this far north, it could not be operated more than six months in the year, ow-ing to the terrible winters experienced in this latitude ; but in practical contradiction of this theory, the fact is announced that, while so many roads further south were blockaded by snow during a greater portion of that terrible winter of 1879–80, the Northern Pacific was not blockaded a single day. It was said that the region through which the line was to run was a bleak, snowy, inhospitable desert, where nothing in the way of farm or garden products could be made to grow, and where stock, as well as human beings, must inevitably perish from cold. But the hundreds of prosperous farms, the beautiful crops, and the large and successful stock ranches all along the route, far up toward the Rocky Mountains, give us ocular demonstration of the fact that the desert has been made to blossom as the rose. And not only has it been found possible to build a railroad and till the soil in this latitude, but the Canadian government is building a trans-continental road on a line two to three hundred miles north of this, that promises equally favorable results.

We arrived at Bismarck at six o'clock in the evening, and stopped over night.

Mr. John Leasure, an intimate friend of former days, whom I met here, entertained me very pleasantly during the evening with an account of a hunt in which he participated, in the Musselshell country, a few years ago. The party killed a number of grizzly and cinnamon bears, elk, mountain sheep, deer, etc. He says it is one of the best localities in the West for game of this class. He is a frontiersman of several years' experience, and a skillful and successful hunter.

We left Bismarck at six o'clock the next morning for Glendive, the then terminus of the road; passed through a beautiful series of valleys, including the Hart, the Curlew, the Knife, the Cannonball and others, through each of which flow streams of water, varying in size as well as quality— some of them being pure and others tinctured with alkali. But there is plenty of sweet water for agricultural purposes, and the land is as finely situated for farming or stock growing as any one could desire.

We passed through the world-famous Bad Lands, bordering the Little Missouri, during the afternoon. These have been described so often by various writers that I will not here detain the reader by adding anything to what has already been said, and besides no one, though he may read volumes of descriptions of this marvellous region, can form any conception of what these Bad Lands are like. They *must* be

seen to be intelligently understood. General Sully's description of them, however, will bear repetition here, for it is
multum in parvo. He tersely characterized them as "hell
with the fire out." Some idea of the expense of building a
railroad through this country and along these winding streams
may be derived from the fact that there are 473 bridges on
the Missouri division, which is only 221 miles long.

We arrived at Glendive at 7:30 o'clock in the evening,
and were cordially greeted by Major Bell and Lieutenant
Slocum, of the Seventh cavalry. Mr. T. C. Kurtz, who is in
charge of the company's store at that place, fed and lodged
us in a most hospitable and comfortable manner. As soon as
I arrived, I commenced to figure on the means of getting
from there to Miles City and Fort Keough. Fortunately I
formed the acquaintance of Dr. G. E. Bushnell, an army surgeon, who was *en route* to Fort Ellis, *via* Fort Keough, and
who was coming through in an ambulance. I drew on my
ample supply of cheek, and requested permission to accompany him, which he kindly granted. Accordingly we left
Glendive at seven o'clock the next morning, on a construction train destined for Cabin Creek, fifteen miles further on,
where the Doctor's ambulance was awaiting him.

We reached it in good time, hastily transferred ourselves
to it, and our baggage to an escort wagon, and were off for a
seventy miles drive up the Yellowstone. The mules were in
good condition, the drivers gave them the buckskin vigorously, and the cloud of dust we left behind us showed the
other voyagers in the valley that we were not disposed to
waste any time making the journey. We arrived at Captain
Snider's camp, at the mouth of Powder river, at four o'clock
in the evening, where a relay awaited us. The captain invited
us to a sumptuous lunch, which we discussed with a relish,
while the fresh teams were being hooked on. When these

duties had been performed, we resumed our seat in the ambulance and again spun away over the plains.

The doctor was accompanied by his good wife, who is
pretty, witty and vivacious, and her conversation added
greatly to the enjoyment of the trip.   We passed through
Miles City at half-past ten, and a few minutes later arrived at
Fort Keough, which is situated two miles further up the river.

I proceeded at once to the quarters of my old friend,
Captain Borden.   He had retired for the night, but a ring at
his door bell brought forth a stentorian " Come in," from his
sleeping apartment.   I obeyed the order, and as I entered, I
could discern in the darkness the white-robed form of the
genial captain coming to meet me, and could hear the thump-
ity-bump of his bare feet on the floor.

I announced myself, and he replied in his cordial, whole-
souled way, " Well, bully for you, Coquina, I'm devilish
glad to see you."   ·

" How do you make that out," I said, " you *haven't seen*
me yet."

" Well, I'm glad you've come, all the same, and I *will* see
you as soon as I can strike a light."

This accomplished, we sat down and had a " big talk,"
which lasted into the early hours of the morning ere peace
was declared, and we both sought our couches.

The next day being Sunday, we spent it in looking about
the post and city, and in friendly intercourse with the various
officers at the post.   I was shown three elk that are in one of
the corrals here—two bulls and a cow.   The bulls are just
beginning to rub the velvet from their horns.   The three
were sold to a railroad officer a few days ago for fifty dollars,
and will soon be shipped East.   Capt. Borden had a pet
antelope that one of his men brought in in the spring.   It is a
graceful, handsome little creature, and made a beautiful pet.

There were a number of valuable dogs at the post, several of the officers being sportsmen. General Whistler, the commanding officer, has a pack of greyhounds that are unusually fleet. His son, a young man of seventeen, is very fond of the chase, and under his management the pack caught ninety-three antelopes that season. This record cannot probably be excelled by any other pack in the country.

There was a large herd of buffaloes, only twenty miles north of the post, and I was pained to learn that a large party of *butchers*, not hunters, were camped near there, and were slaughtering them at the rate of nearly a hundred a day. Only the skins were saved, and the carcasses left to rot. Even the fur was worthless then. The skins were shipped East, and tanned as cowhide and calfskin, and used as such in the manufacture of boots and shoes. It is a burning shame and a disgrace to every citizen of this portion of the country that they should allow this infamous and damnable traffic to be carried on under their very noses, when they have the law, the courts, law officers, and every necessary means at their disposal, to stop it. It only needs some one to make a complaint and testify against the butchers, in order to have them severely punished; but no one has nerve enough, or feels interest enough in the matter, to go to this trouble, and so the slaughter will go on until the last of the noble bisons will fall a prey to these human coyotes, and then the "law-abiding citizen" will awake to a realization of the loss that his stupidity has entailed upon him. He will bemoan his loss, but I will tell him: "It serves you right, you had ample warning, and would not act; now you deserve to be deprived of meat of any and every kind all the days of your life." Congress should pass a law to prohibit this slaughter, and place the execution of it in the hands of the army. Then, and not till then, will it be stopped.

During the day I called on General Whistler, and made known to him my wish to visit the Big Horn mountains, when he kindly offered me a packer and a number of pack mules to transport my provisions, camp equipage, etc. Of course I gladly availed myself of such a generous offer, and at once began preparations for the start. I also procured the services of Mr. L. A. Huffman, the popular and skillful photographer of Miles City, to accompany me.

I desired to limit the party to the smallest possible number, in order to have as little plunder to transport as possible, and so reduced the party to these two men and myself. Three pack mules were thought a sufficient number to carry our outfit. Capt. Borden generously placed at my disposal a saddle pony, which completed the necessary outfit for the expedition, and Tuesday morning, August 30, 1881, found us with provisions, blankets, tents, etc., packed, our rifles slung to our saddles, and all ready to mount and go.

CHAPTER VII.

IN THE YELLOWSTONE VALLEY.

HOW I SHOT A DUCK — AN AUGUST THUNDER-STORM — MENU FOR AN
EPICURE — ROSEBUD RIVER — AN OLD BATTLE FIELD — LAME DEER
CREEK — CUSTER'S LAST CAMPING GROUND — SCARING A COYOTE —
DOG-IN-THE-MANGER MEANNESS OF CROW INDIANS.

WE left Fort Keough on the morning of the 30th of August.
Our route took us up the Yellowstone some twelve miles, through
a series of as picturesque bad lands as are to be found anywhere in the West. Their bold, rugged, ever-changing forms
and outlines rendered an otherwise uneventful ride interesting in the extreme.

After leaving the Yellowstone, we took a southwesterly
direction across a series of high mesa or table lands, following a well-beaten wagon road, and jogged along at a rattling
pace till three o'clock in the afternoon, when we went into
camp near some water holes, having covered, in six hours,
thirty miles. While we were preparing dinner a teal duck
came and lit in one of the water holes within a few yards of
our camp. I picked up my rifle and said I would try and
get it.

"Yes," said Huffman, "you see that you do get it, and
I'll have it in the frying pan before it's done kicking."

I walked up so that I could look over the bank into the
water, and saw the duck in the midst of a bunch of grass. I
could not see his head plainly enough to shoot at it so I had
to take his body. At the crack of the rifle one of his wings
flew as much as twenty feet straight up into the air and other
pieces went in different directions. Then I remembered that

I had put in an explosive ball. I picked up what was left of the poor little teal, but all I could find was the head and tail, held together by a narrow strip of skin along what had once been its back. All the rest had vanished into thin air, as did Huffman's dreams of broiled teal when I showed him the wreck.

About this time I noticed a black cloud approaching from the west, and a few minutes later we heard distant mutterings of thunder. I asked Huffman if we shouldn't put up a tent. He said no, it wasn't going to rain; that it rarely rained in this country at this season of the year. I was the more willing to believe him, for I remembered that General Hazen, our present chief clerk of the weather department, had told us some years ago that the Yellowstone valley was an arid, barren desert and that no rains ever fell there except in the late fall and early spring months. But all signs, or at least most of them, fail in wet weather and just as we got dinner ready, the sky became suddenly obscured with low, dense clouds of inky blackness, that rapidly changed near the horizon to a light colored, foamy, smoky looking mass, that whirled and rolled as it approached like the column of steam from one of the great geysers, indicating that it was accompanied with a high wind. The lightning played through all parts of the heavens, from dome to horizon, with such vivid fury as to almost blind us. The artillery of heaven pealed forth in volumes that almost shook the earth beneath our feet; rolling, echoing and reverberating among the neighboring hills and over the vast prairies, as if sent to awaken the dead from their last sleep. While we were watching and listening to these demonstrations, transfixed with amazement at the unusual and almost unnatural phenomenon of a thunder storm here in August, the rain burst upon us with such violence and in such a dense body as almost to prostrate us at the first shock. Huffman and Jack Conley, our packer, sought shelter under a large sheet of canvas that they had hastily spread upon the *apparejos* to protect them from the storm. I quickly drew on my rubber coat, preferring to stand out and watch the grand play of the elements. Our poor mules and my pony turned their heads toward the storm and stood and took it like veterans The storm lasted about half an hour and was as violent as any I ever saw. When it subsided, the coulee near which we were camped and in which before there were only a few pools of water, was now alive with a roaring torrent. The country all about us was drenched and washed, and General Hazen, or any one else, need never tell us again that it don't rain in the Yellowstone valley in summer.

Now that the storm was over, we began to look about to see what had become of our dinner. We had no shelter to put it under, and were obliged to leave it to the mercy of the storm. We collected the fragments together, reconstructed them to the best of our ability, and sat down to a repast, of which the following is about the

MENU.

SOUP.

Cold rainwater.

MEATS.

Breakfast bacon, rainwater sauce.

GAME.

Teal Duck, all shot away.

Seven up, } After dinner.
Poker,

ENTREES.

Pork and Beans, soaked in rainwater.

VEGETABLES.

Fried Potatoes, ditto.

BREAD.

Hot biscuit, ditto.
Hard tack, ditto.

DRINKS.

Coffee, diluted with rainwater, three to one.
Rainwater straight.

After dinner we put up our tent, just as some men lock up their barn after their best horse has been stolen. We went to a hay-stack near camp, and got hay for our animals and for beds, and slept comfortably.

At noon the next day we reached the Rosebud river, a stream that has been rendered famous by the Indian campaigns of Generals Terry, Crook, Custer and Miles. Their trails may still be seen at frequent intervals, leading into or out of the valley, and remains of their old camp-fires may be found on every available camping-ground. The Rosebud is a narrow, deep, clear, swift-running stream, that looks as if it might bear bass, pike and other game fishes, but I am told that the catfish is the only species known to inhabit its waters. The valley is broad, level, fertile, and will eventually all be turned over by the plow and produce good crops. There are no settlements on it yet, with the exception of two or three cattle ranches. Several other ranches have been located, but the "shacks" have not yet been built. The valley is enclosed on either side with a range of hills that are down on the map as the Rosebud mountains, though they are scarcely of sufficient magnitude to entitle them to such distinction. Nearly all the peaks or buttes are capped with red, fire-baked clay, and the stream takes its name from the fancied resemblance these hills bear to rosebuds. The immediate banks of the stream are covered with a light growth of timber, mostly cottonwood. It make good fuel, and this is about the only use that can be made of it, though an inferior quality of fence posts and railroad ties may be manufactured from it. None of the trees are large enough for lumber. The only game found on this stream, now, is deer; and they are scarce, owing to its having been hunted so persistently both by soldiers and Indians.

At noon on the 1st of September we passed a point further

up the river, where the Bozeman expedition, a party of citizens who left Bozeman in 1874 to explore the Yellowstone valley, were corraled by Sioux Indians and besieged for several days. The party numbered one hundred and thirty men, and the rifle pits which they constructed and occupied are still intact. They lost a large number of horses in the fight, the bones of which still lie bleaching on the field. The Indians finally abandoned the siege and withdrew, after sacrificing several of their number to the deadly aim of the white hunters' rifles. None of the whites were injured.

During the afternoon, we found a covey of eight sharptail grouse in the sage brush near the road, and got seven of them with our rifles before they got out of reach. Our large bore rifles cut them up pretty badly, but we managed to save the breasts of them all, and they made us a good supper and breakfast. This was the first game we had found on the trip.

That night we camped near the mouth of Lame Deer creek, on the scene of Gen. Miles' fight with a band of Minne Conjoux and Ogelalla Sioux, under chief Lame Deer, in 1878. The Indians were defeated and captured. Lame Deer was cornered in a coulee, and seeing there was no chance of escape, came out and surrendered. He walked up to Gen. Miles' ostensibly to deliver his arms to him. The General sat upon his horse, and, when within a few feet of him, Lame Deer suddenly raised his rifle, aimed it full at the General's breast, and fired. The General kicked the muzzle of the gun to one side just in time to save his own life, but the ball passed by him and killed his orderly, who sat on another horse just behind him. The treacherous red skin then started to run, but a volley from the soldiers' carbines filled his worthless skin full of bullet-holes, and sent him over the divide forever.

During the forenoon of the 2d of September we passed the

place where poor Custer made his last camp. In the early morning he had sighted the Indian village in the valley of the Little Big Horn, from the top of one of the peaks of the Wolf mountains, thirty-five miles east of here, and rode from there to this point on the Rosebud, where he halted only for his men to make coffee — it can scarcely be called a camp, strictly speaking — and as soon as they had swallowed their frugal meal, they remounted, rode all night, and struck the Sioux village at daylight; with what fatal consequences to himself and his brave band we all know, alas! too well. The remnants of their camp-fires still lie scattered over the river bottom, as melancholy relics of this, their last supper. Poor, brave boys! little did they think, as they sipped their coffee and ate their hard bread around these fires, that the morrow's sun would shine upon their lifeless forms, and that not one of them would live to tell the world how his comrades fell.

The two branches of the Rosebud unite here, and the locality is called the "Forks of the Rosebud." We continued our march up the south fork, as it would take us into the mountains farther south than would the north fork. As we rode leisurely along, about the middle of the afternoon a coyote broke cover some two hundred yards ahead of us, and started on his long, shambling trot across the prairie. We turned our artillery loose on him, and to use a frontier phrase, literally set the ground afire all around him. We didn't take the trouble to dismount, but sat in our saddles and "fanned" him just for fun. We fired no less than twenty shots at him, and, though none of them hit him, we made it so hot for him that he scarcely knew which way to run. Occasionally a ball would strike just in front of him, plowing the dirt into his face, when he would change his course, and no sooner get started in another direction than a repetition of the offense would give him another whirl. Then three bullets would strike on as many sides of him at once, and he would jump as if trying to get out of his skin. Finally, when he did get out of our range, he did some of the tallest running I have seen done in many a day, and I don't believe he stopped before dark that night.

Just before going into camp that evening, we saw five deer standing near the foot of a hill, about six hundred yards away, looking at us. We all dismounted, knelt down, adjusted our sights carefully to what we judged the distance to be, and fired at the largest buck. As our smoke cleared away, we saw him turn a somersault, and fall dead. We made camp, went and brought him in, and from that time on had plenty of fresh meat.

The Crow Indians had burned the grass all along the Rosebud and Little Big Horn rivers, and on the intervening table-lands, so that we often had great difficulty in finding grazing for our animals. The country in question is covered by their reservation, and it is supposed that they have burned it to prevent the white ranchmen from grazing their cattle, or making hay on the reservation. They are becoming hostile toward the whites, and have ordered several parties of white hunters, haymakers, etc., off their land. They have even gone so far as to burn several stacks of hay that had been cut on the reservation contrary to their wishes. By these and other hostile demonstrations, they are brewing a storm over their heads that will burst upon them one of these days, and they will be driven off their lands as the Sioux, Utes, and other tribes have been in the past. The fact of ranchmen or military parties cutting hay on their lands is not a matter they should object to at all, for the grass is there, they (the Indians) will not cut it, and if not cut it rots or is burned on the ground. It is better for all concerned that it should be harvested and utilized, and this dog-in-the-manger policy of the Crows is making violent enemies of all the ranchmen in the surrounding country.

As to game, there are thousands of heads of it on the Crow lands, and they rarely kill any except buffalo. So long as they can draw rations and annuities from the government, they will not take the trouble to hunt, further than to go out once or twice a year, and butcher a lot of buffaloes.

CHAPTER VIII.

AT THE FORKS OF THE ROSEBUD.

GOOD LUCK WITH THE GROUSE — INTERVIEWED BY A CROW SCOUT—FIRST
SIGHT OF THE BIG HORN MOUNTAINS — THREE DEER KILLED WITH
FOUR SHOTS, "DEUCED CLEVAH!"— FANNING THE COYOTES — ALL
LOADED FOR BEAR — KILLED, BUT LOST AFTER ALL — WET GRO-
CERIES FOR BREAKFAST.

WE camped at the forks of the Rosebud on the night of
the 2d of September near the sight of General Crook's fight
with the Sioux, on the 17th of June, 1876. The rifle pits are
still well preserved ; the position Crook occupied can easily
be traced by these, and various other relics that remain on
the field.

A covey of sharp-tailed grouse came within a few yards of
our camp late in the evening, and with a few lucky shots we
took the heads off of five of them. They were large and fat,
their food being abundant on the plains this season. Their
craws were full of grasshoppers. The feathered life of this
region includes several varieties of hawks common to the
Western plains, the night-hawk, magpie, Canada jay (commonly called meat bird, or butcher bird), red-headed woodpecker, golden-winged woodpecker, Carolina dove, brown
thrush, catbird, red-breasted robin, blackbird, two or three
varieties of owls; the rose-breasted grosbeak, and two or
more varieties of sparrows. The woodpecker must here return
to first principles, to the habits of his forefathers, and become
again an insectivorous bird, for there is not a particle of grain
raised within a hundred miles of here. In the settled districts he has almost entirely abandoned his natural food, and

become wholly a grain eater, grain being procured with less labor on the farm than insects; but the individuals of this species who live on the frontier seem content, like the pioneer of the human species, to forego the luxuries of civilization for the sake of carrying the standard of their race into the wilds of the far West.

During the afternoon we passed the camp of a band of Crow Indians, under Chief Two-Bellies. A scout came out from the camp and rode two or three miles with us, endeavoring to find out who we were, where we were going, and what our object was in thus trespassing on their reservation. He could not, or at least pretended he could not speak or understand a word of English, and the conversation was carried on with him by signs. After he had obtained the information he came for, he asked us where we were going to camp that night, and said he would like to eat with us, but we told him . we were going to ride fifteen miles yet before camping, and thinking that would be rather a long ride for the sake of obtaining a square meal, he turned and rode back to his village. We expected that another party would be sent after us. to order us off the reservation, but were agreeably disappointed. We should not have obeyed such an order if it had come, but preferred not to antagonize the lordly proprietors of the soil.

Wild fruits were very plentiful along the Rosebud, after we got well up toward its head, and we feasted on plums and choke-cherries; both being large, thoroughly ripe, and of delicious flavor.

Having followed the Rosebud nearly to its head—to where it was a mere rill that one could easily step across—we left it early the next morning, and started across the divide to the Little Big Horn. We reached the top of the divide at ten o'clock in the forenoon, and here, for the first time, we saw with eager eyes what we had so long been seeking, the towering walls and snowcapped peaks of the Big Horn mountains. As they loomed up against the western horizon, clothed in green and white, and enveloped in blue and smoky haze, they presented a scene so grand, so beautiful, so enchanting, that we felt as though we could stay there and gaze upon them forever. We dismounted, took out the field-glass and surveyed with wrapt interest and admiration the beautiful scene.

First there were the foothills, bold, rugged and picturesque, through which tumbled many a clear mountain torrent, and next were the great mountains, whose sides were covered with alternate areas of evergreen timber and vast meadows. The golden-hued grass, which grew in these parks, waving in the bright sun, looked like fields of ripe grain; and great ledges of red sandstone or white limestone that cropped out here and there, seemed to be the well-appointed farmhouses and barns that one would naturally look for in this picture of agricultural luxuriance. Farther up were the tall peaks, towering far toward the heavens, piercing the clouds in their upward strides, and already draped in spotless white. It produces a strange sensation in the mind to stand here under this burning sun, with vegetation green and flowers blooming all around us, birds singing in every bush, and look upon these vast fields of snow only fifty miles away. "In the midst of summer prepare for winter" must be the motto of any one who starts on a tramp to the mountains, and we are glad when we remember that we have a full supply of heavy clothing and blankets with us.

Between ourselves and the mountains lies the broad, level valley of the Little Big Horn, the silvery sheen of whose crystal fluid, glimmered and glistened in the clear sunlight as the river wound in and out among the groves of green trees that skirted its banks.

But the objects forming this lovely picture are yet far away, and many a weary mile must be ridden, many a tortuous coulee or gulch must be threaded, and many a steep hill climbed ere we shall set foot on the happy hunting ground that now unfolds itself so invitingly before us. So Jack and Huffman take a pull at the ropes to tighten up the loads on our pack mules and we spring into our saddles and ride away at a brisk trot, down the long slope on the western side of the divide.

There are some fine agricultural lands on this slope. The soil is light but rich, the ground just rolling enough to carry off the water readily, and in nearly every one of the many coulees with which it is drained there runs a stream of clear, cold, pure spring water.· By means of these the tablelands could easily be irrigated, if necessary, and there is a .good supply of timber along the small streams for fuel. Bunch or buffalo grass stands thick and heavy here, affording the best of grazing. We crossed Owl creek near its head. Its waters are very clear and cold and it doubtless bears trout, though we didn't stop to investigate the matter.

As we were riding down a hill toward one of the coulees, three mule deer jumped out of the brush, dashed over the next ridge and were out of sight before we could get a shot at them. We put spurs to our animals and galloped to the top of the ridge, but they were nowhere to be seen. We knew, though, that they must have hidden in the next coulee, as they had not had time to go farther without our seeing them when we reached the top of the ridge, so we separated, Jack riding to the head of the coulee, Huffman toward the mouth, and each dismounted to wait for the game to come out. I rode down to the coulee and followed it up to where Jack was without jumping any game ; then we both rode down on opposite sides and when within a short dis-

tance of where Huffman stood the game broke cover and
started over the next ridge, but at the crack of Huffman's
rifle the leader, a magnificent buck, staggered, stumbled,
swayed to and fro, and after a dozen or more jumps, fell with
a bullet through his shoulder. Ping! went Jack's carbine,
and the doe turned completely over with a broken neck.
My old pill-driver woke the echoes among the far-away foothills, and as the smoke cleared away I saw the dust and
stones waltzing around in the air just beyond where the deer
had been, but he was going toward the top of the ridge with
something like the speed of the late comet. In my haste I
had shot over or under him, I couldn't tell which, but the
next shot proved more lucky, for just as he reached the top of
the ridge an explosive bullet caught him high up in the
shoulder, splintering both shoulder blades and breaking his
spine. He was a good-sized spike buck. We formed a
mutual admiration society at once and proceeded to con-
gratulate each other on our good shooting. It certainly was
" deuced clevah," for here lay three deer within fifty yards
of each other, killed with four shots, and all on the jump.

We reached the Little Big Horn at four o'clock in the
afternoon, and went into camp near the mouth of Pass creek.
There had been a large band of Indians encamped at this
point only a few days before, and we were afraid they had
driven the game all out of the valley, but were agreeably disappointed, as the sequel will show. Early the next morning,
September 4th, we moved up the Little Big Horn, and during
the day jumped at least twenty deer, but did not shoot at
them as we had all the venison we wanted. We also jumped
three coyotes during the day, and never let an opportunity
slip to fan them. We killed the third one at two hundred
yards or over. We were all shooting at him, but from the
appearance of the hole in his ribs when we held the *post mortem*

examination, we decided it was made with Huffman's .44 caliber Kennedy. The pestiferous Crows had burned the valley all over, and we had trouble in finding a spot that had escaped the fire, where our poor animals could graze during the night.

We at last found a small patch of grass, however, that had escaped the fire by being surrounded with thickets of green hazel-brush, through which the fire would not run, and here we made camp. Just before reaching this place we saw the first bear sign of the trip. This caused our temperature to rise several degrees, for bear was the very game we most desired to find. We "hadn't lost no bar," but still we were all loaded for bear, and were anxious to find some. We corraled a covey of prairie-chickens just before going into camp, and got seven of them. We made our camp on the top of a ridge, near a small stream that empties into the river. The weather was clear and beautiful, so we thought it unnecessary to put up a tent.

While the other boys were getting dinner I took a stroll up the little creek on which we were camped, and saw plenty of bear sign. They had bent or broken down nearly all the choke-cherry and plum trees, and their tracks were numerous at every place where the ground was soft enough to show them. Plums and choke-cherries are abundant all along the river, and the bears are coming down from the mountains now to harvest them. We feasted on the plums all along the trip. When I got back to camp Huffman was singing;

> " Shall we gather at the river,
>   Yes, we shall gather at the river."

"What shall we gather at the river?" I asked.

" Plums," said he.

"That will just cost you fellows thirty days in the guard-house when we get back to the post, and don't you forget it," said Jack.

After dinner we started out in different directions to look for game. I went up the river about a mile, and then turned into the thickets. Bear signs were plentiful at every turn, and many of them fresh. I felt sure I should find old big Moccasin Joe, as they call him out here, before night. I hunted along down the river till just at sunset, when I saw a large cinnamon-bear on the side of a steep bluff upon the opposite side of the river, turning over rocks and rustling for his chuck. He was about two hundred and fifty yards away, and there was a large swamp between us, so that I could get no closer without going a long way around the swamp. I was afraid to undertake that for I should have to lose sight of him awhile, and fearing he might stray off during that time, I decided to shoot from where I was. I elevated to what I judged the distance to be, knelt down and fired. I didn't see the first ball strike, and so concluded it must have passed over him and gone into some brush beyond. He paid no attention to it. I held a little lower and fired again. This time I saw the ball strike just under him and explode. I think a piece of the bullet must have struck him, or else the explosion knocked a small stone against him, for he jumped and disappeared in the brush close by. I supposed, of course, he was gone, and took out my field-cleaner to wipe my rifle, but before I got through with it he returned to the same place, and went to work again. I now had my elevation exactly, and I knew that I could hit him this time, so I took a careful aim, just behind the shoulder (he stood broadside to me), held about eight inches higher on him than at the last shot, and when old pill-driver spoke to him this time he reared up, turned half around, plunged forward, then fell backward, and rolled with a crashing, thrashing noise that I could hear distinctly where I stood, down the hillside, and disappeared in the thick brush. I slipped another cartridge into my rifle and started after him. I first went to the right of the slough, but encountered a jungle that was well nigh impassable, and returning, circled around it to the left. This was a long, tedious, and difficult route, but by hard work I at last got through one of the thickets, waded the river, and then after another siege of crawling, climbing and cutting my way, during which every minute seemed an hour lest my game should escape, I at last reached the place where old Joe stood when the battle opened. His pathway through the brush, where he rolled down the hill, was strewn with blood. I followed it, hoping to find him dead at the foot of the hill, but unfortunately there was a wide fissure in the rock near the foot, about thirty feet deep, into which he had fallen. I could plainly see the lifeless form of the great monster lying there among the rocks at the bottom of the cavern, but the walls were perpendicular, with scarcely any projections, so that it was impossible to reach him, and I was compelled to return to camp empty handed.

We compared notes around a bright camp fire for an hour, and then turned in. About midnight it clouded up, and a quiet, but steady, heavy fall of rain set in. Huffman and I awoke and surveyed the situation, but we had a large, heavy piece of canvas spread over us, and after discussing the probabilities for a few minutes, concluded we were safe, and went to sleep again. Later in the night we were again awakened by the water running under us, and our blankets were saturated, but it was too dark and damp to get up then, so we laid like a warrior taking his rest, and weathered the storm till daylight, when we all got up, wrung the water out of our blankets, or as much of it as possible, and packed up. The heavens continued to weep, and we had wet groceries for breakfast, mostly. The alkali mud stuck to our feet, as we tramped around, like warm wax, and large quantities of grass, mixing in with it, our feet looked more like bales of hay, than like the pedal extremities of human beings. Our poor mules shivered in the cold rain, and were anxious to get started.

We moved out at eight o'clock, and at three in the afternoon camped among the foothills, within a mile of the mouth of the canyon of the Little Big Horn river, where it comes out of the mountains.

CHAPTER IX.

THE HAPPY HUNTING GROUND.

HUFFMAN KILLS A GRIZZLY — A NIGHT IN WET BLANKETS — A RACE FOR THE AXE — GRAND SPORT — HUNTING THROUGH THE SNOW — EFFECTIVENESS OF THE EXPLOSIVE BULLET.

IT was with feelings of the greatest delight that we built our camp-fire near the head of the Little Big Horn river, for we were well aware that we had now reached the happy hunting ground for which we had been toiling through hot sands, over barren plains and fruitless bad lands for these many days. From this time forward, for at least ten days to come, we were to be in the midst of the haunts of large game, and if we did not succeed in taking a reasonable quantity of it we could only blame our lack of skill in hunting it.

After we had made camp, Huffman and Jack got out some fishing tackle, and took a few magnificent mountain trout from the stream within a few rods of our camp, and we dined off them with a relish begotten by the day's labor and the fresh·mountain breeze that swept down the valley. After dinner Huffman and I took our rifles and sallied forth in search of game — Huffman going up the stream and I down.

I returned to camp shortly after dark, empty handed, but was glad to learn that Huffman, who preceded me, had been more fortunate, having killed a large grizzly bear before he had gone a mile from camp. He had jumped the old planti-grade on the bank of the river. The bear showed fight at the first shot, but some lively music from the Kennedy rifle soon quieted his belligerent propensities, and laid him a corpse at the feet of his foe.

It has rained nearly all day to-day and continues to rain to-night, so that there is no possibility of drying our blankets, as we had intended to do, and we have no alternative — there is no escape from it — we must sleep in wet blankets to-night. It is a gloomy prospect, and no mistake. The cold chills run up and down our backs as we think of it, and whenever any one mentions it, a groan escapes from the other two. The mercury has crawled down (or would crawl down if there were any mercury in this region) to the freezing point, and a violent snow-storm has set in. The wind sucks down through the canyon just back of our camp, and moans through the cottonwoods, driving the snow in blinding clouds through the brush, over the hills, and heaping it on our fire in such quantities that it soon drowned it out.

"Well, what shall we do now?"

"Go to bed, I suppose," said Huffman, drawing a deep sigh, and proceeding, with the aid of a forked limb, to extract his boots, which were as wet as the snow and water in which he had been wading, could make them. I struck a match and looked at my watch. It was nine o'clock.

"Well, Huffman," I said, "we shall only have nine hours to wait until daylight, and then we can get up and make a fire again."

"Nine hours in those wet blankets, this cold, stormy night!" said he, with another sigh. "I wish the man who invented hunting was in Greenland, and had to sleep on an iceberg to-night."

"And I wish we were all in Florida," said Jack.

We had made our camp where a band of Crow Indians had camped a few days before. They had left some of their wiciup poles in position, and we had spread our canvas over them, thus making a very close, comfortable shelter, if not as roomy as we might wish for. Huffman and I crawled

into our wiciup, and Jack into his. Our clothing was all
soaked with water from being in the rain the most of the day,
and tramping through wet brush and grass on our evening
hunt. We kept it all on, removing only our boots and hats.
Our blankets were so wet and heavy that they stuck to us like
a bathing-suit. Our bones ached and our teeth chattered,
and, if we hadn't been so cold we couldn't talk, we might
have made some remarks about the weather that wouldn't
look well in print.

We finally got reconciled to our fate, however, and went
to sleep, if being stupefied from the effects of hard work and
cold water can be called sleep. Along in the night some-
time—I should think about one or two o'clock—Huffman
woke up, shivering and groaning some more. He seemed to
have a relapse of cold. He said he couldn't stand this sort
of luxury any longer, and was going to get up and start a
fire. I told him he couldn't start a fire, that the wood was
all covered with snow and ice; but he said he'd try it, anyway, so he got up and did try it, but it was no go. The cold
air outside was worse than the wet clothing and blankets
within, and he was soon glad to plunge into the shack and
bury himself in them again.

"C-c-c-con-d-d-d-dem such a c-c-c-condemned c-c-c-
country as th-th-this, anyway!" said he, his teeth chattering
like the "music" of a snare drum. "If any man ever
c-c-catches me starting to these d-d m-m-m-mountains
again, I hope he'll p-p-put me in the g-g-guard-house for six
months."

I really felt alarmed for him, for I feared he might have
a conjestive chill, or something as serious, but he finally became more comfortable, and dozed off to sleep again. We
hailed the first dawn of day with a sigh of relief, and as soon
as it was light enough to see to get about, we were all out

pulling on our frozen boots. Usually, every man in camp shuns the axe, but this morning there was a race to see who could get hold of it first, for we all felt that it would thaw us out quicker than anything else; we took turns at chopping, carrying wood and running until we got a fire started, and then piled on dry cottonwood logs and limbs until we soon had a roaring fire, and were standing around it drying and warming ourselves.

We made a pot of coffee so strong that it swelled our ears; baked some bread, broiled some choice venison steaks, and were soon discussing a most wholesome breakfast. As we became comfortable, and even jovial, we enjoyed the scene around us. The snow-storm was premature. The leaves had not yet fallen from the trees. The wind had ceased early in the night, and the snow had piled up light and feather-like upon the leaves until the boughs were bent down by its weight. The mountain sides are covered with a thick growth of pine timber, the tops of the ridges being bare. All these trees were heavily clad in their mantle of spotless white, and the contrasts between green, gray, brown, golden and other colors, furnished by the autumn foliage, and the snow, made a grand picture.

While we were preparing breakfast, a fawn, attracted by the noise, came to the top of the long ridge, on the right of our camp, and gazed curiously down upon us for several seconds. Outlined against the gray sky he made a beautiful picture. I was chopping wood some distance from camp when he first appeared, and called to Huffman and Jack, who were near the fire. They sprang for their guns as soon as they saw him, but by this time his curiosity was satisfied, and he bounded away and disappeared behind the hill before they could get a shot.

Breakfast over, Huffman and I hurried into the timber in

opposite directions to utilize the heavy snow in tracking game. We had not gone half a mile before I heard three shots from his rifle in quick succession, followed by a shout of exultation, which I knew meant that he had drawn a prize. I hurried in the direction whence the sounds came, and soon found

HUFFMAN'S PRIZE.

him leaning complacently on his rifle, gazing admiringly on the prostrate form of a monster bull elk that had fallen a prey to his deadly aim.

After hastily examining his trophy, and, congratulating him upon his skill and good luck, I turned away down the stream, leaving him and Jack, who had also been attracted to the spot by the noise, to take the game into camp. I found deer signs very plentiful in the fresh snow, but didn't follow any particular trail, as I felt confident of finding game as soon by keeping straight ahead as by trailing.

I had walked perhaps two miles, when, as I was passing over a low ridge, three deer jumped from their beds in some hazel brush at my right and started across an open swale toward the heavy timber, which was about two hundred yards away. The deer were about a hundred yards from me when I first saw them. I paid my compliments to an old buck first, then to a yearling buck, and as these two went to grass in short order, the third, a handsome doe, stopped broadside to me to wait for her companions. I dropped on my knee to make sure of her, but in the excitement of the moment forgot to make any allowance for the fact that she was seventy or eighty yards farther away than the others when I shot at them, and, firing without any elevation, had the gloomy satisfaction of seeing the snow fly just beyond her in a position that told me at once my ball had dropped below her. In a second more she was out of sight in the thick brush.

I then went to where the old buck was when I first fired and saw hair scattered over the snow in every direction, some of it ten feet away. I glanced eagerly along his trail, and where he lit on the first jump after the ball struck him I saw blood. At the second jump a perfect shower of blood had been blown from his nostrils, crimsoning the snow on both sides of his trail, while a stream had also spurted from the wound.

"That settles it," thought I. "Through the lungs and he can't go far."

I moved eagerly forward, but before I had gone a dozen steps I fairly stumbled over his lifeless body, where it lay all doubled up in a clump of thick bushes. I then retraced

and counted his tracks.   He had made just four jumps from
where the ball struck him, and had fallen stone dead, for the
snow where he lay showed that he had not moved a foot after
he fell.

So much for the effectiveness of the explosive bullet.   I
examined the wound and found that the ball had entered his
flank just behind the last rib (he was running quartering from
me) had exploded on entering the body, blown a large hole
through the skin a few inches ahead of where it entered, and
passing on diagonally through his chest, had lodged near the
point of the opposite shoulder.   With this same shot from a
solid bullet, he would have run anywhere from three hundred
yards to a mile, but with this explosive missile his intestines,
lungs, liver, and other internal improvements were so mutilated, that if he had been a buffalo or a grizzly he could not
have survived the shock much longer than he did.   And this
was done with a .40 caliber rifle, which brother Van Dyke
protests is no account for anything larger than a jack rabbit
or a woodchuck.

I next took up the trail of the young buck, and when I
reached the place where he was when I shot, was rewarded by
finding plenty of hair and two or three small pieces of flesh
on the snow.   Ten feet further on, the crimson fluid had
gushed from the wound in a stream that showed unmistakably
that that animal's career was soon to be drawn to a close also.
But I had not given him so dead a shot as the other one, and
he led me a most tedious chase through the thick underbrush
before I succeeded in overtaking him.   When I did reach
him, I found that I had also hit him in the flank low down,
and, as he was running broadside to me, the ball passed
through him at right angles, coming out on the opposite side.
It had exploded when it struck, however, and torn a hole
through him that you could easily have passed an ordinary

teacup through. So large was the opening, in fact, that a fold of one of the larger entrails dropped through on the side where the ball passed out, and dragged in the snow until the deer fell, when I came up and dispatched him. And yet nothing short of a .65 caliber cannon, with an expansive bullet, is fit to shoot deer with! Oh, no, of course not!

I went to camp, when Jack put an *apparejo* on one of the mules, and we returned and brought both of the deer in. Later in the day we dragged the elk and bear both in by means of a rope made fast to the pommel of a saddle, and when arrayed before our wiciups they presented an array that caused our hearts to swell with pride.

We then skinned the game, took the choicest cuts of the meat, and after partaking of a hearty dinner, broke camp and began the ascent of the mountain.

The clouds had now entirely disappeared, and the sun shone forth from a clear sky, giving a most brilliant effect to the scene before us, but the bright glare soon became painful to our eyes.

CHAPTER X.

THROUGH THE CANYON OF THE LITTLE BIG HORN.

AN ADVENTURE WITH NIG — THE PHOTOGRAPHIC OUTFIT IN PERIL —
HUFFMAN FRANTIC — NIG LANDS THE CARGO SAFELY — HUFFMAN
GRUMBLES, I PHILOSOPHIZE — A HERD OF MULE DEER — GROWTHS
OF PINE TIMBER — FINE SPORT WITH A MOUNTAIN BUFFALO — THE
IDEAL HUNTER'S CAMP.

IN our windings through the canyon of the Little Big
Horn, we were obliged to cross the stream several times
during the afternoon. It is a veritable torrent here, boiling
and foaming over its rough bed of boulders and broken
ledges of red sandstones. Its pure liquid is as clear as crystal
and as cold as ice. You would never recognize it as the
same dull, leaden-hued stream along whose banks we have
been wending our weary way for several days past.

And this recalls to my mind an incident of the trip that
must not be overlooked. Soon after leaving the forks of the
stream, we reached a point where it became necessary to cross
it in order to avoid a long detour around a bend. We therefore selected the most favorable point we could find—a place
where the banks were low and the water not more than two
feet deep—and started in with Huffman in the lead. I
followed him with Blinkie, my white pony, and the pack
mules followed me, Jack remaining for the time in the rear
to drive them across. Chicken, one of the pack mules,
crossed and climbed the bank all right, when Nig, a large
black mule, who was always disposed to be willful and contrary, and who was never willing to follow his file leader
when he saw an opportunity of making an annoying

THE RAGE OF HUFFMAN AND THE CALMNESS OF NIG.

CHICAGO ENG. CO.

"break," walked down the first bank into the water, then turned and waded slowly and deliberately down the stream toward a deep hole that lay a few yards below the crossing. His load consisted principally of Huffman's photographic outfit, camera, dry plates, dark tent, etc. ; and when Huffman saw that they were placed in jeopardy—that the dry plates were in imminent danger of being transformed into wet plates by a process that would render them utterly worthless to him—that the camera was liable to be soaked with water and ruined—he became frantic.

He dismounted and rushed madly down the bank of the stream, yelling, throwing clubs, trying in every possible way to head Nig off; but the ugly brute would not head worth a cent. He looked mildly at the woe-begone artist out of his left eye, stopped and drank a few swallows of water, took a step or two, and looked again, first at Huffman and then at Jack, who was on the opposite side of the river, shouting, and throwing clubs, rocks and other *débris* at the long-eared vandal.

"Jack !" shouted the artist, "drive that cantankerous brute out of that deep water, quick, or he'll drown my photograph gallery ! Jump in and catch him—quick ! Blank blank that blanked long-eared son-of-a-gun to blankety blank ! "

"Jump in yourself," said Jack, "I don't want to get my feet wet."

And still the mule moved slowly down the stream, every step taking him into deeper water, bringing his precious load, valued at three hundred dollars, nearer and nearer to the destroying element, while an artist to the mountains bound cries, "Conley, do not tarry and I'll give thee a silver dollar to drive that doggoned mule o'er the ferry."

"Now, who be ye would cross Big Horn, this deep and muddy water?"

"Oh, I'm the artist from Miles City, and this my precious plunder. And fast upon these saddle mules three days we've rode together, and should he wet them in the creek they wouldn't be worth a feather."

Outspoke the hardy Emerald wight, "I'll go, my chief, I'm ready. It is not for your dollar bright, but for some pretty pictures; and by my word, that cussed mule in the water shall not tarry,—so though the waves are raging white, I'll drive him over the ferry or break his blanked neck! G'lang, Nig, git out of there, you son-of-a-gun!" But still, as wilder blew the wind, and as the artist grew madder, adown the stream walked that pesky mule where the water still was deeper.

"Oh, haste thee, haste!" the artist cries. "Though tempests round us gather, I'll meet the raging of the water, but if I lose that outfit I'll walk home to-night."

The mule has left a sultry land, a cool bath is before him, when oh! too strong for human hands, he don't care how many clubs come o'er him. And still they howled amidst the roar of waters fast prevailing, the artist reached that fatal shore, his wrath was changed to wailing. For sore dismayed through storm and shade his mule he did discover, one lovely hand he stretched for the bridle but, oh, he couldn't reach it.

"Come back, come back," he cried in grief across this muddy river, "and I'll forgive the wayward cuss, my donkey, oh, my donkey." 'Twas vain; the loud waves lashed his sides, return or aid suggesting, the waters wild kind o' frightened him, and he turned and came out on the bank o. k.

We took his load off, opened it, and found that though the lower corners of both boxes were wet, the moisture had not reached their contents. We congratulated Huffman on the fact that his dry goods were still dry—that his stock had not been watered, so to speak—and went on our way rejoicing.

During the afternoon of September 6th we toiled up through canyons and over divides and ridges, still climbing higher and higher, until the atmosphere became so rare that neither we nor our animals could walk more than a few rods at a time without stopping to rest. We walked and led our saddle animals nearly all the afternoon, owing to this fact and the extremely difficult nature of the trails over which we were passing. At about four o'clock we reached an open park on the top of one of the highest ridges in that part of the range, and finding there a good, heavy growth of grass which, fortunately, had not been burned, we decided to make our camp there. There was no water near, but the snow, which covered the ground to a depth of six inches, furnished a very good substitute.

We found an abundance of dry pine-knots and whole trunks of fallen pine-trees on the rocks near us, and in a few minutes had a roaring fire, and our wet blankets hanging all around it. We didn't care to take a cold bath in them that night, and so watched and turned them attentively all the evening, until they were thoroughly dry. Our animals ate snow to quench their thirst, and then pawed the snow away so that they could get at the grass. They had all seen plenty of this kind of life in years past, and so lost no time in looking for better fare, but went vigorously to work, and before dark their protruding sides showed that they were in tall clover.

We melted snow to do our cooking with, and for water to drink. Our position gave us a fine view of the surrounding country. We could trace the route over which we had traveled for several days past through the warm, green valley of the Little Big Horn, across the broad divide and far down the now beautiful valley of the Rosebud; over all of which the low, descending sun threw its golden light, forming a most fascinating picture, and one in strong contrast to the bleak, snow-covered hills around us.   Away to the north stretched the valley of the Big Horn, and with the aid of a powerful glass we could easily see the tents and buildings at Fort Custer, nearly sixty miles away.

To the south our vision followed the eastern base of the range, across the headwaters of Tongue and Powder rivers to Fort McKinney, and away toward the Union Pacific railroad.

"What," said I, "will the officers at Fort Custer think if they see our camp-fire to-night? They will think it a party of Crow Indians, will they not?"

"No," said Huffman, "they know that no Crow is fool enough to be caught in such a country as this over night. They'll know it's some crazy white men, and don't you forget it. Ah, what a fool a man will make of himself for the sake of a little fun. The idea of tramping over these dry, hot plains, climbing these mountains, wading snow, eating snow, sleeping in snow, and half freezing to death for the sake of killing a few deer and bears. It's too high for me."

"Well," I said, "the game is worth to me all it costs. If we could stand in our front door and kill these animals in our yard, we would think it no sport at all, but the . harder you have to work for your game the more you appreciate it when you get it. And if we found no game, the novelty of our mode of travel, the grand scenery, the health-giving exercise, the invigorating atmosphere would well repay me for all the labor and hardships we endure."

> "These scenes in glowing colors dressed,
> Mirror the life within my breast,
>   Its world of hopes;
> The whispering woods and fragrant breeze,
> That stir the grass in verdant seas,
>   On billowy slopes,

" And glistening crag in sunlit sky,
   'Mid snowy clouds piled mountain high,
      Are joys to me;
   My pathway o'er the prairie wide,
   Or here on grander mountain's side
      To choose all free."

As the shades of the evening deepened, we gathered large quantities of pine-boughs, spread them upon the snow, laid our blankets thereon, turned in and spread the heavy canvas over us. Although the temperature went far below the freezing point during the night, we slept comfortably and soundly. The next day we continued the ascent of the mountain, after Huffman had made some fine views of scenery in the canyons near our camp. During the forenoon we saw plenty of deer sign and some elk sign. We killed during the morning several mountain grouse (*Tetrao obscurus*), the first we had seen on the trip. In the afternoon as we were crossing a series of beautiful parks—that is, small open prairies in the pine forest, we jumped a herd of six mule deer. Jack and Huffman were riding in front at the time, and I in the rear, so that they got all the shooting. Huffman got a doe and a large fawn, and Jack a fine large buck.

We took their entrails out and loaded them on the pack mules. We bore to the southward to some coulees, in hopes of finding water, but were disappointed, and had to make another snow camp for that night. After dinner I went west about a mile and saw numerous signs of buffaloes and elk, though I did not succeed in getting a shot, but felt great hopes that we should in the morning.

We made an early start on the morning of the 8th, moving in a northwesterly direction, and at about a mile from camp passed a boundary post showing the territorial boundary line between Wyoming and Montana, and showing us that we had spent the night in Wyoming. We now, however, passed back into Montana again. The mountains are thickly covered along the eastern side with pine timber, mostly small, from three to twelve inches in diameter, and six to fifty feet high. This timber would be useful for fence posts, railroad ties, telegraph poles, etc., if it could be gotten out, but will probably not be used for many years to come on account of the great labor and expense that would have to be incurred in getting it out. There are no streams large enough to raft it on, and hauling by teams down through the mountains would be slow and tedious, not to say hazardous. To build a railroad to this locality would cost so much that it will be a long time before capitalists will be found to furnish the funds for such an undertaking. In some localities the timber runs larger than that I have described. We have seen a few trees that would cut several hundred feet of clear lumber each, but they are not numerous at this high altitude. The numerous small parks or meadows, which are covered with a superior quality of grass and surrounded by this thick growth of timber, make this a favorite resort for large game in the winter season. The only drawback to its being a fine grazing country for cattle is the heavy snow-falls in winter at this altitude.

Near the top of the range we found a fresh track of a mountain buffalo. We dismounted, picketed our animals, and followed his trail. When we found that we were very near him and saw by his track that he was feeding, we deployed, Jack going to the left of the trail, I to the right, and leaving Huffman to follow on the trail. I made a bee line for a high crag a quarter of a mile ahead, and had no sooner reached the top of it than I saw him quietly grazing and browsing on some weeds among the rocks, about a hundred and fifty yards to my left. I dropped on one knee, drew a bead on him and pulled. I distinctly heard the dull "whack" of the ball as it struck him, and saw his tail switch quickly over his back as if he were "shooing" a fly away. He turned and plunged madly over the rocks in the opposite direction, when the sharp "ping" of Jack's carbine from

AFTER THE RACE.

that quarter, and the "crack," "crack," of Huffman's rifle from below, all told that he was on very hot ground. He turned and made a few lunges toward me again, but his leaden load was already too heavy for him to carry, and he fell and expired within twenty feet of where he stood when I gave him the first round. He was a large, finely-formed, noble-looking animal. His fur is finer, darker and curls more than that of the plains buffalo, and he usually ranges alone or in pairs, while his cousin of the prairies is strictly gregarious

From the top of the peak on the left of and near where our noble bison fell we enjoyed one of the grandest scenes in the Western country. Away across to the south and west we see the snow-capped peaks of the Wind River mountains already mentioned, while to the west rise the great domes, walls and peaks of the Rocky range. Blue and smoky though they seem, still we can plainly see the snow, and through the glass can distinguish the timber from the bare rocky earth above the timber line. We can locate several of the peaks in and surrounding the national park, a hundred and thirty miles away. To the north and west loom up the Snow mountains, and still further north the Crazy mountains — all belonging to the Rocky system. Intermediate between us and them flow, besides the streams already mentioned, the different branches of Pryor's river, Clark's fork, Rocky fork, and others, all of which empty into the Yellowstone, whose course we can trace far up toward its source and away down toward its mouth.

We saw signs of mountain sheep during the day, but none of the "critters" themselves. We moved northward along the top of the range, and in the afternoon crossed down on to the western slope, where we found a large spring and camped. To our surprise our mules and pony were not thirsty at all, notwithstanding they had lived two days and nights without water, having eaten snow only as a means of quenching thirst. They drank but little here, and seemed to care very little whether they drank any or not. But for ourselves we were delighted to get a drink of straight spring water again after our long dependence on its best substitute.

We made an ideal " hunter's camp" that night.   Built a large fire of pine knots in the midst of a dense pine thicket, and were as comfortable as we could wish to be under the circumstances.   We slept better on our bed of pine boughs than we could have slept on a feather bed or hair mattress at home, without the toil, the mountain air, and the sport of that day.   Another heavy fall of snow during the night, which continued through a greater portion of the day.   After breakfast we talked of a programme for the day, but the boys said they didn't care to go out while it stormed so hard.   I was loth to lose any time, however, and so started about six o'clock to see what I could find.

CHAPTER XI.

A GRAND DAY'S SPORT.

THE first signs of sport I saw as I journeyed forth alone were those of half a dozen mule deer, commonly (but erroneously) called on the frontier, black-tail deer. The tracks showed that the deer had been ranging about leisurely feeding. I selected the track of the largest buck, and, following it perhaps half a mile, jumped him, but in thick brush so that I failed to get a shot. He bounded away through the thicket and broke cover at a distance of half a mile from me. As he passed over an open ridge I saw that he was a remarkably large, fine buck, and that his capture would well repay a long and arduous chase. I had often heard it asserted that a hunter who possessed sufficient power of endurance, enthusiasm and "sand" could run a deer down; that the largest and strongest of the species would not run more than twenty to thirty miles until he would become so exhausted that he would lag, lie down, and thus give the hunter an easy opportunity to approach and kill him.

I stopped and contemplated the chances of such an undertaking. A stern chase is always a long chase, and when the slow and steady stride of a man is matched against the fleet-footed bound of the wild and wary stag it must indeed be doubly so. But think of those noble antlers added to my collection of trophies and specimens at home.

How proudly would I hang my hat upon them in the hall as I returned at night from my day's work at the office. And how serenely could I rest upon that glossy coat as it formed a covering for my favorite easy-chair. I am hooked up for a long tramp. It is early in the morning, and I have eaten such a breakfast as only a man can eat who has been campaigning in these mountains, and who sits down in the early morn to a plate smoking with the fruits of his own rifle. The weather is cold, the air clear, bracing and exhilarating, and I decide here and now to settle the question to my own satisfaction, as to whether I at least can run down and kill a deer in a fair chase.

I took up the trail and followed it across the ridge, through sage-brush, for a mile or more to where it entered a body of pine timber. Up to this point the deer had kept up his long jumps of about fifteen feet each, but as soon as he entered the timber he slackened his pace to a walk, and a few hundred yards further on stopped and turned to look back. I made no effort to steal up and get a shot but walked briskly on, only taking note of the trail sufficiently to follow it. As soon as he obtained sight of me, or heard me approaching he again bounded away, and, now appearing to realize the fact that he was pursued, he plunged swiftly on, as if bound to distance his pursuer and make good his escape at a single effort.

He took a southerly direction, keeping just below and on the west side of the crest of the range, and for two or three miles I followed the trail before I saw any evidence of his slackening speed. But at last the jumps began to grow shorter, gradually dropping into a trot and finally into a walk. This was kept up for another mile, when I came to where he had again stopped to take breath. From this point a repetition of the long jumps showed that he had again taken alarm at the sound of my coming and skipped out.

Now more thoroughly alarmed than ever, and convinced that desperate measures were necessary in order to elude me, he changed his course to the westward and started for a great canyon that opened near the top of the range. He plunged wildly forward through sage-brush, greasewood, scrub-pine thickets, heavy pine forests—through windfalls and over rocky barrens until he reached the verge of the north wall of the canyon, where he paused to see if I were coming before taking the plunge. His inquiry was soon answered, for, hearing me approaching, he wheeled and leaped down the almost perpendicular wall at such a reckless rate of speed that he lost his footing at the very start and rolled and tumbled fifty feet through the brush before he could recover.

When I reached the spot from whence my quarry had taken this fearful leap I paused and debated in my mind whether I should risk my life by following him into this awful abyss. The wall was so nearly perpendicular that I could and did reach out and break off a twig from the top of a pine-tree forty feet high, and which stood that distance below me on the side of the wall. I looked into the bottom of the canyon and my brain reeled as I thought of the danger and the folly of trying to descend into it. It was 2,000 feet deep if it was a foot, and large trees that stood at the base of either wall looked from where I stood like mere saplings. Rocks that I knew would weigh many tons looked like boulders such as we often see built into fences or stone walls. The rapid mountain stream that plunged through the canyon looked to be a mere rill.

But why parley? My game has gone down this wall, and while I stand here querying whether it is possible to follow

him or not, and at the same time almost lost in admiration of
the grand panorama spread out before me, he is rapidly
speeding away from me.   Of course it is possible to follow
him.   A man can go anywhere that a deer can if he (the man)
only have "sand" enough.   And, awakened by this reflection, I grasped my rifle tightly in my right hand, made a
spring, and next touched the earth twenty feet below where I
jumped from.   By catching firm hold of a sapling I was
enabled to maintain my footing and steady myself for the
next bound.   It was not necessary to pay close attention to
the trail of the deer, for between falling, sliding, plowing
through the snow, and rolling down detached rocks, he left a
trail that might almost have been mistaken for that of a small
avalanche.

He soon tired of this perpendicular flight, however, and
began to tack like a vessel sailing against the wind.   This
enabled me to gain rapidly upon him, for by holding on to
trees and bushes, a faculty he did not possess, I could continue my descent in a straight course.   Several times we
encountered perpendicular ledges of rock cropping out of
the main wall and towering to a height of fifty, seventy, and
even a hundred feet.   In passing some of these it was necessary to make long detours.   Then there were chasms and
fissures from five to twenty feet wide.   Some of these I could
jump across, but was compelled to round many of them.

Still I kept on and on, until at last the frightful descent,
with all its dangers, toils and vicissitudes, was accomplished,
and I stood upon the bank of the clear, cold mountain torrent
that flowed with a wild, roaring, echoing music through the
canyon.

Into this the buck had plunged, and had evidently waded
down it.   This was another trick by which he hoped to evade
me, for here I could not trail him.   I followed down the

right bank perhaps 200 yards, watching both banks closely, when I saw his trail emerge and lead out on the opposite side. I waded the stream, whose icy waters almost paralyzed my limbs, took up the trail which wound through the brush, first up and then down the stream, until, finding that I was still following, he started directly up the opposite wall of the canyon.

But here he began to show unmistakable signs of weakening. In making this ascent he would stop every few rods, and would frequently lie down. He made frequent doubles on his trail, by which he evidently hoped to elude me; but, though these clever ruses often succeed with a hound, who runs entirely by scent, they did not trouble me in the least, as I could readily see in every case where he had broken off on the return; so that I could take up the trail here and save all the distance he had traveled on the double. This gave me a decided advantage, for it enabled me to press him all the harder.

The wall which we were now ascending was as steep, rugged and difficult as the one which we had just descended, and though climbing up was much harder work for me than jumping and sliding down, I consoled myself with the reflection that it was also much harder for my antlered fugitive. An hour of this toil landed me again on top of the south wall. Here was a wide plateau partly covered with pine timber, the remainder with sage brush. Over this the frightened and now weary stag circled, doubled, crossed and recrossed, trying, but still in vain, to mislead me. He moves now almost altogether in a walk. Occasionally, when I approach closely, he takes fresh alarm and makes a few spasmodic bounds, but he is too far exhausted to continue them, and soon relapses again into a slow, dragging walk, keeping just far enough ahead of me all the time to be out of sight.

7

At last, finding that he can't shake me off his trail by these tactics, he strikes straight south again. I follow, and after a walk of a mile I find that his trail leads me to the brink of another canyon as deep, bold and rugged as the one I have just crossed. "Great heavens!" thought I, "can it be possible he is going into this?" "Yes, my brave hunter," he seemed to say, as he paused on top of the wall and looked back to see if I were coming. "I must now bid you good day. I have been playing with you thus far; but now I have other business to attend to and must leave you. Besides, I am getting tired and must go and lie down awhile. I have given you one dose of canyon and I don't think you will want another. So here goes for the bottom of this one. Good-by, my lad." And his trail showed that he had surely enough taken that awful plunge again. I hesitated but a moment as to whether I should follow, and then my mind was made up. "Not much, my fine buck," said I. "I haven't taken this tramp for my health. I'm after that handsome coat of yours, and I'll have it if I have to camp on your trail to-night and renew the chase to-morrow.

So saying I let go, and away I went again at break-neck speed, down, down, down, over rocks, chasms, fallen trees, and through thick brush, until the foot of the wall was at last reached. Here the trail wound and twisted again. Here were new doubles and crosses. Here were frequent "standing tracks" where he had stopped to rest, warm beds in the snow every few rods where he had lain down, all showing unmistakably that the quarry was far exhausted. In following the track across a level strip of bottom in the canyon I came upon the track of a large she bear and two cubs. But it was not fresh, so I did not leave the trail I was on to follow it, but I promised the buck then and there that if he would in his meanderings lead me upon this new game I would give him his liberty and take their scalps instead. But he heeded not my promise and kept on down the canyon. Here a new danger presented itself to my mind. The snow even here in the canyon was much lighter than on the mountains, and so light in places that it was difficult to follow the trail, and I knew that a short distance down the canyon it opened out into the Big Horn Valley, which was an open prairie and entirely below the snow-line.

And the wily buck seemed to understand this fact as well as I, for without further ado he headed straight down the canyon. I followed briskly, hoping to get within sight of him and obtain a shot before he should get beyond the snow. As I emerged from the timber and looked out upon the dry, hard ground of the prairie in the valley, my heart sank within me, for I thought after all my toil, my tramping, climbing, wading and crawling, I was outwitted and left. But placing my field-glass to my eyes and scanning the ground closely I saw a gray bunch of something with a white spot at one end of it, closely ensconced under a cluster of greasewood. I examined it closely and carefully, and finally satisfied myself that it was my buck. By changing my position slightly I could plainly distinguish his antlers. His head lay flat upon the ground, as if dead, and his tongue protruded to almost its full length. Knowing that I could not track him on the dry, hard prairie he had gone far enough from the snow to be, as he thought, safe, and, concealing himself under this clump of bushes, doubtless considered himself beyond all possibility of discovery. Indeed, I probably never should have found him without the aid of a field-glass.

He was about eight hundred yards from where I stood, but I knew that I could get an easy shot at him as he was off his guard, so I stepped down the side of the hill until I got a low ridge between him and myself, when I crept cautiously to the crest of it, which brought me within about a hundred and fifty yards of him. Here I leveled my rifle at him and turned her loose. At the report he sprang into the air, made two or three convulsive bounds, and fell dead.

In a moment I was at his side and my knife was hissing through his hide. I threw him out of it in short order, cut a favorite roast from his loin, and started for camp. At the creek which flows through this canyon I stopped and took a drink in honor of the event from the cold crystal fluid that comes fresh from the snow. I looked at my watch, and found that it had been seven and a half hours from the time I struck the trail of the deer in the morning until I killed it. As I had made a good three-mile gate all the time, I must have ran him something over twenty miles.

As I passed up the canyon on my return to camp I again came upon the trail of the bear and her two cubs, and here it was fresh. They had been feeding on the choke-cherries that grow here in abundance, and had passed over this spot not twenty minutes before me. It was now the middle of the afternoon and I should have to hurry to reach camp before dark, but here was a temptation I could not resist. I had rather camp in the canyon alone to-night than miss this opportunity of corralling three bears in a bunch; so I took up their trail and followed it. In a few minutes I heard the cubs calling to their mother making a noise something like the squealing of a pig. I could also hear the mother grunt and growl at them in reply. They were not over a hundred yards from me, but the brush was so thick in this locality that I could not see a tenth of that distance in any direction.

I dropped the trail and started for the noise, which the cubs kept up nearly all the time. I crawled through thickets on my hands and knees and climbed over great masses of broken and disordered rocks, until I found myself within thirty feet of the monster old plantigrade and her two young hopefuls. She was a large savage-looking grizzly, and her cubs were about half-grown. I felt perfectly secure, however, for I was loaded for bear, even to the size and number of the party I was looking at. I have one cartridge in the chamber of the rifle and three more in my left hand ready for immediate use, should the first fail to bring her down. As a precautionary measure, however, I have taken a strap from my pocket, tied one end around the breech of my rifle and the other to my belt, so that if compelled to tree, my gun will go up with me.

The old she-bear, when I came in sight, at once raised on her haunches to take a look at me. As she did so I took a dead aim at her breast and fired. At the report she reeled, staggered and fell; but recovered strength enough to regain her feet and started toward me. By this time I had another cartridge in my gun, and a quick aim, a steady hand and a pull just at the right instant planted a ball just above her left eye, at which she dropped dead almost without a struggle. The ball exploded when it struck and carried away a piece of the skull from just above the ear nearly as large as my hand, scattering her brains in every direction. The first ball, I found on examination, had passed through her heart, tearing it into a shapeless mass, but so great an amount of vitality and brute force do .these animals possess that they will withstand the effect of such a shot as even this several minutes before death will ensue.

To dispatch the two cubs was but the work of as many seconds—one shot to each being sufficient to lay them out. The only trophies I could save from these were the claws of the old one, as it was getting so late that I could not take time to skin them, nor could I carry the skins home if I did.

When I reached the top of the canyon wall the sun was

low in the west. I had at least fifteen miles to walk yet to reach camp, but a brisk walk, and for a portion of the way a dog-trot, landed me there at nine o'clock, tired, wet and hungry enough to eat four men's rations.

CHAPTER XII.

A BUSY DAY.

SCORING A MISS — HUFFMAN PHOTOGRAPHS A SCENE — SHAKSPEARE IN THE MOUNTAINS — A GRIZZLY "RUSTLING FOR CHUCK" — A RACE FOR LIFE — BRUIN FALLS — A SEVERE ATTACK OF PUNNING — BUTTER SIDE DOWN — A HERD OF ELK — MORE SPORT.

HUFFMAN had been out during the afternoon and made a few exposures on some fine scenery. We experienced another cold night. While eating our breakfast next morning, ice formed on water we had brought from the spring but a few minutes before. We moved at nine o'clock A.M., keeping northward along the west slope of the mountain. At three P.M. we made camp near some large springs and in the edge of a group of pines. On the little park in front of our camp the grass was thick and furnished capital grazing for the animals.

Just as we halted for camp, five mule deer, three bucks and two does, jumped from the grass about two hundred yards from us, and started up a hill toward the timber. We built a smudge after them, tore the ground up all around them, and finally knocked one down.

After dinner we went to some springs near us to watch for elk, as signs were very plentiful there, showing that they had been coming in there to water and feed every night. We hoped they might show up this evening before dark, but they did not. The next morning, while packing up two more deer, a buck and doe came into the meadow within a few rods of our camp. Jack caught up his carbine and knocked one of them down. In the afternoon, as we were passing

through a heavy body of timber, we sighted our first elk—a
bull and cow. They were about a hundred yards ahead of
us, and saw us about the same time we saw them. Jack slid
off his mule and opened on them bringing the bull down
with his second shot, while on the run. At this the cow
circled around us so as to give us each a shot. I scored a
miss, but Huffman, who was in the rear, hit her in the flank
with his first shot, missed with his second and third, and
finally brought her down with a broken shoulder on the
fourth round.

Later in the day, as we were passing another of the small
parks, I saw an object under the low hanging branches of a
small pine tree that looked like a deer—a buck with large
antlers standing facing us. I pointed it out to the other boys
and asked them if it were not a deer, but they thought not—
thought it was only a log with dead limbs on it. The ground
was bare of snow there, and the dense shade caused by the
green foliage of the pine tree rendered the figure very indis-
tinct, still it looked so much like game that I told them I
would try it one any way. As I turned the old pill-driver
loose, the deer—for such it proved to be—made one leap into
the air and was out of sight in the brush. Then we saw five
or six others leap across an opening about ten feet wide,
between two clumps of scrub pine. As they went we fanned
them, and when the circus was over we went down there.
One handsome buck lay dead within twenty feet of where the
performance took place, with a hole in his shoulder where a
bullet had entered, and one among the short ribs on the
opposite side where it had passed out.

Huffman unpacked " Nig " and exposed a plate on this
fellow, after placing a large elk skull and antlers that lay near
the spot in the rear of the " subject " to fill in the back-
ground.

Soon after leaving this point we passed out of the timber entirely onto a high, open plateau—a broad stretch of prairie tableland. Over this we were slowly wending our way, when we saw at a distance, about a mile and a half ahead of us, a large dark object moving slowly about, evidently feeding. I took out my field glass to try and determine what the strange apparition was, that here upon this blasted heath stopped our way with such peculiar motions. Huffman said it was a buffalo. Jack said:

"No, it's a horse with a saddle on. There must be a camp not far off."

By this time I had adjusted the glass and taken an observation.

"It's a bear," said I, "and a big one, too."

"Well," said Huffman, "If that's a bear it's the biggest one in the mountains."

I passed him the glass. He looked, still doubted my assertion; but we resolved to settle the question of its identity in short meter, and as we put spurs to our animals, Huffman shouted in tragic tones:

> "Angels and ministers of grace defend us!
> Be thou a spirit of health, or goblin damn'd,
> Bring with thee airs from heaven, or blasts from hell,
> Be thy intents wicked or charitable;
> Thou com'st in such a questionable shape,
> That I will speak to thee,
> With this old paralyzer of mine."

As our mules tore up the sod and filled the air in our rear with pulverized grass and mud, the distance between us and the mysterious apparition rapidly diminished, and we soon saw plainly enough with the naked eye, that it was a large grizzly engaged in turning over rocks and clawing up the ground in search of worms; or as the Western slang expresses it—"rustling for his chuck." We now halted and laid our

plan of attack, which was, that Huffman and Jack should go
to the right of him to keep him from getting into a canyon
on that side if we failed to bring him down, and I to the left
in order to cut off his retreat should he attempt to reach a
canyon that lay on the left of him, or a body of timber near
by.

We rode rapidly, taking care to keep on the lower ground
and out of his sight, as much as possible.   When I got within
about a hundred and fifty yards of him, I dismounted, knelt,
and turned "old reliable" loose on him.   As her voice rang
out over the mountains and echoed through the canyons, he
reared up, looked quickly round him, saw us, took in the
whole situation in a second, and then started for the timber
at a rate of speed that astonished us all.   I never would have
believed that a bear could run as that bear ran if I had been
told about it.   But he seemed to realize that he had been
caught in a hard shower and was a long ways from shelter,
that he was largely in the minority and would stand a poor
show in a fight, that discretion would in his case prove the .
better part of valor, and that by making the best use of the
little time that was left him for this world, he might possibly
reach the timber to the south, and be permitted to die alone
and in peace.   I think that if Goldsmith Maid, Bonesetter,
Maud S., Iroquois, Dexter, Foxhall and the whole lot of those
fast horses had been there and seen that bear run, they would
have kicked their hind shoes off and quit the turf in disgust.
I slipped a second cartridge into my rifle, took a running shot
at the old monster, but forgot that I was shooting against the
speed of a comet, and my ball struck about ten feet behind
him.   I then mounted old Blinkie, gave him the steel, and
started for a race with Bruin.   It was nip and tuck for a short
distance, but the grizzly's strength soon failed him, and when
he saw that he could not escape, he turned and came for me.

The pony didn't like this first-rate, but still didn't make as big a fool of himself as most horses would under the circumstances. I dismounted, and was just ready to pull on the bear again, when he stopped and sank to the ground.

I waited for reinforcements before going up to him, and when Jack and Huffman came up I advanced very cautiously,

THE DEAD GRIZZLY.

keeping the enemy covered with my rifle lest he might be only "possuming" and would charge me when I got too close to retreat. But not so. I found him stone dead, shot through and through, just behind the shoulders.

We found on examination that my bullet had exploded as soon as it passed through the skin, had riddled the lungs until

they were scarcely recognizable, and passed out, breaking two
ribs on the side where it went in and three where it came
out.   He did not run more than a hundred yards, and this
was the only shot that hit him.   A forty caliber that will
break a grizzly up like that is slick enough for me ; brother
Van Dyke's opinion to the contrary, notwithstanding.

We made camp in the edge of the timber near by, and
after dinner Huffman made several good views of the critter.
Then we skinned him, and now when I step out of bed these
cold winter mornings, instead of landing with my bare feet
on the bare floor as other newspaper men have to do, I step
proudly on the soft warm skin of that bear.   In other words,
the bear skin keeps my bare feet off the bare floor.   It is
barely possible that some of my readers may see this threadbare pun.   If I thought they would bear more of this sort of
stuff, I would prolong the discussion, but I forbear.

The old fellow was very fat.   I took a large quantity of
the fat and fried it out in our frying pan by the camp-fire
that night.   I brought home a canteen full of it, and it fits
my rifle first-rate.

The snow had all disappeared from this plateau, and we
had difficulty in finding enough in the timber for the stock
and for cooking purposes that night — there being no water
in the vicinity.   We spent the next day in winding among
the canyons of this locality, trying to find a trail by which
we could get out and down into the Big Horn valley, but no
sooner did we cross one of these terrible chasms, each of
which was from a thousand to three thousand feet deep, than
we found our way impeded by another.

We had crossed one of them and was toiling up the opposite wall of it, picking our way over rocks and among crags,
where you would not suppose, to look at it, that a dog could
go in safety, when we met with what might have proved a

a serious accident. One of our pack mules — a little sorrel, called Scotty — was blind in his left eye. At one point, a ledge of rock projected over the narrow trail from the right

BUTTER SIDE DOWN.

hand side to such a distance as to leave barely room for the pack mules to pass without their packs catching on the shelving point. Scotty saw this obstruction with his good eye, but could not see the danger that beset him on his blind side, and as he approached the crag he naturally shied off to dodge it, just as a book agent shies away from a cross dog that is chained up in the front yard. He swerved a little too far from the path of duty, and with a crashing, rattling, smashing racket he went rolling, turning, sliding down the the almost perpendicular wall, a distance of forty feet or more, and landed, *butter side down*, in the creek at the foot of the wall.

"There goes our Dutch oven," said Huffman, "smashed all to thunder, I'll bet."

"Yes, and there goes our flour and sugar, all wet, and turned to dough and molasses," said I.

"Darn your Dutch oven and grub," said Jack, "there goes Uncle Sam's mule, all ground into sausage meat. If we ever save any of his load, we'll have to walk and carry it ourselves from this on."

We hurried down to where the wreck lay, as fast as possible, and to our surprise found the poor creature still breathing. We waded in, and unlashed his load as quickly as we could, pulled one of the boxes away from him, so that he could turn over, and with our help he struggled to his feet. We found that, though badly cut and bruised, he had sustained no serious injuries — that he was much worse scared than hurt — that he was slightly disfigured, but still in the ring. We examined the rocks over which he had fallen, and found that only a small chunk was broken off here and there; that further than this they, too, were uninjured.

We next carried the boxes ashore, and unpacked them. The Dutch oven, our dearest treasure of all, was safe. The potatoes and canned beans ditto. The sugar was decidedly damp, and much of its sweetness had been wasted on the desert air. The flour had fortunately been put on one of the other mules that morning, and so these were the only casualties. We led the erring brother back onto the high and narrow way, adjusted his burden upon his willing back, and once more slowly wended our weary way toward the goal.

We camped near a fine spring that night, on the same plateau and only a few miles from the scene of our former night's camp. All night we could hear elk whistling around our camp. They wanted to come to the spring for water, but the sight of our white canvas, our mules, etc., kept them back. Along toward morning I saw one large bull standing on the top of a ridge about seventy-five or eighty yards away. There was no moon at that hour, but the stars shone brightly, and his majestic form was plainly visible by their light. I crawled out of bed, took my rifle, and started to crawl up toward him, but he saw or heard me, and vanished into thin air before I could get near enough for a sure shot.

We were up at 5 o'clock A.M., had an early breakfast, and moved at six. After we had gone about half a mile from camp, we looked back and saw a small band of elk coming over a ridge away to the southwest, heading directly for the spring we had just left. Huffman and I dismounted, left Conley in charge of the mules, and ran down into a coulee out of sight. Then began a long, tedious, laborious still hunt. The elk were on higher ground than we, and were moving, slowly, cautiously, warily toward us, stopping at frequent intervals to scan the ground and sniff the air in search of danger. We had a broad expanse of level prairie to pass over yet before reaching the cover of the brush, and we knew that in order to get a shot we must needs be in the thicket before the elk got there. To get over this open prairie without letting the game discover us was an undertaking of no small magnitude. We laid down and crawled through the grass a distance of a hundred yards or more to a

low swale, where, by stooping low, we were concealed behind
a ridge between us and the game. Here we rose to our feet,
and ran up this swale as far as it went in our direction.
Then we paused to watch the elk. They were still moving
slowly toward the spring, from the south, and we from the
east. Another tedious crawl of twenty minutes, that seemed
to us like so many hours, brought us to the edge of the
thicket of quaking-asp.

Here we took a breathing spell, for we were now safe
from observation, and had plenty of time to reach the spring
before our competitors in the race could get there. Then we
moved cautiously up through the brush to the opposite edge,
near the spring where we could look through, and our race
was ended. The band was yet two hundred yards away, and
we had plenty of leisure to watch them. They were strung out
in single file, led by an old cow, followed by her calf. Next
came an old bull, then another cow and calf, then two young
bulls, and so on to the end of the line. The leader, with
true motherly instinct, watched every moving blade of grass,
and every leaf in the thicket, as they rustled in the wind,
frequently turning to her calf and caressing it, as much as to
say: " Come on, little one, I will take care of you."

They were evidently the same band that had been there
during the night, else they would not have been so cautious
about approaching their usual haunt, but they had doubtless,
from their distant lookout, seen us move away with our train,
and thought we were out of sight long ago. But a feeling of
danger seemed to hang over them still, and they showed the
care and caution of an Indian warrior in approaching an
enemy. It was interesting to study their movements, their
wary, cautious advance. At last they reached a point within
fifty yards of us, and stopped again. The wind was in our
favor, and even at this short distance they could not scent us.

It was now time to open the ball. The lead cow stood
broadside to me, and I drew on her side just back of the
shoulder, Huffman at the same time taking a bead on the
largest bull. Our rifles cracked simultaneously. The cow
sprang forward, then wheeled, started back toward the herd
and fell dead. The bull dropped on his knees, then raised,

SKINNING THE ELK.

plunged forward a few feet, staggered, and fell very near the
cow. The other animals dashed away in opposite directions,
but stopped suddenly, turned, and stood looking at each
other, and at their fallen companions. We remained concealed, but did not care to continue the slaughter. We fired a
shot in the air to watch its effect upon them. They were

8

panic-stricken, and would not run, but huddled together and stood there trembling. Then we walked out into the open ground, and when they saw us, and knew from whence the danger came, they turned, and went over the prairie with the speed of a courser.

I found on skinning the cow that my bullet (an explosive) had passed directly through her, ranging a little forward, and coming out at the shoulder. It had broken two ribs where it went in, and shattered the shoulder-blade where it came out. This was from a forty caliber rifle, mind you, and it would seem from this shot to be about as effective a weapon as brother Van Dyke's sixty-five caliber cannon.

CHAPTER XIII.

FROM CUSTER TO KEOUGH.

IN THE BIG HORN RANGE — THE BLACK CANYON — A PERILOUS DESCENT—
JACK LOADED FOR BEAR — BEAR LOADED FOR JACK — HUFFMAN'S
TRAIL — SCALING A MOUNTAIN WALL — CUSTER'S GRAVE — UP THE
BIG PORCUPINE — FLAGGING THE ANTELOPE — ANTELOPES AS CURIOUS
AS WOMEN — NO COUNTRY LIKE THE BIG HORN FOR SPORT.

At about eleven o'clock next morning we reached the Black
Canyon, one of the grandest in the Big Horn range. It is
from two thousand to three thousand feet deep, and from an
eighth to a quarter of a mile wide. Its walls are precipitous,
almost perpendicular in many places, great ledges of white
limestone and red sandstone cropping out here and there, and
towering hundreds of feet toward the heavens, their faces split
and waterworn into fantastic shapes resembling the ruins of
some ancient mosque or castle. Through the bottom of this
canyon runs one of those clear, cold, rapid mountain streams
that poets love to linger over, and that always fills the heart of
the true sportsman with rapture when he beholds its crystal
fluid and listens to its joyous music. This one is ten to
twenty feet wide at this point, and very swift. It boils and
foams over large boulders and beds of snow white gravel. Its
waters are so pure and cold that not a particle of moss or
fungus of any kind can be found on the rocks or logs that lie
in its pathway.

On either side of the stream are beautiful little parks
where green grass grows luxuriantly, and these are surrounded
and shaded by tall, handsome pines, cottonwoods and other
varieties of timber. We halted on top of the wall, and

gazed down upon the scene of enchantment. We were enraptured, delighted, intoxicated with its beauty and grandeur.
We longed to live in this fairyland, to feast our eager eyes
always on such a picture.

But this could not be.

Our time was growing short, and we must soon bid the
mountains farewell.

Huffman went ahead to seek a passage-way into the canyon.
There was only a game trail where we entered it — no evidence that any human being had ever risked his life by
descending the wall where we were about to descend it. After
Huffman had gone down some five or six hundred feet, he
fired a shot as a signal that we were to come on, that he had
found a route that was practicable.

The report caused an echo that almost alarmed us.   It
resounded, reverberated and rolled back and forth from wall
to wall, up and down the canyon for miles, and still came
back again and again in echoes as loud as the first. It seemed
to linger and mutter as if loth to leave the scene of its birth.
It gradually receded and finally, after what seemed to us a
long time, it began to grow fainter and fainter and at last
died out, and the great chasm relapsed again into its virgin
stillness.

A few minutes later a large band of elk, probably a hundred
and fifty, alarmed by the report of Huffman's rifle, broke from
their cover and trotted off across one of the parks in the bottom
of the canyon. It was a beautiful sight. We watched them for
several minutes, but they were so far below us that they looked
no larger than sheep. We started on our descent, and it
fairly made our heads swim to look over the dizzy heights and
through the narrow defiles that we were to pass. But by slow
and patient toiling, picking our way and tacking like a ship
sailing against the wind, we finally reached the foot of the

JACK LOADED FOR BEAR.

117

wall in about two hours from the time of starting. We turned down the canyon, and as we passed the mouth of a smaller canyon that puts into the main one, we saw an ugly old grizzly on the side hill some distance away. Jack was riding at the head of the train, and the moment he sighted the game put the rowels to his mule, and went tearing through the brush in pursuit of it. When near the spot where the bear had disappeared in the brush, he dismounted, threw his lariat around a sappling and waltzed bravely forward. As he neared a clump of pine trees, bruin raised on his haunches to size up his pursuer before commencing to make a meal off him.

Jack brought his carbine quickly to his shoulder, glanced nervously along the barrel, and fired. When the smoke lifted he saw the bear coming toward him at a 2 : 17 gait, his mouth open and his eyes glaring vengeance. Jack thought he who shoots and runs away may live to shoot another—bear, and accordingly made tracks (about two to the rod) for tall timber. He had not more than thirty yards to run across an open space to a friendly tree, but when he reached it old grizzly was so uncomfortably close that Jack declared afterward he could feel his warm breath through his heavy cavalry boots. Jack said he never felt so pale in all his life as he did when he was reaching for that tree, and that he never saw a tree seem to run from him as that one did. But he finally reached it, and swung into its branches just in the nick of time, having offered up his hat and gun to his hungry foe on the way. As the bear reached the tree and halted for a moment, a ball from Huffman's rifle doubled him up, and another rolled him over.

Jack was loth to come down from his perch until he saw us go up and take hold of Bruin, to convince him that there was no further danger.

We proceeded down the canyon about three miles and

BEAR LOADED FOR JACK.

made camp at three o'clock. Huffman went out and made some views of the grand scenery of the canyon. Jack went down the stream a few rods and caught some beautiful mountain trout, weighing from one to two pounds each.

The next morning we made an early start, our next hard task being to get out of the canyon. We went out by what is known as "Huffman's Trail," our artist having discovered it some two or three years ago, when with Captain Baldwin of the 5th Infantry, and a detachment of troops exploring for timber. It was only a game trail at that time and he piloted the command over it. It has since been improved by the troops at Fort Custer and is now a respectable looking trail. But oh, how our backs and legs did ache before we reached the top of that terrible wall! Three long hours we labored with it, and when we had at last scaled it, we landed on another of those broad, level plateaus, where we found a good, plain wagon road leading direct to Fort Custer. Our hard work was at last over, for the descent from here was gradual and easy. That night we camped on the bank of the Big Horn river, fifteen miles below old Fort C. F. Smith, and two days later landed at Fort Custer. From here we visited the Custer battlefield, where sleeps that noble little band who went down under the bloody hands of Crazy Horse, Sitting Bull, and their followers, on the twenty-fifth of June, 1876. A handsome granite monument has been erected on the ground, by order of the Secretary of War, and on it are inscribed the names of General Custer and all those who fell with him. May their memory ever be kept green in the hearts of their countrymen.

The only event of interest that transpired during our four days' ride down the Yellowstone valley from Custer to Keough occurred on September 19th. We were passing over a high piece of tableland overlooking the valley of the Yellow-

stone and the lower part of that of the Big Porcupine. We
had heard from some ranchmen along the way that the
buffalo herd was at this time grazing about fifteen to twenty
miles up the Big Porcupine, and knowing that antelopes are
nearly always found hanging on the outskirts of every large
herd of bison, we were on the lookout for them, for it would
not be at all strange to find them near the stage trail on
which we were traveling. We scanned the country closely
with the field glass and were finally rewarded by seeing a
number of small white spots on the dead grass away up the
Porcupine, that seemed to be moving. We rode toward
them at a lively trot for perhaps a mile and then stopped to
reconnoitre again. From this point we could plainly distinguish them, though they looked to be about the size of jack
rabbits. We again put the rowels to our donkeys and rode
rapidly up to within about a mile of them, when we picketed
our animals in a low swale, took out our antelope flag—a
piece of scarlet calico about half a yard square—attached it
to the end of my wiping stick, and were ready to interview
the antelopes.

I crawled to the top of a ridge within plain view of the
game, and planted my flag. The breeze spread it out, kept
it fluttering, and it soon attracted their attention. They
were then near the bank of the river, grazing quietly, but
this bit of colored rag excited their curiosity to a degree that
rendered them restive, anxious, uneasy, and they seemed at
once to be seized with an insatiable desire to find out what it
was. An antelope has as much curiosity as a woman, and
when they see any object that they don't quite understand,
they will travel miles and run themselves into all kinds of
danger to find out what it is. They have been known to
follow an emigrant or freight wagon with a white cover
several miles, and an Indian brings them within reach of his

arrow by standing in plain view, wrapped in his red blanket.
Some hunters "flag" them by lying down on their back,
holding one foot as high as possible, and swinging it to and
fro.   A piece of bright tin or a mirror answers the same
purpose on a clear day.   Almost any conspicuous or strange
looking object will attract them, but the most convenient, as
well as the most reliable at all times, is the little red flag,
such as we employed in this instance.

Huffman went to the top of another ridge, to my right,
and some distance in advance, and Jack crawled into a
hollow on the left, and well in advance, we three forming a
half circle, into which it was our intention if possible to
decoy the game.   When they first discovered our flag they
moved rapidly toward it, sometimes breaking into a trot, but
when they had covered half the distance between us and
their starting point, they began to grow suspicious, and
stopped.   They circled around, turned back, walked a few
steps, and then paused and looked back at the, to them,
mysterious apparition.   But they could not resist its magic
influence.   Again they turned and came toward it, stopped,
and gazed curiously at it.   The old buck who led the herd
stamped impatiently, as if annoyed at being unable to solve
the mystery.   Then they walked cautiously toward us again,
down an incline into a valley, which took them out of our
sight, and out of sight of the flag.

This, of course, rendered them still more impatient, and
when they again came in sight on the next ridge, they were
running.   But as soon as the leader caught sight of the flag
he stopped, as did the others in their turn when they reached
the top of the ridge.   There were seven in the herd, two
bucks, three does and two fawns.   They were now not more
than a hundred yards from me, and still less from the other
two of our party.   Their position was everything we could

FLAGGING AN ANTELOPE.

wish, and though we might possibly have brought them a few yards nearer, there was a possibility of their scenting us, even across the wind, which, of course, we had arranged to have in our favor, and I decided that rather than run the risk of this and the consequent stampede, I would shoot while I had a good chance. It had been arranged that I was

THE ROUND UP.

to open the ball, so I drew my peep and globe sights down very finely, taking the white breast of the old buck for my bull's-eye, and pulled. Huffman's Kennedy and Jack's carbine paid their compliments to the pretty visitors at almost the same instant, and for about two or three minutes thereafter we fanned them about as vigorously as ever a herd got fanned under similar circumstances. The air was full of leaden missiles; the dry dust raised under and around the fleeing herd as it does when a team trots over a dusty road. Clouds of smoke hung over us, and the distant hills echoed the music of our artillery until the last white rump disappeared in the cottonwoods on the river bank.

When the smoke of battle cleared away and we looked over the field, we found that we had not burned our powder in vain. Five of the little fellows, the two bucks and three does, had fallen victims to their curiosity. The two fawns had strangely enough escaped, probably only because they being so much smaller than their parents, were less exposed.

This closed our hunting for the time being. We arrived at Fort Keough on the twenty-first, tired and hungry, but feeling well pleased with the result of our long, hard ride.

To sportsmen in quest of large game I can heartily commend the Big Horn country as the very place for them to go to. Besides our own experience, I have the testimony of a number of old frontiersmen to the effect that it is one of the best game regions in the whole Northwest. Dr. J. C. Merrill, post surgeon at Fort Custer, informs me that he spent two weeks in the Big Horn mountains last June, collecting ornithological specimens, and that during that time he saw as many as five or six bears in a day, and that in one day he saw eleven. He states that deer, elk, mountain sheep and other large animals were equally plentiful. Several others with whom I spoke gave testimony to the same effect.

Persons who may contemplate a trip to the Big Horn mountains, or any portion of the great Yellowstone country, or National Park, should not forget that the most direct and speedy route to that country from the East and South, is by way of the Chicago, Milwaukee & St. Paul, and the Northern Pacific railroads.

CHAPTER XIV.

TEN DAYS IN MONTANA.

MONTANA A VERITABLE WONDERLAND—SPORT FROM THE BAGGAGE
CAR—ALKALI BEDS NEAR CRYSTAL SPRINGS—"WHY DID YOUR
AUNT ELOPE?"—RESOLVED TO KILL A BUFFALO OR GET SCALPED—
JUDGE SOUTHER—IN LUCK—IN THE CUSTER VALLEY—"YOUNG
MAN'S BUTTE"—CUSTER'S LOOKOUT!—PRAIRIE-DOGS—BAD LANDS
—TOO BAD TO BE DESCRIBED.

EVER since the days of my childhood I have longed to
see the great plains of the Far West. My highest ambition,
my fondest dream, has been to hunt the buffalo on his native
prairies, to see the antelope, the Rocky mountain sheep, the
elk, the black-tail deer and the coyote roam at will in their
favorite ranges. I have longed to see the famous " bad
lands " of which authors, journalists and travelers have told
us so much ; which artists have attempted in vain to portray
on canvas. I have longed for the privilege of ascending the
tall buttes, and viewing with one sweep of the eye as much
territory as is inclosed within the boundary lines of one of
our eastern states.

All these desires I have at last been permitted to realize,
and their realization has far exceeded all my anticipations.
These western territories, at least Dakota and Montana, the
ones I have visited, are indeed a veritable wonderland.

I left Chicago at ten A.M. of September 15th, on the Chicago, Milwaukee & St. Paul railroad, arrived at St. Paul at six
A.M. of the 16th, covering a distance of 409 miles in twenty
hours, and enjoying a comfortable night's sleep in the
meantime in one of this company's commodious and well-

appointed sleepers.   I spent the day at St. Paul, and improved the opportunity of taking a good look at this, one of the liveliest and most enterprising cities in the Northwest.

At twenty minutes past six P.M. I boarded the westbound train on the Northern Pacific railroad, disposed myself in the sleeper "Fargo," and at a seasonable hour wrapped the drapery of my couch about me, and laid down to pleasant dreams.   The night was bright with the light of the full moon, and an occasional glance through the windows showed that the country through which we passed during the night was not thickly settled, nor, generally speaking, good land. Most of the soil is too sandy to be valuable for agricultural purposes, though there are occasional tracts of a better quality, and on these there are good farms.   After passing Brainerd we enter a good country, a rich black soil.   Here vegetation grows luxuriantly, and the farmers are in good circumstances.   At Perham we enter the lake region.   From here to Moorehead the country is dotted all over with lakes of various sizes.   Nearly all of them afford good fishing and duck shooting.   Wild rice grows in most of them, and ducks breed numerously all through this part of the state.   On nearly every lake or pond we passed we saw large numbers of them.   They are very tame.   They pay but little attention to the noise of the passing trains, and frequently sat within twenty feet of the track while we passed.   Even when some of the passengers shot at them with revolvers they would not fly.   Conductor Doyle told me that sportsmen often stand in the door of the baggage car and kill large numbers of them as the trains pass them.   Chicken shooting is also good all along the line of this road from Brainerd west to its terminus.   Deer are found in goodly numbers in the timber belt about Detroit, which is ninety-two miles west of Brainerd.

Near Crystal Springs, a station one hundred and thirty miles west of Fargo, we saw the first alkali beds one meets with on the line of this road. There are three of them, covering in the aggregate probably five hundred acres. In the wet season these are lakes of water, but as the dry, hot season progresses, the water all evaporates, leaving a deposit of pure alkali. Within eighty rods of one of these beds is a lake of pure fresh water in which there is no particle of alkali.

After leaving Jamestown the train men told us we were likely to see antelope at any time, that they were frequently seen within a few hundred yards of the track. I strained my eyes all day long looking for them, but did not catch sight of one. Toward night a man in the seat just in front of me looked out of his window and shouted "Antelope." I ventured to ask him why did his aunt elope? Were the old folks opposed to the match, or did the young couple simply get up this kind of a scheme on account of the romance of it? He looked at me a minute or two and then shook his head and sighed, as if to say, "Poor fellow, I'm sorry for you." Soon after this a crow flew along opposite the train for a mile or two, keeping just even with the car we were in. My neighbor in front turned around and asked me if I knew how far a crow could fly without stopping to rest. I said no, I was not well up in crow-nology, and was always getting my dates mixed up. He looked at me again intently for a few minutes and then went forward and told the conductor there was an escaped lunatic in the rear coach, and he ought to be taken into the baggage car and taken care of.

There were four Pawnee Indians on the train from St. Paul to Bismarck. They were *en route* to their home, or camp, which is with the Rees, near Fort Berthold. They told us that a roving band of Chippewas had invaded the Rees reservation a few days ago, and stolen several ponies. A

number of Rees warriors turned out and followed them, overtook them and recaptured the ponies, killing six of the
Chippewas and losing four of their own men.   The Pawnees
were feeling good over the success of their friends, the Rees,
and the defeat of the Chippewas, who are their bitter enemies.
We arrived at Bismarck at half-past six in the evening,
twenty-four hours ride from St. Paul, and as there was no
train west on the extension until next morning, I put up at
the Sheridan House, which is said to be the best hotel in the
place, but if this be so I pity the others.   After supper I took
a walk round to the gun store, to interview the proprietor
thereof as to game out along the extension.   He told me I
could find all the antelope shooting I wanted in the Curlew
valley, about twenty-five miles west.   This was just what I
wanted, just what I had come for.   But he said if I wanted
larger game I could get it ; that a man just in from Green
river, one hundred miles west, reported having seen several
large herds of buffaloes only forty miles south of that station
two days before.   Shades of Nimrod !   Could it be possible
that I was within one hundred and forty miles of a herd of
buffaloes?   And I was going to Green river, and should then
be only forty miles from them.   I resolved at once to kill a
buffalo before I returned or get scalped in the attempt.   But
then how was I to make that forty miles?   And who would I
get to go with me for company and to help keep the Indians
off?   Well he said I could probably hire a man at Green
river to take me down there on a buckboard, but that two of
us couldn't do much toward keeping Indians off in case we
should run across a party of them.   Well, I said, I would go
for the buffaloes any way, and take the chances on meeting
the Indians.

The construction train was to leave at half-past five the
next morning for " end of track."   That was the way my

ticket read, and that was where I wanted to go, so I told the clerk to call me when the lark flew down from his roost. At breakfast the next morning I had the pleasure of meeting Judge Henry Souther, of Erie, Pa. There was only us two at early breakfast, so the Judge introduced himself to me and I introduced myself to him. He asked me where I was going. I said to the end of the track, if not farther. I fired the same question at him, and he said to the end of the track and from there into the buffalo country; that he was to meet a party of friends at Mandan, just across the river, who had everything cut and dried for a big buffalo hunt. I asked him if there was any chance to get counted into that party, and he said he was only a guest, but thought he could arrange it for me all right. This was more good news. We got into a box-car and rode up to the ferry, four miles above town. The water in the "Big Muddy" is at a low stage at this season of the year, and the ferry had great difficulty in making the landings. However, we succeeded in getting over, were switched into the train on the other side, and left Mandan at ten o'clock that morning for the front. At the depot Judge Souther introduced me to Mr. James Bellows, of the firm of Walker, Bellows & Co., railroad contractors, and to Mr. B. J. Van Vleck, their cashier and paymaster, who had made up the party for the buffalo hunt. They received me kindly and gave me a cordial invitation to join their party, which invitation I of course eagerly and thankfully accepted. There was another hunting party on board the train bound for the buffalo country. A man from Custer City had been to Bismarck and employed four men at thirty-five dollars a month and board, and they were going out to kill buffaloes for the skins. They declined to tell us where they expected to find the herd, but, as will be seen later on, we found it before they did. They got off the train at Green river.

Thirty miles out from Mandan we entered the Curlew valley,—a very handsome country, by the way, which will one day be a rich farming district. The Curlew river is a small, clear stream of pure water, and will be useful for stock raising. At this point we saw our first antelope. There were two of them grazing on a hillside about four hundred yards from the road. As the train came in sight they stood and looked at it for a minute and then turning their white rumps to us, skurried away over the hills out of sight. From this point west we saw them almost every hour in the day. This valley is a famous feeding-ground for them. The conductor informed us that there is a herd of from twenty-five to forty that graze here all the time. He said that some days they would all be together, on other days scattered out in small herds. Beavers are plentiful along this stream and its tributaries, and since the railroad has been built they are making trouble in some instances by cutting away the piles under bridges and culverts.

Soon after entering the Curlew valley we were shown a ranche owned by a man named Warns, who has lived here about ten years. His house stands on the top of a high rocky bluff or butte, and is stoned up on the outside in such a way as to render it bullet-proof; in fact, it is a stockade, or fort, on a small scale. It is said that the Indians have tried several times to kill or capture him, but he has always been able to hold his position against them. He refuses to say whether he has ever killed any Indians or not, but says that if General Custer were alive he could tell where several of them are buried, not far off. He is said to have been a warm personal friend of Custer's.

Near Eagle's Nest station our attention was called to "Young Man's Butte," a high peak, so named from the fact that some years ago a young lieutenant of the army, who

was killed in a fight with Indians near the butte, was buried
on its summit, and about a year later, when his friends from
the East came to exhume his body and take it home for
burial, it was found to be completely petrified.   Before his
death he weighed but one hundred and sixty pounds, and
when taken up weighed three hundred and ninety pounds.
About two miles to the northwest we were shown another tall
butte, the tallest in all this section of country, called " Custer's Lookout."   It is said that the lamented commander used,
frequently, during his Indian campaigns, to ascend this peak,
and with the aid of his field-glass scan the surrounding country in search of hostile Indians.

We reached Green River, one hundred miles west of Bismarck, at two o'clock P.M., and had to wait there for a new
train to be made up to take us to the front.

On Saturday, the 18th, our party having some business to
transact at Houston, that would take up the greater part of
the day, I took my rifle and walked out four or five miles from
camp to try and flag an antelope.   I saw three during the day,
but they had been hunted so much near camp that they knew
what a red flag meant, and would not come near it, so I did
not get a shot.   I saw two carcasses of antelopes that had been
killed by hunters, but had gone so far after being hit that they
had not been recovered.   The coyotes had eaten all the flesh
from their bones.   On my return to camp I passed a large
prairie-dog town.   While I was yet half a mile away the dogs
set up a lively barking, and kept it up until I was in the
midst of their village.   I undertook to shoot some of them,
as every tenderfoot does who goes to the plains.   I had read
and been told often that they would always drop into their
holes when shot, but thought that possibly a large caliber
rifle-ball with a high velocity might possibly knock them away
from the hole, and that I might thus be able to secure a speci-

men for mounting. I killed several, but although the force of the ball did knock them across the hole, they invariably fell back into it, and I could not get them. I then tried shooting into the dirt just under them, thinking that I might be able to thus kill, or at least paralyze them by the concussion, and perhaps throw them away from the hole; but though I could throw them up a foot or more into the air, they invariably tumbled back into their hole, so I gave up the task and returned to camp. On the way back I found some very fine specimens of petrified wood, of which there are great quantities all through this region of country.

Mr. Bellows had arranged to go over the line of the road from Houston to the Yellowstone, and pay off his men who were engaged in grading, bridge building, etc. After completing this duty we were to leave the line at the most favorable point, and strike the buffalo with as little delay as possible. He accordingly provided teams at Houston to take us through. They consisted of two buck boards and a light platform-wagon. On these were loaded our tent, blankets, provisions, guns, ammunition, and other equipments necessary for the expedition, and besides comfortable seats were provided for all the party to ride on them. Three extra ponies were led for use when we should reach the buffalo country. In addition to this complete and comfortable outfit, General Merrill sent with us an escort of five men and a non-commissioned officer, as a safeguard against roving bands of hostile Indians, with whom we were liable to meet at any point along the line.

Our expedition left Houston at eight o'clock A.M. of the 19th, and after driving five miles we entered the famous "bad lands," through which the Little Missouri river flows. An accurate description of these bad lands—such an one as will present to the eye of the reader a fair picture of them—is one of the impossibilities of the English language. Geologists who have examined them have various theories as to their origin; but the most common one, and that which appears to me most tangible, is, that at some remote period there were great internal convulsions of the earth, something of the nature of earthquake, that, owing to the existence of extensive subterranean caverns, at no great distance below, the crust or surface gave way and dropped, to distances varying in different localities, from two hundred to five hundred feet. The bases or floors of these caverns must have been very uneven. Apparently there were, in places, great ledges or pillars of granite or other solid formation, towering to great heights from these floors. On these projections this falling mass must have struck, and portions of it were held in suspense, while the remainder passed on down to the general level base of the caverns. The general surface passing down left these portions of it which first met with resistance protruding through, and thus were formed great buttes, peaks, mounds and pryamids, of all sizes, heights, shapes and colors that the most speculative mind could possibly imagine.

Then, either before or after these great convulsions, internal fires have raged, perhaps for ages. Rich deposits of coal or lignite have in some manner become ignited and burned away, leaving other cavities which have in turn been filled up by the sinking crust. There are many distinct and well defined craters, long since extinct, around which lie masses of lava, scoria, lime and baked clay. Some of the buttes where these extinct craters are found are covered all over with red clay, baked to the consistency of brick or pottery, and broken into small pieces, looking as if thousands of crates of pottery might have been broken up and piled there by the hand of man. Then, since these scenes were enacted, another destroying element, water, has wrought its ravages, uninterrupted and unimpeded, perhaps for many hundreds of years. Great gulches, canyons and ravines are cut out between these buttes. The sides of the buttes, mounds and turrets are washed into fantastic shapes, and are still changing in shape and appearance every year. The various strata of each butte are plainly visible, owing to the absence of vegetation on their sides, and we see here a tall butte with half-a-dozen beds of clay of various colors and as many more of sand, while within fifty feet of it we see another standing lower down in the valley, whose head only reaches to the level of the base of this one, and which contains the very same strata as in the one just mentioned. The average level of these bad lands, as above stated, is from two to five hundred feet below the adjacent prairies; and as one stands on a ridge of the prairie overlooking a tract of these lands perhaps thirty to fifty miles in circumference, a scene is presented to the eye that for grandeur and sublimity cannot be excelled on this continent, if on the globe. After all that can be said in the way of describing these wonderful bad lands, no more correct idea of them can be given than that conveyed in the few words of General Sully, who, when asked what the bad lands were like, replied, "They are simply hell with the fire out."

I predict that when the Northern Pacific railroad is completed through to the Yellowstone, people will come here from all parts of the civilized world simply to see the bad lands, and consider themselves richly repaid for their time and trouble when they have beheld them.

CHAPTER XV.

LIFE ON THE PLAINS.

TWELVE miles west of Houston we halted at Lord, Fogarty & Co's camp and were there joined by Mr. John Fogarty, Mr. S. J. Hill, and their driver, John Kelly. This increased our number to seven men all told, and completed our party.

We reached the Little Missouri river Sunday evening at six o'clock, and were warmly welcomed by Colonel Clough, chief engineer of the Missouri division of the Northern Pacific, S. M. Keith, resident engineer, R. C. Sattley and C. H. Hurley, his assistants, and by Major Comba, Lieutenant Roberts, Lieutenant McCoy, Surgeon Miller, Post Trader Moore, and other officers of Major Comba's command who are stationed here.

These railroad and military officers render life on the plains much more agreeable than we in the States might imagine it could be made. The railroad people, even those who live in tents and move frequently to keep up with their work, provide themselves with nearly every luxury that the Eastern markets afford. Even ripe fruit, fresh oysters and new vegetables find their way out here within ten days after their appearance in the Eastern markets. Cows are kept with each camp and fresh butter and milk greet the hungry traveler as he sits down at the hospitable board. Then, added to all these, they spread before you game of a dozen different varieties and all cooked to a turn. Buffalo hump, buffalo tender loin, elk steak, roast loin of venison (mule deer and Virginia deer), antelope chops, roast duck and broiled prairie-chicken . are a few of the delicacies with which our palates have been tickled since we came west. Good cooks are employed in these camps, the best that can be had in the Eastern cities for money, and in many instances the cuisine equals that of the Palmer House or Grand Pacific. What is said here of the railroad people is generally true of the military. Major Comba and his command are living in comfortable log houses, floored and ceiled with dressed pine lumber. The rooms are well furnished. Ingrain and Brussels carpets, walnut bedsteads, bureaus, dressing cases, cast iron cook and heating stoves are among the items of furniture one sees in these quarters.

The Little Missouri is one of the best game countries on the line of the road; that is, the largest variety of game is found there. The bad lands furnish excellent cover for large game. There are timbered coolies all along the river and some timber along the banks of the river itself. There is good grazing and plenty of fresh water all through this region, and these conditions cause the game to congregate here. These bad lands are a favorite winter resort for the buffalo. In the deep cuts and canyons they are protected, in a great measure, from the severity of the weather and by pawing the snow away can always find plenty of good tender grass. At other seasons, however, they prefer the open plains. The Rocky Mountain sheep, elk, mule deer, Virginia deer, red fox, beaver, otter, mink, wolf and coyote are all found here in large numbers. Four mule deer, two elk, and two Rocky

Mountain sheep were killed and brought into Major Comba's camp within two or three days previous to the time of our visit.   Two cinnamon-bears were killed here in winter, and others have been seen lately.

They have a pet fawn of the mule deer species at this camp, that was caught by one of the Indian scouts last spring.   It is now about half grown, and is very handsome.   Its neck, back and sides are a dark lavender color; belly and legs lighter, with a white spot on rump; tail white, with black tip; ears large; eyes dark, lustrous, and very expressive.   The scouts caught several fawns last spring, but there were no cows in camp then, and no milk to feed them on, except the condensed milk (or condemned, as the boys call it), and all the others died.   This one was brought in just at the time when the first cow arrived in camp, and has been healthy and happy ever since.   He roams at will about the camp, and is the equal in rank of any one he meets with, from private up to post commandant.

Mr. Keith informed us that one day last fall, soon after he established his present camp, a noble old buck of the " big horn " species came to the top of a tall bluff that stands just back of his camp, some two hundred feet high, and remained for some minutes looking over the camp.   As he stood there looking down with silent disdain upon his natural enemies, his long spiral horns, and heavy, well developed frame outlined against the clear blue sky, Mr. Keith says he presented a picture worthy the pencil of a landseer.   No one disturbed him, and after he had made a satisfactory survey of the camp, he retired.

A good story is told on a couple of officers of this camp and two or three men who were out hunting a day or two before.   They were returning to camp well laden with venison, when they discovered in the water, a short distance ahead, four wild geese. They slipped up within range, and opened fire on them. After a good deal of shooting they succeeded in bagging all four of them. Each member of the party was confident that he had killed one or more of them, and that it was the others who had done so much bad shooting. But the next day a ranchman, who lived in the neighborhood, turned up at headquarters and demanded pay for four "pet" wild geese that the soldiers had killed the day before, and that belonged to him. Then a change came o'er the spirit of their dreams, and each man was confident that he had not killed any of them, that it was the "other boys" that had done the good shooting; that he was a little off that day. Finally, by a preponderance of testimony, the geese, and likewise the cigars, were saddled onto Lieutenant McCoy, for it was pretty clearly shown that he had killed them all. The event was duly celebrated the night we were there, in an extemporaneous song by Mr. Howard Eaton, of Pennsylvania, which brought down the house, and some more cigars.

The Little Missouri bad lands are also rich in fossils, petrifactions and other geological specimens. I saw stumps of trees there seven or eight feet in diameter, and two to three feet high above the ground, that were perfectly petrified, and thus preserved intact. In some cases the bark remains on them as when in the full vigor of life.

The roots can be traced into the ground several feet. There are numbers of these scattered along the line of the road, and many of them will eventually be dug up, shipped East, and placed on exhibition in museums, parks, and private grounds. I saw many fine specimens of marine fishes, mollusks, crustaceans, etc., that the engineers and others had collected, and also found a number myself, which I brought home, and shall value them above almost any others in my collection, owing to the fact that they were collected while on my first buffalo hunt. We pulled out early on Monday morning, the 20th, and a drive of five miles took us out of the bad lands and on to a most beautiful tract of rich, fertile prairie. Just on the margin of this prairie the trail passes through a very large prairie-dog town, or rather "republic." It covers some two or three hundred acres. As we came in sight of it we saw a hundred or more of the little spike-tailed republicans skurrying hither and thither, each making for his own house. When they had found these they stopped, sat up on their haunches and commenced barking at us. Those nearest the trail disappeared as we approached them, but those at a little distance away held their ground, and kept up their noise. We got out and took a few shots at them. Mr. Van Vleck killed a very large one, the largest we saw on the trip, and probably the president of the republic. Fortunately, too, the force of the ball knocked him off the bank where he sat, and he died before he could reach his hole, so we recovered him. I skinned him, and have sent his skin to Dr. Velie, secretary of the Chicago Academy of Science, to be mounted.

We saw large numbers of antelopes during the day, but did not stop to shoot at them. We arrived at Camp McIntosh, on Beaver creek, about sundown, and found Major Bell, Captain Borden, Lieutenant Defries, Surgeons Black and Ewing, and Post Trader Leasure as glad to see us as if we had been their paymaster and his escort.

After the first interchange of congratulations we inquired eagerly as to the whereabouts of the buffalo, and received in reply the welcome news that they were in the vicinity of Cabin Creek, about fifty miles south of this camp; that a scouting party had lately returned from that locality and reported the prairie black with them in every direction. The Major said the scouts had had difficulty in getting any water in that region fit for themselves or their ponies to drink, that it was all so strongly charged with buffalo manure and urine as to be unfit for use. He said furthermore that he wanted some fresh meat for his men, and would be glad to join us on the hunt, that he would take with him an escort of ten men and a team or two to bring in the meat. By the time these matters were arranged supper was announced, and we repaired to the Major's mess tent, where a spread awaited us that would have done honor to a king's table. There was venison steak, antelope steak, broiled buffalo tenderloin, Saratoga potatoes, baked sweet potatoes, stewed tomatoes, corn, vegetables, fruit, pastry, desserts, and other articles too numerous to mention. Imagine six hungry men arrayed before such a lay-out as this, six men who had ridden all day across the plains with a September wind fanning their manly brows — and appetites ; six men whose appetites had been sharpened for the last two hours by such news as we had been listening to ; and these six men being ordered by their host to "pitch in." But, reader, if you have never been there, your imagination, however vivid, will fail to picture the scene correctly. The onslaught was furious, our victory was complete, and when we withdrew from that hospitable board the table looked as bare as the plains were reported to be, where the great herd of buffaloes had grazed over them.

Supper over, we retired to our tent, where the Major, his subordinate officers and Mr. Leasure again joined us. They entertained us with reminiscences of frontier life, Indian warfare, hunting yarns, etc., till the night waned into the wee sma' hours. Then they left us, and we retired to our bunks. But how is a man to sleep under such circumstances, with his mind full of such fancies as filled our minds that night ?

Here we are, away out in Montana, more than a thousand miles from the stately edifice in which these lines will be put in type. There is more than an hour difference between the time at this point and Chicago. We must wait a whole hour after you have daylight there to-morrow morning ere the sun will deign to smile on us here. When we first see him here the early riser in Chicago will have eaten his breakfast, and will be on his way down town.

Well, there's no use lying here — I can't sleep — so I turn out and take a stroll about camp. The moon is at the full, and in this clear, rarified western atmosphere, her light is so strong that I can even see to read the smallest type in a news-paper. The vigilant sentinel, pacing his beat in front of our .tent, challenges me as I approach him, in a friendly tone, however, for he knows by my meek and lowly appearance that I am only a tenderfoot and that I have no blood in my eye. I recall some of my long-forgotten knowledge of mili-tary matters, and answer him in a manner that proves satis-factory, and then I proceed to buzz him awhile. Among other questions, I ask him if there are any Indians in this part of the country now.

"No," said he, "there are none now. There was a band of five Sioux through here a week ago. I was out on a scout with an officer and thirty other men, going over toward Powder river, and we struck their trail about forty miles from here. The lieutenant detailed Sergeant Deavron and ten of us boys to follow that trail while he continued on his course. Two Cheyenne scouts were sent with us to trail them. They laid down alongside of their ponies, their heads as near the ground as they could get them, in order to be able to see the trail, and struck out at a lively trot. This was in the morn-ing. All day long they followed the trail without difficulty, while for the greater portion of the time we could see nothing of it. Whenever we came to the top of a ridge the scouts would take the field glass with which they had been provided,

and scan the country carefully as far as they could see.   Late
in the afternoon they spotted the Sioux crossing over a ridge
about ten miles away.   We could barely see them with the
aid of the glass, and would not have guessed them to be
Indians, but our scouts shouted ' Sioux, Sioux, five Sioux!'
We had ridden hard since morning, our horses were tired, and
the sergeant ordered a halt here for a rest and lunch, but our
Indians wouldn't have it.   They kept shouting, ' Sioux, Sioux,
soldier heap damn lazy!   Come on!'   So the sergeant told
them to go and we would follow them.   Then they patted us
on the backs and said, ' Soldier heap bully; come on.'   At
this they dropped the trail and made a bee line for the top
of the hill where we had seen the Sioux.   We rode this ten
miles under the spur, took up the trail again on the hill, and
followed it into a timbered ravine.   The scouts now told us
that we were close to them, and that they had not yet see us.
We rode cautiously and carried our carbines at a "ready."
Finally we sighted them at about five hundred yards, and
before they knew that they were followed at all we gave them
a volley, killing one of them and wounding two others.

They returned the fire and then skipped out.   As our
horses were badly worn out with the long chase, and their
ponies comparatively fresh, we knew it was useless to follow
them.   When we fired the volley our scouts disappeared.
We didn't see which way they went nor how they got out of
sight so quick; but in about half an hour they returned with
three ponies that they had captured from the Sioux.   One
had probably belonged to the Indian we killed, and they had
been leading the other two.   They then went for the dead
Indian's scalp, but the sergeant wouldn't let them scalp him.
After grazing our horses a few minutes and making coffee, we
started back to the command.   Pretty soon our scouts were
missing again but that night they turned up and one of them

had the dead Sioux's scalp. They also had about a dozen little scalps that they had cut off, after they got the main one, and these they gave to us boys.

It was now about time for the relief guard and the sentinel said I must retire from his beat. Besides, he said, I had better go to bed and sleep if I were going on a buffalo hunt to-morrow. So I bade him good-bye, and after taking a further stroll about the city of tents for half an hour, crawled into my blankers and went to sleep.

I was out again at daylight, walked about camp and waited patiently for nearly an hour ere the welcome sound of reveille rang out on the clear morning air. . Then all was bustle about the camp. The men turned out to roll call, then stable call sounded and they went forth to feed and groom their horses. The civilians of our party now began to stir out and from this on I had company. The morning was clear, cold and frosty; just such a morning as sends the blood tingling through the veins of the sportsman if he rises in time to get the benefit of it.

Our plans were made late the previous night—after tattoo had sounded and the men had retired; but the detail for our escort was announced early that morning and the busy notes of preparation were heard throughout the camp as the men packed the Major's tents, mess chest, cook stove, cooking utensils, provisions, etc., into the wagon. They packed their own blankets and shelter tents, filled their haversacks, cartridge belts, and, in short, made every necessary preparation for a five days' scout. It took a greater portion of the forenoon to fit out the expedition, but when we did move it was in a style that the general of the army, had he been a member of the party, would have felt proud of.

CHAPTER XVI.

AFTER THE BUFFALOES.

WE START WELL EQUIPPED — CAMP AT BEAVER CREEK — THE ANTELOI E
HARD TO KILL — DR. BLACK "ALL BROKE UP" — TAKES HIS SUPPER
STANDING — GOOD MORNING'S SPORT — A BREAKFAST FIT FOR THE
GODS — BUFFALOES AT LAST — "LET THEM HAVE IT" — THE
BUFFALO TAKES A GOOD DEAL OF KILLING — SHARP'S RIFLES.

MAJOR BELL, mounted on his large handsome iron-gray charger, led the van, followed by Sergeant Deavron, Corporal Brown and ten picked men from Company F, of the famous Seventh Cavalry. Their horses are all fine large animals, in good condition, high spirits, perfectly groomed and caparisoned. The men are armed with the improved Springfield carbine. Our party on the buck-boards and spring wagon followed the escort, and the military wagons brought up the rear.

Each member of our party carried a Sharp's rifle. Several of us had large navy revolvers for use when we should choose to hunt our buffalo on horseback, and Judge Souther carried a Parker gun which came in good play several times, in bagging a few ducks and sharp-tail grouse, by way of variety.

When we got about five miles from camp the major through out flankers or hunters to ride a mile or two to right and left of the trail in search of antelopes. Three of our party mounted their ponies and rode on the left flank with Major Bell. They saw several antelopes during the day, but they were wild, having been hunted so much near the trail, and it was difficult to get a shot at them.

We who kept the trail met two different parties during the

10   145

afternoon coming in from the railroad work on the Yellow-stone river, both of whom reported having seen several small herds of buffaloes along the trail in the forenoon. They reported one herd within fifteen miles of where we then were, and thought we would be very likely to strike them before night. But night drew on and no buffaloes had been sighted by our horsemen, nor had they even succeeded in bagging an antelope. We began to think we should be without fresh meat for supper and breakfast, but just as the sun was sinking behind the hills we heard a shot away off to the right, and ten minutes later the Major came up to the column with a fine young antelope swinging from the pommel of his saddle.

We went into camp at the head of Beaver Creek, twenty-seven miles from camp McIntosh, at six o'clock, put up our tents, our Sibley heating stoves in them, collected a supply of dry wood, and made fires that heated the large wall tents as hot as we wanted them. While we were doing this, Mugler, the Major's cook, had set up his cookstove and prepared a supper that made us all feel glad we enlisted. As we partook of the juicy and delicate antelope steak the Major spoke of the great amount of vitality this animal possesses — of the amount of shooting it takes to kill it. He said he once shot one through the heart and it ran a hundred yards before it fell; that he cut it open and examined its heart, and the bullet had passed directly through the center of it, tearing a hole nearly an inch in diameter. He said he shot another one that stood with its tail toward him. The ball cut off one hind leg and then entered its flank, cutting a long slit and letting a large portion of its entrails out, ranged forward, and cut its liver all to pieces; that after all this it ran two hundred yards, and that nearly as fast as his horse could run. He says he considers them the hardest animal to kill that there is on the plains, except the buffalo and grizzly.

The only man in the party that is not happy to-night is Dr. Black. He has been riding to-day, for the first time, a very high-spirited horse, who insists on traveling all the time in a trot or canter. The Doctor has lately entered the service, fresh from college, and is not much of a horseman at best. He has whipped and spurred this noble animal ever since we left camp, trying to tame him down to a walk, and of course the more the Doctor plies his whip and spur, the more the horse won't walk. Moreover, he trots very roughly; at each step he throws the Doctor about eighteen inches into the air, and then meets him half way as he comes down. The result may be easily imagined. The Doctor is "all broke up," and says he is 'sorry he enlisted. He takes his supper standing to-night, and wants to trade places with the driver of our spring wagon for to-morrow.

As the first streak of daylight appeared in the east on Wednesday morning, September 22d, I took the Judge's gun and went down along the creek to shoot a few ducks, while Mugler prepared breakfast. I bagged six, five mallards and a teal. I also killed a young, half-grown beaver, and saw several others, but could not get a shot at them. This creek is the home of large numbers of them. There are two new dams within a few rods of where we camped, and they may be found at short intervals all along the stream. It would be a good field for a trapper this coming winter. I returned to camp at a little after sunrise, and we partook of a breakfast prepared by Mugler's skilful hands, and such as one rarely sits down to in camp. Imagine a breakfast out here on the plains, and while on the march, consisting of hot biscuits, baked potatoes, venison and antelope steak, apple sauce, baked sweet potatoes, and coffee with real cream in it. And yet such was our bill of fare on this occasion, and with suitable variations at every meal during the whole time we were out.

Just as we finished breakfasting an antelope appeared on top of a ridge half a mile away, and one of the " 7th " boys picked· up his carbine, ran to the brow of another ridge within about two hundred yards, fired, and knocked it down. He started to go up to it, when it recovered from the shock sufficiently to get up and run. He fired two more shots at it as it ran, one of which hit it, but still not fatally. As he had only taken three cartridges with him, he was compelled to give up the game and return to camp, but as the animal had taken the course upon which our route lay, we overhauled him soon after leaving camp, and a ball from the Major's rifle finished him.

While we were striking tents and packing up preparatory to the start, we saw a lone horseman coming from the east. It proved to be Mr. Hill, who had become separated from us the evening previous while on the march. He had been unable to find us again before night set in, and spent the night on the prairie, alone, with the broad canopy of heaven for a tent, and the cold, cold ground for a bed. He said there was one advantage in staying out all night — that a fellow was sure to get up early in the morning, but he preferred to camp with the other boys in future, even if he didn't wake up quite so early.

· We resumed the march at eight o'clock ; Major Bell threw out scouts to right, left, and in front, with instructions to cover as much ground as possible, and whenever they sighted buffalo to come in and report to him at once. We moved along at a good gait until half-past ten o'clock, when we saw the half-breed scout and one of the soldiers on top of a tall butte, about two miles ahead of us. They had stopped and dismounted. We knew at once that they had sighted game, and we were in a fever of excitement to know what was ahead. They mounted, rode back to us, and imparted the welcome

news that at last we had reached the buffaloes! They said there
were five very large ones grazing in a valley just beyond the
butte where they had halted, and that the lay of the ground
was such as to give us every advantage in approaching them.

We plied spur and whip, and in a few minutes were as
near the quarry as it was safe to go with the teams.   Here we
dismounted, gave the teams in charge of Kelly, and the saddle horses in charge of a man detailed to hold them.   Major
Bell then crawled to the top of an adjacent ridge to recon-
noiter.   When he returned he said we were within two hundred yards of them, and that they had not yet discovered us;
that we were squarely to leeward of them, and that a friendly
rise of ground near them would enable us to shorten the distance by at least one half before they could possibly discover
us.

We then formed in line and started for the top of this
ridge.   We moved cautiously, slowly, silently.   No one
spoke above a whisper.   The soldiers held their triggers back
while cocking their carbines, so as to perform the operation
in perfect silence.   Those of us who had hammerless rifles
pulled the safety triggers back so carefully that they gave forth
no sound.

We are now so near the apex of the ridge it is necessary
to stoop low to conceal ourselves from the game; but still we
press silently, breathlessly forward.   Now we are as near the
summit as we dare go without giving the alarm.   We pause,
raise our heads, and peer cautiously over.   And what a sublime, what a magnificent sight greets our eager eyes!   There,
down in that little swale, within less than a hundred yards of
us, stand five of as noble specimens of the American bison as
were ever seen upon these plains.   They are all large bulls, old
patriarchs of the herd, and they have not yet seen, heard or
scented us.   They are quietly grazing, totally unconscious of

danger. Little do they dream that within the next thirty
seconds each one of them is to feel half a dozen leaden mes-
sengers of death crashing through his majestic frame. And
still we pause. We are unwilling to break the spell—to destroy this grand picture—this picture to look upon which men
would come and have come from all parts of the civilized
world. Yes, to gaze but for a moment on this picture—on
these grand old bisons, roaming at will here upon their native
heaths, would well repay a trip from the remotest part of
Europe or the Orient. It is the event of a lifetime. It is a
privilege for which men would give hundreds, yes, thousands of
dollars, and yet it is a privilege which but one man in a
thousand ever enjoys.

But our reverie is interrupted by the voice of our leader:
"Let them have it," he says, and the response is spoken by
our rifles. Spat, spat, spat, go the bullets into the huge carcasses of the buffaloes; at square broadside, and they break
into their heavy, rolling run. They are all hit, and perhaps
fatally ; but he who looks to see a buffalo fall from the first
shot, or even the first volley, is sure to be disappointed. We
slip in fresh cartridges and give them another round, and another, and another, until they are out of range. Then our
horsemen mount and pursue them. One of the wounded
animals turns out of the file and circles away to the right.
The great gouts of blood issuing from his nostrils, tell us
plainly that he has been shot through the lungs, and cannot
go far. After running, perhaps a quarter of a mile, he stops,
and a bullet from Mr. Van Vleck's rifle finishes him. Major
Bell, with characteristic courtesy, orders four of his men to
pursue the other wounded animals and not to shoot at them,
but to turn them back, if possible, that we, his guests, may
further enjoy the sport. But they are so thoroughly panic-
stricken that, although the gallant troopers ride directly

alongside of and around them, firing their revolvers in the air and shouting, the infuriated animals refuse to change their course, and in a few minutes are miles away.   And thus ends our first set-to with the buffalo.

The reader will justly wonder that we did not kill more of them, that we allowed any of them to escape.   We, who had never before hunted buffaloes, were at first surprised our-selves; but when we remembered what we had read and been told about the amount of shooting necessary to bring down a buffalo, we marveled no longer.   Subsequent experience proved that it takes, on an average, five to ten bullets to stop one within a reasonable distance, depending on the portion of the body through which the balls pass.   Of course, one ball through almost any part of the trunk of the animal will cause death eventually, but the great amount of vitality he possesses will enable him to travel miles ere he succumbs.   That we did not kill the others dead in their tracks was not owing to bad shooting.   We could plainly hear our bullets strike the animals, and see them flinch as they felt the effect of the shot. The soldiers who pursued them said they saw blood streaming from every one of them when riding within a few feet of them, and they had no doubt but that every one of them would die before night.

The one we secured had nine bullet holes in him, and the majority of the balls had passed entirely through him, which fact spoke highly of the hard-hitting qualities of our Sharp's and Springfield rifles.   The reader will pardon me for digress-ing here to state for the information of those concerned, that a large majority of the frontiersmen I met with — in fact, nearly all of them — used Sharp's rifles.   I saw probably a hundred of these in my travels, and only three or four of any other kind.   I questioned a great many of the men who use them, as to their effectiveness and adaptation to frontier use, and they all pronounce them the best arm in use, all things considered, for that purpose. Nearly all now in use are of the new hammerless model, forty-five caliber. The troops, of course, are armed with the improved Springfield, and it is well adapted to both military and sporting purposes.

After cutting up the bull we had killed and taking out such portions of the meat as were edible; we resumed our way. A few miles from this point we entered the Cabin creek valley. The soil here is so strongly impregnated with alkali as to give it much of the appearance of ashes. It is said that in the wet season the decomposition of chemical matter in the soil renders it so soft and slushy as to be almost impassable for man or beast. We found here some good specimens of mica, gypsum and other crystals. The water in Cabin creek is strongly charged with alkali, but not so much so as to render it wholly unfit for use. We were very thirsty when we reached it and drank heartily of it without any serious consequences.

CHAPTER XVII.

TWO HUNDRED THOUSAND BUFFALOES.

JUST before reaching the creek we struck the Keough stage trail, a tolerably fair road leading from Bismarck to Fort Keough. There is a line of stages, so called, buckboards in fact, running between these two points, which carry the mail, express matter, and any passengers who have courage enough to risk their scalps in making the trip. They run every day so that Fort Keough, Miles City, and other towns situated from three to five hundred miles west of Bismarck, get daily mails when the weather or Indians don't interfere. During the winter, however, the line is frequently impassable for weeks at a time, and at other seasons of the year much trouble is experienced from the Indians. Since the opening of the line several drivers and station keepers and a few passengers have been killed and a good deal of stock stolen.

There are feeding stations every seventeen miles and relay stations every thirty-four miles along the line where fresh ponies are supplied. These stations consist merely of a log cabin, or "shack," a stable and a stack of hay. The garrison consists of one, and in some cases two men, and the armament consists of a rifle for each man. The passenger tariff on this line is fifteen cents a mile and the passenger runs his own risk of being scalped. We went west on this trail from Cabin Creek and at three o'clock P.M. reached Pennell station, about 225 miles west of Bismarck, and went into camp.

We were then in the immediate vicinity of several small herds of buffaloes and we broke up into small parties and went in various directions in search of them. Major Bell went west, Mr. Bellows, Judge Souther and Messrs. Fogarty, Van Vleck and Hill went north, parties of soldiers in various directions, and I went south. After walking about two miles I reached the top of a high ridge that commanded a fine view of a vast stretch of country to the south and west. At a distance of two miles from where I stood I saw two herds, one of about thirty and the other of seventy-five to eighty; but the sun was then setting and I knew that before I could reach them it would be too dark to see to shoot accurately, so I reluctantly returned to camp where I arrived soon after dark.

My friends had reached camp before me, and reported having had grand sport. They had found a herd of eleven, out of which they had killed five; Mr. Bellows, the Judge, Fogarty, Van and Hill each selecting an animal, following him up and pumping lead into him until he was brought to the earth. The Major saw two small herds, but as he was with us more as leader than as hunter, and preferred to leave the greater portion of the sport to us, he made no attempt to get a shot at them.

Lance, the Major's orderly, and the half-breed scout did not return until after ten o'clock. We all supposed they had lost their course and camped alone, but just as we were retiring they rode in and reported having struck the main herd about twelve miles to the north of us. They reached it just at sunset and said that as far as they could see, to the right, left, and in front, the prairie was black with buffaloes. They estimated the herd to contain at least two hundred thousand!

The half-breed is a native of the plains. Lance has seen several years' of frontier service, and consequently both are accustomed to seeing and hunting buffaloes. It is not likely, therefore that they overestimated the size of the herd. They killed several choice young bulls and heifers and said they could have slaughtered a hundred of them had they chosen to do so. But they only killed such a number as the teams could take care of the next morning.

This is said to be about the only great herd of this noble animal now remaining in the Northwest. Twenty years ago such herds could be found in every valley, in every good grazing district in all the great West, but the constant and yearly increasing slaughter by market hunters, those who kill them merely for their hides, has reduced them to this one herd in the North and one or two smaller herds in the South. The progress of civilization westward is yearly curtailing their range, and the building of railroads into the very heart of their country is rendering the killing of them for marketing purposes still more lucrative. In view of all these facts I repeat that he who would kill a buffalo or even see one alive on his native range, must do so within the next five years, or the opportunity will be forever past. I believe that ten years hence they will be almost entirely extinct if not protected.

On Thursday morning, the 23d, I crawled out of the tent at daylight without disturbing my companions, and, equipped for action, I made a bee-line for the place where I had seen the two herds the night before. But when I reached the top of the ridge from which I had seen them and eagerly scanned the valley to the north, south and west as far as I could see, I was sadly disappointed to find that they were nowhere to be seen. They had left for parts unknown. But while looking for them I saw two very large bulls grazing in the valley half-a-mile below me, and proceeded to lay my plans for stalking

them. I saw at once, however, that this would be very difficult to do, for they were on the top of a small ridge that
commanded a full view of all the ground within three or four
hundred yards of them, except one very small cooley. If I
could get into this I could approach within short range of
them. But how to get there was the question. I made a
wide detour to get to leeward of them, keeping far enough
away to prevent them from seeing me. When the wind finally
blew squarely in my eye as I looked at them, I commenced
the approach. I sought the lowest ground I could find, but
go where I would I was in full view of them. Finally I
reached a low swale, in which, by lying down, I could conceal myself from them. Here I crawled, prone upon the
ground, through cactus, sage brush and sharp, flinty stones, a
distance of three or four hundred yards. This at last brought
me to the cooley or ravine that I so longed to reach. Up
this I moved rapidly but stealthily until within about three
hundred yards of my game. Here the cooley turned squarely
to the left and would not carry me any closer if I followed it
further. So I must shoot from here or crawl again.

Which shall I do? I can hit one of them from here, but
am somewhat tired and nervous from my long and laborious
crawling, and whether I can put the first ball where it will do
the most good is a serious question. Then after the first shot,
the subsequent ones must be made on the run, and the distance will render these still more uncertain. So I will crawl
again. But the sun has risen, is shining brightly, and as I
emerge from the cooley and start up the swale, though I lay
perfectly flat, my shadow is thrown strongly against the side
of the ridge on the opposite side of the cooley. Will they
not see this, and take the alarm? Well, I can only hope not,
for there is no other course open to me. I move very slowly
now, frequently stopping and peering cautiously over the

short grass, to see if I am discovered. But no; they are still feeding, and I move on. Now I look again, and sure enough one of them *has* seen my shadow. He has stopped feeding and is looking intently at it. Now is my last chance. Not a moment is to be lost. I measure the ground with my eye quickly and see that perseverance has accomplished its object. I am now within a hundred and fifty yards of my game. I select the largest of the two, raise on my elbows — the "Bodine position" — and hold, not for his heart, but for a larger target, his lungs, which lie just above and in front of the heart. I pull, and as the voice of "old reliable" rings out upon the clear morning air, I hear the bullet "spat" against the tough skin of the old monarch. He lashes his tail, bounds convulsively, and he and his mate break into their heavy, rolling, shambling run. I put in another cartridge and give him another shot, and then another, both of which I plainly hear strike him. By this time they have passed behind a hill and are out of sight. I run to the top of this hill, and on the way cross their trail, which I find marked with blood. Yes, it is from his nostrils, too. My first shot did its work well — it went through his lungs and he cannot go far. As I reach the top of the hill I see them standing some three hundred yards beyond.

I was now certain of the wounded bull, and turned my attention to the other. The first shot hit him, and as he ran I gave him two more, but although badly hurt he carried away my lead. The one I first shot followed as far as he could, but after running about a quarter of a mile he stopped, swayed to and fro, staggered, and fell heavily to the earth.

I walk deliberately up to the dead monarch and gaze upon him in silent admiration for several minutes. This is, indeed, one of the proudest moments of my life. This is my first buffalo. Moreover I have killed him alone and unaided — there is no lead in him but my own.

Now that the excitement is over I realize the fact that I am over three miles from camp and entirely alone. I remember that we have all along been on the lookout for Indians and have been prepared to meet them. The Sioux, of course, know where these buffaloes are as well as we do, and that bands of them are likely to be out here laying in their winter's supply of meat, is the most natural conclusion in the the world. I instinctively feel for the top of my head, but then I reflect that bald-headed men don't make good scalps, and I feel a little safer. However, I felt that I ought to go to camp at once for it was breakfast time, so I went. When I arrived there my friends had finished eating, hitched up the teams, and were waiting for me to join them in another hunt.

I ate a very hearty breakfast in a very short space of time, and we were off again, the Judge and Mr. Bellows on one buckboard, the Major and I on the other, and the boys on horseback. We drove southwest about fifteen miles, but did not succeed in finding any game. We returned to camp at three o'clock in the afternoon, when Corporal Brown and I took one of the teams and went out to skin the buffalo I had killed in the morning. We found it a very difficult task. He was an unusually large and very old one, and the skin about the head and neck was from a half to three-quarters of an inch thick. The fur was in fair condition, much better than it usually is at this time of year.

When we commenced the operation the corporal reminded me that it would be prudent to load our rifles and lay them close at hand, for said he, "We never know in this country when we are going to be jumped by Indians, and we make it a point to always be ready for them." As we proceeded with the work we frequently stopped and looked cautiously over the surrounding country, but seeing neither Indians or other game and becoming more deeply interested in our work, we became less vigilant. We were working with a will and had almost entirely forgotten our self-imposed duties as sentries when we heard a voice, and looking suddenly in the direction from which it came, we saw three men emerging from a ravine within thirty yards of us! They were white men, for which fact we felt devoutly thankful, for had they been redskins they might easily have had our mules, our rifles and our scalps. We felt considerably chagrined at having allowed ourselves to be caught so entirely off our guard, and our visitors appreciated the joke all the more that they had not tried to steal the march on us at all, but had walked briskly along conversing in their usual tones. They proved to be the party of market hunters I had met on the train from Bismarck to Green river. They had come through from the latter place by team and encamped in the vicinity of our camp. They had not yet found any buffaloes, and we treated them to a liberal supply of "hump" from the one we were at work on, for their table. They came just in time to give us a hand at turning the carcass over, a thing the corporal and I should not have been able to do alone without first cutting it up. They estimated that the animal would weigh fourteen hundred pounds, gross.

At about six o'clock we finished our task, rolled up the skin and put it on the buckboard, cut out the best of the meat, and started for camp. On the way in Corporal Brown made a very fine shot at an antelope, cutting him down clean at three hundred and fifty yards.

Fogarty, Van Vleck, and Hill, who had ridden south about fifteen miles, came in late and reported having struck a herd of about two hundred, besides several smaller herds. They only killed two, as they were so far from camp that they could not bring in the meat, and as we had decided to move north the next day, should not be able to send the teams for it.   Some of the soldiers who had been out north reported having seen a very large herd moving toward Beaver creek. We felt sure we should find them on the morrow, as that was the direction in which we had arranged to move.   We retired to rest late at night, well pleased with the day's sport as a whole, having killed three buffaloes and an antelope.

CHAPTER XVIII.

THROUGH AN EXTINCT HELL!

ANOTHER HERD OF BUFFALOES — AN UNUSUAL EXPERIENCE — A GRAND
LEAP FOR LIFE — PURSUING THE HERD — BACK THROUGH THE BAD
LANDS — BLACK-TAIL DEER—STILL AFTER THE BUFFALOES — DE-
FEATED — MORE SPORT — CLOSE QUARTERS — THE BISON YIELDS —
THE HUNT IS UP.

WE awoke on Friday morning, September 24th, to find a
raw, cold, northwest wind blowing, accompanied by a rain
that seemed to wet us, even through our heavy rubber suits.
Truly a bad day for our business, but time was precious with
most of us, and we had journeyed too far to waste any of it
lying in camp waiting for fair weather, so we struck tents,
packed up, and pulled out for Beaver creek on our return to
Camp McIntosh.

At about five miles from Pennel station we again entered
the Cabin creek bad lands. As we halted on the margin of
the prairie overlooking this valley it seemed folly to attempt
to cross them with our teams. Here were abrupt hills,
gullies, buttes, rocky precipices, gulches, canyons, extinct
craters, great heaps of scoria and *débris* of various kinds, all
mixed and jumbled together in an indescribable and almost
indiscernible mass. How on earth could any human being
ever find a passage through this extinct hell (as General Sully
termed it) on foot? And if such a feat seemed impossible
how were we to make the passage with our heavily-loaded
teams? There was no trail, and no evidence that any man
or body of men had ever crossed through here, yet Major Bell

said we could do it, and we simply said we would go where-ever he told us to go.

At this juncture we sighted a herd of about two hundred head of buffaloes, grazing on the creek bottom two miles ahead in the direct line of our march, and started for them. The descent into the valley was comparatively easy, the worst portion of the bad lands lying beyond the creek. Still we had to pick our route very cautiously, and our progress was slow and tedious. Finally we reached a point as near the herd as we could drive the teams, and dismounted. Unfor-tunately we were on the windward side of the herd, and as a broad level plateau stretched away beyond them it was im-possible for us to approach them from the leeward. A few of our party succeeded in getting within range, however, and gave them a volley. Then were we treated to a spectacle that only falls to the lot of a professional plainsman to witness once in a lifetime. Perhaps not one in ten thousand who go from the States for a buffalo hunt would ever see it. It is a thing we have read of in our boyhood days ; a thing we have seen delineated on canvas, or on steel, but we never hoped to see it enacted in real life.

At the first volley the herd stampeded. Not only did the reports of our rifles alarm them but they winded us at the same time, and, as they started to move, our horsemen charged them, firing as they ran. The consternation of the herd was complete. They took a westerly course over what appeared to be a perfectly level stretch of ground for two miles down the valley. Little did they expect to meet with any obstacle to their flight. Like chaff before a gale, they fairly flew. Only the fleetest horse could successfully cope with them in speed. They had gone perhaps a quarter of a mile — just far enough to become thoroughly warmed to the flight — their excitement at fever heat — when suddenly the leaders of the

herd, several of the largest and fleetest bulls, were seen to plant
all four of their feet firmly in the ground and throw their
huge bodies backward upon their haunches in a vain endeavor
to stop.   What is it that can thus check their mad career?
We look quickly ahead of them, and a single glance explains
it all.   There, just ahead of them, under the very feet of the
leaders, is a perpendicular precipice seventy feet high.   Great
heavens, must they go down this?   Must they take this dizzy
plunge?   They will be dashed to pieces, mutilated beyond
description or recognition.   But there is no help for it.
Their momentum exceeds all their great strength.   Besides,
those in their rear rush headlong against them, impelling them
irresistibly to destruction, and losing their footing they fall
headlong, summersaulting through the air, down this frightful
precipice !   They piled up at the foot of the embankment
three, six, ten deep, in a struggling, writhing, surging
mass. .

A few of those farther back in the herd, when they saw
their leaders halt and plunge out of sight, wavered, checked
their speed in time to save themselves and, sheering off to the
left, went down a ravine, and thus escaped the fate of those in
front ; but not until seventeen of them had taken this fearful
leap was the line broken.   We rushed to the brink of the
precipice fully expecting to find all, or nearly all, of those who
had gone over lying dead in a heap, but to our utter amazement not one of them was killed.   Fortunately for them, there
were no rocks there for them to fall on, but on the contrary a
large alkali bed, of about the consistency of mortar.   In this
they were rolling and struggling, and when they finally
emerged from it it would have been difficult to determine to
what species they belonged.   As they galloped away across
the valley, plastered from head to foot with this white mud,
they presented such a ludicrous appearance as to provoke

shouts of merriment from all who saw them. And thus was a tragedy suddenly transformed into a farce.

As soon as we recovered from the effects of the scene we had witnessed, several of our horsemen mounted, pursued, and overtook the herd, charged them, and killed three of them. Then we resumed our difficult and perilous journey through the bad lands. We wound through narrow defiles where there was barely room for a team to move; we drove along the very brink of deep gulches, where a swerve of a foot out of the proper course would have sent team and driver on even a worse plunge than the buffaloes made. We crossed deep gullies, the banks of which were so abrupt that, as we went down, we had to brace ourselves and hang on with all our strength to avoid tumbling over the dashboard, and as the mules started up the opposite bank we could easily take hold of their ears without leaving our seats.

Finally, after four hours of this toiling, we ascended onto the high, open prairie again. There we halted, and with one accord congratulated Major Bell upon the ingenuity and skill with which he had selected the route and piloted us through this seemingly impassable region.

During the passage through this strip of bad lands we jumped several mule deer, but owing to the character of the ground only succeeded in killing one. This is a favorite cover for them, and a large number of them could easily be killed in a day's hunting. This variety of the *cervidæ* is generally known throughout Dakota, Montana, and other adjacent territories, as the black-tailed deer, but this is not its proper name. Judge Caton, than whom there is no better authority on the *cervidæ* of America, proves conclusively that the black-tail deer inhabits Oregon and Washington territories only, and has never been found east of the Sierra Nevada mountains. In the black-tailed deer almost the entire tail is

black, while in the mule deer, the species we killed, it is
nearly all white, having but a few black hairs on the tip.
The mule deer is so called from the large size of its ears and
their resemblance to those of the mule, while in the black-tail
deer the ears are nearly identical in size and shape with those
of the Virginia or red deer.

We arrived at the head of Beaver creek (the scene of our
first night's camp on the outward march) at seven o'clock in
the evening, and were gratified to see a large herd of buffaloes
grazing in a valley only about two miles away. It was too
late to go after them then, but we felt sure they would be
there in the morning, and so they were.

After a sound night's sleep we were up at daylight and
again on the war-path. The herd had moved but a short
distance from where we saw them the night before. We had
ridden but a few miles when we again saw them lying down.
They were sleeping later than usual, probably owing to the
inclement weather. The cold rain of the previous day continued to fall at intervals and the buffaloes dislike to move
about much in such weather. We found it very difficult to get
to leeward of this herd, owing to the formation of the ground.
While attempting to do so they winded us and stampeded up a
valley before we got a shot at them. We knew they would
not go far, so we followed them. When we reached the top
of a high ridge we saw several smaller herds in different
directions. Here Mr. Van Vleck kindly offered me his little
bronco pony to ride for the purpose of taking a run after
them. He had made me the same offer several times before,
but I had declined it. This, however, was to be the last day
of the hunt, and I now gladly accepted. I mounted and Mr.
Fogarty and I started for eight old bulls that we saw a mile
or two to the south. We rode up a valley running parallel to

the one they were in, hoping to pass and get to leeward of them before they should scent us.

Occasionally we rode cautiously up the ridge and peered over to keep the lay of the land, but before we could get favorable ground on which to make the crossing they winded us, sure enough, and started at full speed for the bad lands, which at this point were but two miles away. Then we concluded to try speed with them, although they had the start by a long stretch, so, dropping back over the ridge that our presence might not unnecessarily frighten them, we spurred our ponies and the race began. We hoped to be able to head them off before they reached the bad lands and turn them back in the direction of our comrades. After covering the two miles we wheeled to the right, fully expecting to find ourselves ahead and to charge the bulls ; but, alas ! we had sadly overestimated the speed of our ponies or underestimated that of the bison, for when we reached the top of the ridge there stood the eight old monarchs on the top of another ridge still ahead of us. They were masters of the situation. They were on the very brink of the bad lands, whither they seemed to know we could not follow them. They were drawn up in line like so many knights of old, as if determined to resist our further advance, even to the death. As they stood there facing us, frowning down upon us with disdainful, majestic mien, their mammoth forms outlined against the gray, misty clouds, they loomed up like distant mountains. They seemed to bid us defiance. No artist could ever do that picture justice. We did not fire at them, as we knew it would be useless while they stood with their heads toward us. The only effective shot at a buffalo, generally speaking, is a broadside. We wheeled again, rode round a neighboring butte in hopes of getting a broadside at them yet, but when we again came in sight of where we left them they were not there. They had fled into the bad lands, and nothing remained for us but to acknowledge defeat and retrace our steps.

All this time we had heard firing on our right and knew that the other boys were having their sport. We rode over to them and found that Judge Souther, Hill and Lance had each killed one. We cut them up as quickly as possible, loaded them onto the wagons and again started in the direction of camp. We had gone but a few miles when we saw still another herd of about two hundred. We were already to leeward of these and had no trouble in getting a choice position for the first shot. Nearly all the party dismounted, walked cautiously to the top of a hill within about a hundred and fifty yards of the herd, and gave them a volley. Then a number of other shots were fired in rapid succession before the herd got out of range. When the first volley was fired, I rode quickly to the top of the hill to watch the effect and await a cessation of hostilities, so that I could ride in. As the herd started, at the first round, three animals—a bull, a cow and a calf—fell out of the ranks mortally wounded.

As soon as the firing ceased, I put spurs to my pony and started in pursuit of the herd. A stern chase is a long chase, and so it proved in this instance. No one who has not seen a practical demonstration of it would believe that the heavy, clumsy-looking animal, the bison, possesses speed equal to that of the horse in general, but such is the fact. It takes an unusually fleet horse, and one of good bottom, to catch a sound buffalo, and a horse, that is not superior to his class in speed will get sadly left in the race every time he undertakes it.

Waiting for my friends to get all the shooting they could on foot before I started, had given the herd nearly a quarter of a mile the start of me, but the little bronco, when I gave him the spur and the rein, flew like the wind. The herd started up a long "divide," over ground as hard and smooth as a race track, and as they had about three miles to run before reaching the bad lands, I had every advantage I could wish for. My pony gained steadily on them, and the nearer he got to them the more he became imbued with the spirit of the chase. Finally, he laid me alongside of the herd, but it was stretched out to a great length, running in single file, or nearly so, and those in the rear were the slowest and least desirable animals of all. So I encouraged my pony, and with a renewed effort he carried me up along the line, passing the rear guard, then the center of the herd, and finally well toward its head. What an exciting scene is this! Here I am, riding within ten feet of this vast throng of fleeing, panic-stricken monsters. What if my horse should make a misstep and fall; what if he should become suddenly panic-stricken, too,—become unmanageable and throw me? Then, indeed, would death be my certain lot, for I should surely be trampled into the earth.

But the excitement of the sport outweighs all sense of danger, and I would not for a thousand dollars be elsewhere than just where I am. Finally I selected the animal I wanted,— a young, active, vicious-looking bull—a foeman worthy of my steel. I drew my revolver and fired at him. I saw the dirt fly beyond, and thought I had missed him, but another glance told me that the bullet had passed through his neck. At this he had dropped out of the ranks and circled off to the left. I pursued him, and riding up close to him gave him two more shots, when he stopped suddenly, turned and charged me, as if intent upon wreaking vengeance on me for the wrong I had done him.

My pony was well used to this sort of thing, and needed little direction from me to wheel and bound away out of reach of the infuriated animal. As soon as the bull stopped I wheeled again, rode up to him on the other side, and taking deliberate aim at the region of his lungs, fired again. He turned and came at me again, but little Bronco still kept out of his reach. Another ball went crashing through his ribs, and again he charged me with the same result. I then gave him the last charge I had in my revolver, and still he kept his feet, but was too weak from loss of blood to again attack me. He now stood with his head down, looking moodily and sullenly at me, turning as I rode round him, so as to face me all the time. Finally I unslung my rifle from the saddle, and slipping in an explosive ball, fired it into him and brought him down.

When I first attacked the herd and brought this bull out of it several of those in rear of him became demoralized and left, too. They turned and fled in different directions, and Mr. Fogarty and other members of the party coming up, killed three of them, which with the three killed from the first firing, made six in all that we got out of this herd.

We cut these up, took the best of the meat, and again moved rapidly toward Major Bell's camp, where we arrived at seven o'clock in the evening.

And thus ends the story of my first buffalo hunt. It was a most pleasant and successful one in every respect, barring the weather of the last two days. We killed in all sixty-four buffaloes, seven antelopes and two mule deer, besides a goodly quantity of small game.

Some of my readers may accuse us of slaughtering an undue number of buffaloes, but when I remind them that we saved nearly all the meat, and took it into camp, where the troops made good use of it; that there were nearly twenty men in our party, making the number killed average but little more than three to each man, and that we had ample

opportunities to have killed at least three times the number
we did kill, but stopped as soon as we had all we could take
care of, I trust, dear reader, that you will withdraw the
charge.   Two, at least, of the party traveled over 2,000
miles to engage in this hunt, and in view of this and the
other facts "hereinbefore set forth," we consider three buffaloes to each man a very modest bag.

By prolonging our stay we could have killed hundreds,
but there was not a man in the party who did not express
himself as opposed to any waste of this noble animal. Would
that I could say as much for every man who has ever been on
the plains.   If so, the buffaloes would be almost as plentiful
there to-day as they ever were.

CHAPTER XIX.

THE GULF COAST OF FLORIDA.

JACKSONVILLE — A CITY OF ORANGE GROVES — ON BOARD THE "PAS-
TIME" — MRS. HARRIET BEECHER STOWE'S WINTER HOME — HIBER-
NIA — MAGNOLIA — PALATKA — "THERE'S AN ALLIGATOR!" — FINE
SPORT — LAKE GEORGE — MANHATTAN — WILLIAM ASTOR'S ORANGE
GROVE — AN ALLIGATOR THIRTY FEET LONG — DR. SPALDING'S
TROUT — ST. AUGUSTINE, THE OLDEST CITY IN THE UNITED STATES.

As every sportsman who visits Florida will, of course,
visit Jacksonville, and as he may perhaps wish to know something of this, the commercial metropolis of the State, before
coming here, I shall give a brief description of it.

It is situated on the St. John's river, twenty miles from
its mouth, and has become in the past few years an important
railroad, manufacturing and commercial center. The
Atlantic & Gulf, Jacksonville, Pensacola & Mobile, Florida
Central, and the Atlantic, Gulf & West India Transit railroads, all contribute to its prosperity.

It has grown to its present magnitude almost entirely
since the war. In 1865 it had a population of only 1,800,
and to-day it numbers within its corporate limits nearly
12,000 souls. Much of this growth has occurred even within
the past five years, and a majority of the best residences and
business blocks have a new and fresh look about them that
contributes largely to the beauty and attractiveness of the
place. Nearly every yard in the city is ornamented with
rich tropical and semi-tropical shrubs and plants. Orange
trees are used for shade-trees in door-yards and along the
sidewalks in front. In many places you will see rows of these

trees along either side of the street, laden with their rich, golden fruit, tempting you to partake thereof as freely as you would drink water from the public fountain.

The streets are macadamized, so to speak, with oyster shells, reminding one of the vast quantities of this delicious bivalve that are annually taken from the adjacent waters.

The city is illuminated with gas, and water-works are now in process of construction. She has seventeen churches and four schoolhouses, nearly all built of brick.

The manufacture of lumber is carried on extensively here. There are six large mills in operation, some of them cutting as high as 125,000 feet of lumber per day.

There are eight large hotels, several of which are first-class in every particular. The principal business streets present a scene of energy and activity not excelled in any city of this size in the country. Nearly all the business houses are built of brick and stone, and are furnished with all the modern improvements in architecture. The stocks of goods display taste and judgment in the merchants, and many of the houses do a very large business.

Having taken a hasty look about town, I boarded the good steamer "Pastime," and at ten o'clock A.M. of the 16th, we steamed out upon the broad and placid bosom of this, one of the most sublimely beautiful streams in the world. It flows from the mysterious everglades, in the southern portion of the state, some of its tributaries rising near the famous Lake Okeechobee, vast swamps and morasses are drained by these tributaries, imparting to the water of the St. John's a rich chocolate color. It is one of the few large rivers in the world that flow from south to north. From Jacksonville to Palatka, a distance of seventy-five miles, it has an average width of two to four miles, giving it the appearance of a vast lake more than of a river. Above Palatka it narrows rapidly to a width of one to two hundred yards and becomes exceeding crooked.

The first object of interest after leaving Jacksonville is at Mandarin, twelve miles above, where we were favored with a view of Mrs. Harriet Beecher Stowe's winter residence. Her house is surrounded by a beautiful orange grove and she is willing to present every northern visitor to Mandarin with an orange, *if* the visitor happens to have a dime about his clothes.

Two miles farther up, Orange Park is situated. A large amount of money has been expended here by the owners of the tract of land on which the town is situated, in improving and beautifying it, and as a result a most beautiful picture is presented to the eye of the visitor. Hibernia, Magnolia, Green Cove Springs and Picolata are passed in succession. They are all pleasant little villages, but offer very little of real interest beyond their abundant and prolific orange groves. Next comes Palatka, which we reach about dark and where the steamer very wisely stops over night in order to allow the tourists to make the entire trip by daylight.

This is an old town. It was an important military post during the Seminole war. It has eleven hundred inhabitants and is a very handsome town. Game is abundant in this vicinity. Deer are killed within five miles of Palatka all through the winter, and turkeys are found by going a few miles farther. Quail are abundant and alligators are numerous in the river and adjacent lakes and bayous.

On the morning of the 17th the " Pastime " turned back down the river and we took the " Georgea " for the completion of the trip. At seven o'clock A.M. we were under way. Capt. Schoonmaker, master of the " Georgea," informed us that we would find plenty of game from this point up, so we brought out our guns — Dr. W. his shot-gun and I my rifle. We took up our positions on the quarter-deck ready for business.

We had gone but a few miles when the ladies, who occupied seats in the pilot-house, shouted, " There's an alligator !" We looked in the direction indicated and there, sure enough, was one of the gigantic saurians lazily swimming across the river, some two hundred yards ahead of the boat. The captain said they were wild and that he would not let us come much closer, so I opened fire on him and in quick succession landed three bullets in such close proximity to his eyes that he at once sank out of sight.

A few miles farther up we sighted another lying on a log near the shore about a hundred and fifty yards away. I adjusted my sights to the distance as nearly as I could estimate it, but distance on the water is very deceptive, and my first ball fell a few feet short of him. I elevated a point and the second went a few inches over. I then lowered half a point, and the third went through him just behind the shoulder. Then there was a sport ! He gave us such a gymnastic exhibition as only a wounded 'gator can give. He first tried to stand on his head, then he tried to stand on his tail. Then apparently tried to turn himself wrong side out. Finally, recovering temporarily from the shock, he reached the water, and was lost to our sight forever.

It is a well-known fact that the only place to shoot a 'gator and make him lie perfectly still is in the head, but the distance was so great and the speed of the boat so rapid that I could not choose so small a target. If hit in the body he will invariably find the bottom of the deepest water within half a mile before he dies.

If the explosive bullet be used, however, he may be stopped suddenly if hit almost anywhere, and many sportsmen use this effective missile when hunting them. Captain Schoonmaker gave us some amusing accounts of shots he had witnessed from his boat, when the explosive balls were used.

In one instance he said a passenger was shooting a Sharp's rifle and using the exposive ball. He hit a very large 'gator just back of the ear, and literally lifted the whole top of his head off. In other instances he hit them in various parts of the body, and, as he forcibly described it, "busted them wide open."

During the remainder of the day we had fine sport shooting blue herons, white egrets, blue and white ibises, ducks, cormorants, coot, etc., but owing to the motion of the boat (she made about fifteen miles an hour) I made rather a poor score with the rifle. The Doctor with his shot-gun did much better. Game is very abundant all along the river. We were told by numerous settlers at the various landings above Palatka, and with such candor and earnestness that we were compelled to credit the reports, that the deer actually destroy the crops of corn and "garden truck" to such an extent that the farmers have to hang up white flags and other conspicuous objects in their fields to frighten them away. In some cases they even poison them to save their produce. Most of this damage is of course done at night, but occasionally they come into the fields in daylight. They say no fence will turn a deer; that he will go over a ten-rail fence as easily as over a log. Venison is cheaper all along the river than beef, and there are plenty of "crackers" (native Floridians) who will contract to furnish you any number of deer per week and fulfill their contract to the letter.

If any sportsman wishes to engage in deer hunting all he has to do is to go to Welaka, Norwalk, Mount Royal, Volusia, Blue Springs, or, in fact, almost any of the small landings above Palatka and employ a "cracker" at a dollar a day, who will put him on a run-way and drive the deer to him until his appetite for this kind of sport is appeased. Fire-hunting is the most popular method with the natives,

and the one by which they take most of their venison for
market.

About noon on the 17th, we reached Lake George, a
beautiful sheet of water through which the river flows. It is
twelve miles wide and eighteen miles long. There is an
island in the south end of the lake covering eighteen hundred
acres, upon which is one of the oldest orange groves in the
state. It was planted in 1824. Most of the original trees
are still vigorous and healthy, and are bearing full crops of
fruit every year. There is a house on the island that was
built by John C. Calhoun in about 1835.

About twenty miles above Lake George we find the village
of Manhattan, where William Astor has a large orange grove
and from whence a railroad is being built across the country
to Lake Eustace, the head of navigation of the Oclawaha
river. At six o'clock P.M. we reached Lake Monroe, two
hundred and twenty-eight miles above Jacksonville, and the
head of navigation of the Saint John's river for large vessels.
Small ones have, however, ascended two hundred and
seventy-five miles above here.

We staid overnight at Sanford, a thriving town on the
south shore of the lake, and at six o'clock the next morning
we again boarded the " Georgea " to return to Jacksonville.
A brisk " norther " was blowing this morning, accompanied
by a cold, driving rain that rendered the cabin far more
comfortable than the open deck, so we oiled our guns and
laid them away. But time did not drag, for the captain
entertained us with many interesting stories of life on the St.
John's. He says he frequently has as many as twenty-five
sportsmen on board at once, armed with shot-guns, rifles,
revolvers, etc., and that they make sad havoc among the
water-fowls, 'gators, etc. That if a bird escapes the fusilade
that is opened on him the moment he appears within range,

it can be regarded as only a miracle. The 'gators, he told us, fare no better, and hundreds of each are killed every winter, and still there is no perceptible decrease in their number. Many of the latter are wounded who speedily recover. He thinks there is not an alligator on the river five years old but carries twenty to thirty pounds of lead in his carcass, and he notices that it is very difficult for some of them to swim with even their noses above water, on account of the extra ballast they carry. He told us of one old saurian who lives in and around Lake George, who is nearly thirty feet long, whose back is four feet broad, whose head is as large as a flour barrel, and who when he "bellows," wakes all the natives for miles around. He says he frequently takes in a hog, deer, deerhound or other animal as he attempts to swim across the river, and makes a meal off him.

Under the influence of these stories and other pastimes the time fled rapidly, until at six P.M. we again reached Palatka and tied up for the night. Early the next morning we resumed the voyage. From here we had as a fellow passenger the Reverend Dr. Spalding, of Atlanta, Ga., who is an enthusiastic fisherman. He gave us a most humorous account of an experience he had while fishing in Mobile Bay last summer. He and a friend were fishing for sea trout with excellent success but were greatly annoyed by a large fish that kept breaking their hooks. They procured larger hooks and he broke those. They got the largest the tackle dealer had and he broke those with equal facility. Then they went to a blacksmith, and had him make some hooks of quarter-inch steel wire. These were too much for him, but he now got away by cutting the line. Then they put on copper wires for leaders and used a small-sized clothes line for the main line, baiting with a large-sized mullet cut in two. This time the Doctor said he fastened him sure and no mistake. He

12

was afraid to risk his strength to hold Mr. Fish so he took a
hitch around a convenient pile to let him play.   When
slightly tamed the Doctor and his friend doubled on the line
and hauled in their prize, hand over hand.   When landed he
proved to be an alligator gar six feet long, and weighing a
hundred and sixty pounds.   The Doctor said that thereafter
whenever he lost a hook he at once baited his iron-clad tackle
with a large mullet, and brought the intruder to speedy
justice.   By the time the Doctor had finished his story we
were at Focoi, where we stopped off and took the train on
the St. John's railway, of Florida, for St. Augustine, where
we arrived an hour later.

This is the oldest city in the United States, and a brief
description of it here may prove of interest to those who have
never strolled through its dark, narrow streets and viewed its
antique, strange looking walls.   It is bounded on the north
by the mainland, and on the east by the North river, the
harbor entrance and the Mantanzas river, with Anastasia
island forming the breakwater, and on the south and west by
the St. Sebastian river.   The city is built upon the point that
was occupied by Menendez, who gave it the name of St.
Augustine, as he arrived there on the day dedicated to that
saint.

Its present population is about 2,200.   It has four churches,
one of which was built in 1830 and another in 1832.   There
are four first-class hotels here and several second-class.   There
are four principal streets, extending the entire length of the
city.   These are named Tolomato, St. George, Charlotte and
Bay.   Other and less important streets are called Spanish,
Marine, Orange, Redout, Cuna, Hipolata, Treasury, King,
Artillery, Green, Bravois, Bridge and St. Francis.   These
vary in width from twelve to thirty feet.   The old Spanish
residences are built of coquina, a species of shell-rock, that is

quarried on Anastasia island. Many of them have balconies, or, as they are called here, galleries, all along their second stories, which overhang the narrow streets and give to the city a most quaint and antique appearance. There are, however, many modern style buildings, both residence and business houses, some of the former having large and elegant grounds. One of the most interesting points in the city, and the one first visited by every tourist, is old Fort Marion. It stands at the northeast end of the town, and commands the inlet from the sea. It is also built of coquina, and is in an excellent state of preservation. It was commenced in 1520, and completed in 1756. Its first name was "San Juan de Pinos," which was afterward changed to "San Marco," and upon the change of flags in 1821, it was given its present name. It covers one acre of ground, and has accommodation for one thousand men and one hundred guns. Over the entrance to the fort is the Spanish coat-of-arms surmounted by a globe and cross, while suspended beneath is a lamb. From the interior of the hollow square formed by the walls are entrances to a number of dungeons, in which it is supposed the Spanish authorities confined their prisoners. In one of these the skeletons of two human beings were discovered in 1846, one of which is now in the Smithsonian Institution in Washington, together with the iron cage in which it was enclosed when found. The fort is twenty-one feet high. There are bastioned angles at each of the four corners, which are surmounted with sentry-boxes and lookout towers. The moat or ditch surrounding the fort is forty feet wide and ten feet deep. It was flooded from the St. Sebastian river. There are inner and outer barriers, the barbican, drawbridge, portcullis, wicket and all the appliances of the European castles of the middle ages.

During the Seminole war many prisoners were confined

here, among whom were Osceola and Coacoochee, noted
chiefs.   It was frequently used during the early history of the
state as a place of refuge for the citizens of the town and
vicinity in time of Indian outbreaks.

Another of the ancient landmarks is the Sea Wall, which
was originally built by the Spaniards in 1690, and rebuilt by
the United States government in 1837.   It is also built of
coquina, with a coping of granite four feet wide and about
eight inches thick.

The Catholic cathedral was erected in 1793, and is still in
a tolerable state of preservation inside, though the hand of
time has dealt roughly with the exterior.   It is surmounted by
a quaint Moorish belfry, with four bells set in separate niches,
which, together with the clock, form a complete cross.   One
of the bells bears date 1682, and is supposed to have been
taken from the ruins of a church which previously stood on
St. George street.   At the north end of the city stands the
city gate, another very interesting relic of past ages.   It has
recently been repaired, but portions of it still remain as
originally left by the old Spanish masons hundreds of years
ago.   It is the only remaining relic of a wall supposed to
have surrounded the city in its early days.   It is a most im-
posing and interesting structure—is ornamented with lofty
towers, loop-holes and sentry-boxes, all well preserved.   The
" Plaza de la Constitution," is a small park situated in the
center of the town, with seats, walks, shade-trees, etc., similar to those of our modern parks.   In one end of the square
stands the monument erected in 1812, in commemoration of
the Spanish Liberal Constitution.   It bears an inscription in
Spanish, a translation of which is as follows :

" Just before the session of Florida to the United States,
the king of Spain granted a liberal charter to the citizens of
St. Augustine and of Florida, and this monument is a memo-

rial erected by the Spanish citizens of St. Augustine. The date of this constitution was the 17th of October, 1812.''

In the other end stands the monument to the Confederate dead, erected in 1866.

St. Augustine will for years to come be to the student of antiquity one of the most interesting places on the continent. It is, moreover, a popular resort for invalids, tourists and pleasure-seekers of all classes, and it is estimated that during the winter of 1878–9 it was visited by twelve thousand strangers.

CHAPTER XX.

· THE GULF OF MEXICO.

OFF FOR SARASOTA BAY — A ROYAL KINGFISH LANDED ON DECK — A
WHITE CLOTH BAIT — A HERON ROOKERY — MR. MOORE A REAL
DEER-SLAYER — VARIETIES OF FISH — TAMPA — DR. J. P. WALL — FIVE
HUNDRED AND FIFTY ACRES OF ORANGE TREES — A GRAND CHANCE
FOR SETTLERS — 8,000,000 ORANGES A YEAR — A GRAND RESORT FOR
INVALIDS.

"HAUL in that bow line!" "Let go that stern line!"
"All ready, Pilot, stand out — head 'sou'-west' by west!"

Such were the commands given by Captain Jackson, of
the good steamship "Valley City," to his subordinates, on
Sunday afternoon, November 23d, as we let go the wharf at
Cedar Key and which fell like sweet music upon our anxious
ears, for we were now embarked for a voyage upon the grand
old Gulf of Mexico.

From my boyhood I have read and heard, with increasing interest, of this great body of water which sits majes-
tically enthroned at the southern end of our continent,
between the states of Florida and Texas, and backed on the
north by Louisiana; but never until to-day have I been permitted to view it in its supreme beauty, face to face.

Our destination is Sarasota Bay, one hundred and fifty
miles south of Cedar Key, and we have heard so much of the
vast resources of that locality in the way of tropical fruits,
rich tropical scenery, balmy atmosphere, and, above all, in
fish and game, that our hearts bound with gratitude at the
thought that we are now on the homeward stretch toward it.
However, time does not drag by any means, for a voyage on

the Gulf must always have its charms, and when accompanied by a companion possessing so many of the attributes of a perfect womanhood as does my better-half, who accompanies me on this trip, it is rendered doubly delightful.   Then to add to the pleasures of the trip still more we soon make the acquaintance of Captain Jackson and Purser Swingley, of the "Valley City," whom we find to be gentlemen in the highest sense of that term.   They improve every opportunity to contribute to the comfort of their passengers, and are ever ready to give any desired information regarding points of interest along the coast.

A few miles out of port, as we sat upon the forecastle, enjoying the beautiful scenery before us and chatting pleasantly with the captain, the steward of the vessel came and called us to the quarter-deck to see a kingfish he had caught. We responded with alacrity, and were rewarded with a view of a magnificent specimen of this noble fish which he had just landed on deck.   He was twenty-eight inches long and weighed thirteen pounds.   He is appropriately named, for he is certainly the king of the finny tribe.   He bears some resemblance, in general shape, to the Northern lake trout, but has a slimmer and handsomer head.   His back is of a rich, dark-green tint, changing to a lighter shade along the sides, while the belly is nearly white.   The scales are very small. The flesh is fine in texture and of a delicious flavor.   It grows to a great size, frequently measuring four feet in length, and weighing thirty to forty pounds.   They are frequently caught by trolling from these gulf steamers with one hundred to two hundred feet of line.   No bait or even spoon is used. They are attracted simply by a piece of white cloth tied on the hook.   They are very gamy when hooked and make a most obstinate fight, frequently jumping to a height of ten feet above the water.

We returned to the forecastle and spent the remainder of the afternoon pleasantly. We retired early at night in order to rise early and enjoy that novel and beautiful sight, a sunrise on the water. At one o'clock A.M. we reached Egmont Light, which stands upon a small island called Egmont Key. Here the steamer tied up until day, when the captain sent the steward to call us and say that he would give us an hour to take a walk upon the beach.

We gladly availed ourselves of the opportunity, and after partaking of a cup of hot coffee served in our stateroom, hurried out and beheld a most lovely picture. Egmont Key is a picturesque little isle half a mile wide and one and a half miles long. The government lighthouse and light-keeper's residence are handsome and substantial structures. We found Mr. Moore, the light-keeper, an intelligent, kind-hearted and hospitable gentleman. He gave us some interesting information concerning this island and others in the vicinity. He says there is a heron rockery on the island only half a mile from his house where the birds annually build their nests and rear their young. Last year there were five hundred nests there. He estimates that each nest produced on an average five birds, making the total crop two thousand five hundred. He considers them his pets, and will not allow them to be shot or disturbed in any way.

Mullett Key, two miles northeast, is the home of a large herd of deer, and Mr. Moore goes over there and kills one at any time when he wishes some fresh venison. Mr. Moore is an enthusiastic sportsman, by the way, and I am informed that he has killed one hundred and ninety-three deer in the past two years.

During our walk around the island we found many wonders of the deep in the way of shells, fishes, etc. A cold norther had prevailed for two days previously, and many of the more delicate fish having approached too near the beach in quest of food, were paralyzed by the cold air and swept ashore by the surf. Among the curious specimens we picked up, I note the cow-fish, sea-horse, rock-fish, dog-fish, lamper-eel, three varieties of the toad-fish, etc. We also collected many specimens, shells, coral, sea-moss and sponges.

The time for our departure having now arrived, we reluctantly returned to the steamer. On our departure, Mr. Moore gave us a pressing invitation to visit him on our return and spend several days on the island as his guests. We sincerely hope to be able to accept, for it is a most fascinating place, and we feel confident that we could spend a few days here both pleasantly and profitably.

Five miles up the bay we met the steamer " Lizzie Henderson," of the same line. The two steamers lashed together when we transferred to her our Key West passengers, mail and freight, after which she sailed for that port and we for Tampa, where we arrived at three o'clock that afternoon.

This is a pleasant little city of 1,800 inhabitants, situated at the head of Tampa Bay and mouth of the Hillsborough river. It is the county seat of Hillsborough county, and is one of the most enterprising towns of its size in the state. It is the headquarters of the Tampa Steamship Company, who run a line of steamers from here to Cedar Key, one from Cedar Key to Key West, and one from New Orleans to Havana via Cedar Key, all carrying the United States mails. During the cattle-shipping season the Cedar Key and Key West line also runs to Havana. The cattle interest is a very important one to this portion of Florida. Over 1,500 head were shipped from this point alone during the past summer, besides large numbers from other points a few miles south of here. There are thousands of acres of wild lands lying adja-

cent to the coast, which furnish rich pasturage for cattle
winter and summer.   They are never fed or cared for at any
time.   The owner simply turns his young cattle or breeders
into the woods with his brand on them, and once a year
thereafter—generally in May or June—starts out with a force
of men on horseback, brands the calves, collects and corralls
the fat cattle for shipment.   Several stock-raisers on this
coast have from 500 to 1,000 head of cattle in the woods all
the time.   Havana is their principal market, a few head only
being shipped to Key West each year.   Next in importance
to cattle growing comes the orange trade.

Through the courtesy of Dr. J. P. Wall, editor of the
Sunland Tribune, I took a pleasant ride in company with
him through the country adjacent to the village, and was
thereby given an idea of the extent and number of its orange
groves. We went east on Florida avenue, one of the principal
roads leading into the country, a distance of two miles,
returned to within a mile of town where we entered Michigan
avenue, upon which we went south to Nebraska avenue.   We
then rode east again three miles and returned to town.   In
riding over these few miles we saw about five hundred and
fifty acres of orange trees.   Many of these are young and
have not yet come into bearing, while many others are
annually yielding large crops of fruit.   The majority of the
groves contain ten acres each, though others are much larger,
some reaching fifty or more acres.   Each grove has with it a
neat cottage house, garden, outbuildings, and a few lemon,
lime, banana and other fruit-trees.   New groves are being
planted each year, where the year before stood the tall pine-
trees, bidding defiance to the aggressive hand of the sturdy
woodman, and it is interesting to contemplate what a vast city
will in twenty years from to-day stretch away back from the
beach of Tampa bay, with ten to twenty acres in each lot,

with princely residences, broad avenues and rich orange groves to the portion of each resident.

Such is the certain future of this city, for new settlers are coming in each year, hailing from every state in the Union, and each bringing nerve, energy and money to the task. There are several families here from Maine, others from Nebraska, Illinois, Kentucky, etc. Nearly all are prospering and writing to their friends to come and join them. As an instance of what may be accomplished here: one man took a homestead of one hundred and sixty acres in the midst of a pine forest a few years ago, built a neat cottage house, cleared off acre after acre, and planted each with orange trees. He has recently been offered $6,000 cash for his house and six acres of land adjacent.

Over six million oranges were shipped from this point last year, and the indications are that nearly eight millions will be shipped the present year. Notwithstanding the success these people have achieved, I would not advise any one to come to Florida and engage in orange culture until he has counted well the cost. Many have tried it and failed—some for want of energy and determination, some for want of proper knowledge of the business and others for lack of means to prosecute it to a successful issue. A cash capital of at least two thousand dollars is absolutely necessary to start on if a ten-acre grove is to be made. More than this sum will be needed, but it can be accomplished for this if proper economy be practiced. Then a great deal of hard work will be required. Help can be employed to do this if the settler has sufficient means; if not he must do it himself. Some people may not like the climate—the long summers or the dry, warm winters. When these features are considered I would say to any one wishing to engage in orange growing, who finds himself possessed of the above-mentioned requisites, and who wishes to live in a climate of perpetual summer, go at once to Tampa, or at least to the Gulf coast. I consider it far superior to the eastern coast or the St. John's River district, after having studied both portions of the state impartially.

As a resort for invalids, I consider the Gulf coast also far superior to the eastern. The Gulf winds are much milder and more temperate and the changes of temperature not nearly so sudden or radical. I would, therefore, most emphatically advise all who suffer from pulmonary diseases to visit the Gulf coast in preference to any other portion of the state.

What Tampa most needs is a government appropriation for the improvement of her harbor. There is a bar across the bay near the mouth of the river that prevents vessels of any size from reaching the city wharf. They have to anchor three miles out and transfer freight and passengers in small boats. Colonel J. L. Meigs, under the direction of the Bureau of Navigation, recently surveyed a channel across this bar, and estimated the cost of cutting it to such a depth as to give eleven feet of water at low tide, at $80,000. In view of the importance of the improvement to gulf navigation, Congress should by all means make the appropriation.

A railroad has been in course of construction for several years past from Gainesville, a station on the Transit railroad, to Tampa, a distance of one hundred and fifty miles; but as only a small amount of work has been done each year, the people are greatly dissatisfied with the management and an effort will probably be made to annul the charter at the next session of the legislature and give the right to some other company who will build the road without delay. It is greatly needed by the section of country through which it is to pass, and will prove of inestimable benefit to Tampa, when completed.

This point offers many attractions to sportsmen. Excellent fishing may be had in the mouth of the river and in the bay. Sea-trout, red snappers, mangrove snappers, and sheepshead are the varieties usually caught. Good duck and bay-bird shooting may be had near town, and by going fifteen to twenty miles into the country deer and turkeys may be found in liberal numbers. Judge Mitchell, who is an enthusiastic sportsman, is ever ready to give all desired information regarding the best shooting and fishing grounds.

CHAPTER XXI.

SNEAD'S ISLAND.

GREAT SCHOOLS OF MULLET — SOLID ACRES OF FISH — SNEAD'S ISLAND A
GRAND FISHERY — "THERE'S MILLIONS IN IT!" — WE "SMOLE"
AUDIBLY — ON BOARD THE "SKY LARK" — THE MANGROVE —
MR. WEBB — A PARADISE FOR BOTANISTS — CENTURY PLANTS IN
BLOOM — FISHING — MACKEREL SIXTEEN INCHES LONG, WEIGHING
THREE POUNDS.

WE enjoyed a pleasant sail down Tampa Bay on the
morning of November 27th, on board the steamer "Valley
City." The most interesting incident of the trip was the
great schools of mullet we saw on the shoals off Snead's Island,
near the mouth of Manatee river. Without any exaggeration
there were solid *acres* of them feeding on these shoals, and
they were as close together as they could possibly swim. At
some points they were in such shallow water that their back
fins and the upper rays of their tails were out of the water.
As they feed here, a seine three hundred feet long, skillfully
handled, would catch, at a low estimate, ten to twenty barrels
of fish at every haul, and they were not here in unusual
numbers at this time, either. Captain Jackson informed me
that it is no unusual thing to see twice or thrice the number
at this point, that we saw on this trip. He says he frequently
finds the water literally black with them, for a distance of two
or three miles along this beach.

This story may sound decidedly "fishy," but every word
of it can be corroborated by a dozen people who reside in the
vicinity, and by any of the officers of the Tampa Steamship
Company.

I am astonished that some one has not established a commercial fishery on this island, long ago. Thousands of barrels
of this most delicious fish could be packed here every winter,
at a merely nominal expense, and they always find a ready
market and command a fair price in the northern and eastern
cities. Some enterprising party, with a taste for such a
pursuit, should secure this opportunity without delay. In the
language of Mulberry Sellers, "There's millions in it."

Soon after leaving Snead's Island we entered the mouth
of the Manatee river, up which we made a run of eight miles,
when we arrived at the village of Manatee, a lively little town
of some two or three hundred inhabitants. We stopped over
night at the Turner House, a comfortable hotel, and early in
the morning Captain Harlee, a merchant of the place, sent his
team to take us to Mr. Whitaker's plantation, on Sarasota Bay,
twelve miles below.

The road runs through a belt of pine-woods, dotted thickly
with ponds, covering from one to twenty acres each, the
margins thickly grown with saw-grass, and in the center a
pool of clear water. We came upon the first of these ponds,
within half a mile of town, and saw in it a dozen or more of
the large water birds which are so numerous in this state. I
brought out my rifle and bagged a beautiful white ibis. A mile
farther on we came to another pond. A large white egret sat
near the center of it, about two hundred and fifty yards away.
I drew a bead on him, let go, and he immediately sat down.

The driver, a good-natured negro, got out, rolled up his
pants, and waded in to get the game. The bird proved to be
only winged, and showed fight. He struck out vigorously
several times, but the plucky negro finally secured him, took
him by the head and started for shore with him. Reader, you
would have smiled to see that darky teaching that bird to
follow. It was a most ridiculous sight. We "smole"

audibly   The bird objected to that mode of travel at first, but soon succumbed to the inevitable and followed as obediently as Mary's little lamb is said to have done.   He was a beautiful specimen of the species, and measured five feet nine inches from tip to tip of wings, and four feet seven inches in height.

We passed a dozen or more of these ponds during the day, and at each of them I got a shot, making a very handsome bag, considering that I was "going somewhere" and not on a regular hunt.

We arrived at Mr. Whitaker's house about noon, and remained until the next morning.   Mr. Whitaker is one of the oldest settlers on the Gulf coast, having first settled here in 1844.   He has a large comfortable house, well finished and furnished, a large orange grove, and is extensively engaged in cattle raising.   He has over seven hundred head on the range and sells from two to three hundred head each year.   In the evening I engaged Maurice Lancaster, a boy fifteen years old, son of Mr. Israel Lancaster, who lives five miles below, to take us in his sail boat to Mr. Webb's plantation, twelve miles farther down the coast.   Accordingly, early on Friday morning the "Sky Lark," with Captain Maurice at the helm, landed at Whitaker's beach.   We hurriedly loaded our trunks, other luggage and ourselves into the vessel, spread sail and stood out down the bay under a fair wind and with buoyant hearts, for we were now on that famous portion of the coast of which we had heard so much, from which we anticipated such rich sport, and in which, as the sequel will show, we were not to be disappointed.

Whenever we pass over shoals where the water is less than six or eight feet deep, we see myriads of beautiful fish of various kinds, among which are mangrove snappers, red-fish, sheepshead, mullet, drum-fish, grunters and many others,

Occasionally some of the great monsters of the deep show themselves to our eager eyes. A ray-fish as large as the head of a hogshead, and weighing probably a hundred pounds, is aroused from its bed in the sand by the near approach of our boat and swims rapidly away, dragging after it a tail resembling in form a whiplash. This tail is only an inch and a half in diameter at the base and is from three to four feet long.

Farther on a monster shark, seven or eight feet long, swims boldly alongside of our boat, apparently curious to know who it is that thus invades his domain. If we had had a harpoon on board we could have satisfied his curiosity in a way he would not have liked.

Five miles below Mr. Whitaker's, Maurice landed at his father's house to get his blanket and some provisions for camping, thinking it possible we might be delayed and have to camp out over night.

Two miles below this point we passed Captain Young's boat-house. He builds small yachts, sloops and schooners and sells them to settlers along the coast. About noon we entered the mangrove thickets, which reach clear across the bay at this point, with only narrow passes winding through them, and which at low tide are very difficult to navigate, even with small skiffs. But fortunately we entered them at high tide, and this, together with the fact that Captain Maurice knows every foot of the passes and handles a pole extremely well, enabled us to go through them with flying colors.

This mangrove is a strange shrub. It grows only in or near salt water. The stem grows up to a height of one to two feet when a few limbs branch out ; a few inches farther up two or three roots will put out and seek the earth. Farther up more limbs shoot out, still farther up more roots, and so on until limbs, roots and main stems are mixed up in one almost

13

indistinguishable mass. Where it stands thickly upon the
ground it forms a jungle that even a dog can scarcely penetrate. After passing these mangrove thickets we had plain
sailing for awhile. Just below them we passed some long
sand-bars, upon which were feeding great flocks of Spanish
curlews, both straight-bill and sickle-bill, millet, white-
breasted plover, and other varieties of bay birds.

A good wing shot could enjoy rare sport here, but I am
in search of larger game and will not trouble these birds.

About three o'clock in the afternoon we came upon a
series of oyster bars which extends clear across the bay and
nearly two miles up and down it. The tide had gone out by
this time and we had some very had work poling and occasionally wading, dragging and lifting our boat over the worst
portions of the bars. Perseverance, however, won the battle
and we succeeded in getting over.

We arrived at Mr. Webb's house just as night set in, and
were given a most cordial greeting, although we were entire
strangers to the family. Such kind and hospitable treatment
as we received, and such a clean, wholesome, palatable supper as we were treated to that night, made us glad in our
hearts that we had had the good fortune to be directed to and
finally to reach the home of these kind-hearted people.
They are natives of Utica, New York, where Mr. John G.
Webb, the head of the family, was engaged in the drug business for many years. They came here twelve years ago.
Mr. Webb owns a large tract of land and has a large, comfortable farm-house and ample outbuildings. He has chosen
for his residence one of the most romantic and beautiful
spots in the state, or, for that matter, in any state. It is a narrow point of land ranging from one to two hundred yards
wide and extending into the bay nearly a quarter of a
mile. It contains about five acres of land. There is

a high shell mound near the center of the tract, and
on this mound Mr. Webb's house stands. The point is covered with native and cultivated shrubs, plants, etc. Shades
of Agassiz, what a paradise for a botanist! Within the space
of this five acres may be found West India birch, papaya, two
varieties of palmetto, the date palm, red cedar, live oak,
American aloe or century plant, yucca or Spanish bayonet,
bird pepper, winterberry, Spanish stoppor, mimosa, sea bean,
iponacea, madeira vine, several species of convolvulus, several
of euphorbiaca, two of cactus, mershalline, **verbesina**, verno-
nia, **sea myrtle, grape vine** and ivy of several varieties, big-
nonia, soap wort, sugar berry, prickly ash, sea-ash, matich
plum, crow berry, Indian fig, or India rubber tree, black, red
and white mangrove, buttonwood, sea grape, and many
others. Several of the century plants have bloomed since
Mr. Webb has lived here. In some instances the stock
bearing the flower has grown to a height of thirty feet. In
a few days after blooming, the plant dies.

The windows on the north and south sides of the house
command a beautiful view of the bay, and from those in the
west end you may look away across Sarasota Key and miles
out upon the Gulf. Steamers and sail vessels may be seen
almost any hour in the day. We had scarcely entered the
house when Mr. Webb commenced the task of destroying my
night's rest by telling me that the deer were eating up the
sweet-potato vines at the homes of his two sons-in-law, only a
mile from here in opposite directions, and that they would be
very glad to have them killed off; that sand-hill cranes, white
egrets, ibises, etc., were plentiful around the ponds from one
to three miles from his house; that on South Creek, three
miles away, alligators are numerous; that his two sons who
are now away from home, but will return in a day or two, are
enthusiastic and successful sportsmen, and that they will be

glad to pilot me to all the best shooting and fishing grounds
in the neighborhood; that they will go with me fire-hunting
and fire-fishing at night, and many other things equally in-
jurious to the mental equilibrium of so enthusiastic a devotee
of the rod and gun as myself. We spent the evening
discussing these and other interesting topics, until eleven
o'clock, when we retired for the night. I dreamed all night
of hunting deer and fishing, and many were the noble specimens of the antlered and finny tribe that fell victims to my
prowess that night.

I arose at day light the next morning and called Captain
Lancaster on deck. He responded promptly and accepted
my invitation to remain with me and spend a day or two
fishing. We rigged our tackle and after a square breakfast
hastily eaten, boarded the "Sky Lark," and sailed across the
bay into Little Sarasota Pass, for our first day's fishing. As
soon as we entered the Pass I attached an artificial minnow
to my line and cast out for a troll. I had scarcely reeled out
half of my two hundred and fifty feet of line, when whiz-z-z!
it went across the pass and back to the other side in less time
than it takes to tell it. Maurice luffed up and ran in to shore.
I was using light tackle, and finding that I had a game fish to
deal with, I was compelled to play him a few minutes before
attempting to land him. I soon wore him out sufficiently to
be able to bring him aboard, when I found him to be a handsome specimen of the *Cavalli*, locally known as the jack-fish.
He weighed four pounds, and was seventeen inches long.
This fish closely resembles the pompano, both in outward
appearance and flavor. He is one of the most delicious
fish in the Gulf waters, is frequently served at hotels and
restaurants in the southern cities under the name of pompano,
and none but an experienced palate can detect the difference.
There is a streak of dark meat along either side of the back-

bone that is especially rich and oily, and somewhat resembles
the flavor of the sardine, as we get it, dressed in oil.

After contemplating with pride, for a few minutes, this,
my first prize, we pushed off and I cast again. We had gone
but a few yards when the alarm in my reel notified me that I
had some more business to attend to. I landed this catch
with as little delay as possible, and was surprised and delighted
to find that I had a fine Spanish mackerel sixteen inches long
and weighing three pounds. This fish is too well known to
need any description. Suffice it to say that I relished a piece
of him broiled for breakfast next morning, as I had never before
relished Spanish mackerel. We had scarcely gotten under
way again, with perhaps one third of my line out, when away
she went again. I thumbed the line, struck hard and although
the drag was tight, my fish went down the Pass like a bolt of
lightning, until every foot of my two hundred and fifty feet
was out. I shuddered as I thought of the possibility of the
line snapping, but at this juncture I gave him the butt of the
rod, and succeeded in checking him. Then, what a thrilling
sight met my eager eye ! Whisp ! he went *six feet* into the
air, and shook himself like a wild colt striving to break the
lariat with which he is caught. But no, my mettley little
friend, you are securely hooked. My line stands firm, and
you must abide the consequences. He comes back into the
water with a terrific splash, and starts directly toward me, and
with all possible speed I reel in. He passes me, and by the
time he comes taut above, I have a hundred feet or more of
the line in hand. Then he jumps again, displaying his rich,
silvery form in the bright sunlight, each time increasing my
anxiety to make sure of my prize. As he starts down the
Pass again with the speed of the wind, I thumb the reel again,
but in spite of that and the drag, he takes it all out before he
stops, and again rises high in the air. There is no sulking

here, as with almost every other variety of game fish—it is all *go*, and that of the most vigorous quality. He ran constantly for thirty minutes, before he showed any signs of weakening, but finally was compelled from sheer exhaustion to give up the fight, when I landed him on shore. He proved to be what the natives call the "bony-fish," or "lady-fish," and what the Bahama Islanders call the "ten-pounder." It is by far the gamiest fish I have ever caught, and I have caught nearly every variety of fresh-water fish on the continent. He has greater strength and greater speed than any fish of his size I ever saw. This one was eighteen inches long and weighed five and a half pounds. In form it bears some resemblance to the pike or muskalonge of the northern waters, but is somewhat thicker in proportion to the length. The back is of a pale-blue color, and the sides are of a bright silvery-gray. The scales are as large as those of the mullet. It is not considered eatable at all here, on account of being so full of small bones, but I am inclined to think that it would be very palatable if this difficulty could be gotten over. I caught four of them during the day, and burned several little blisters on my thumb, the marks of which I expect to wear for several weeks, as relics of this, the finest day's fishing I ever enjoyed.

We trolled through the entire length of the Pass, a distance of three miles, and caught fish as fast as we could handle them. At the mouth of the Pass we pulled up to a high bank, where the water was about six feet deep, and saw large schools of mangrove snapper (a fish resembling in shape our black bass) sporting along the bank, but we had no live minnows with us, and no other bait would tempt them, so we were compelled to pass them until another day.

We then pulled across to the opposite side of the Pass, where the surf was running; and fished an hour for redfish. For these we used cut bait (mullet is best) with heavy leads, cast out as far as possible, and let the hook lay on the ground. We caught a number of very fine ones, weighing from four to six pounds, and about three o'clock pulled up and went home, well satisfied with our day's work. We had over a hundred pounds of fish, including, besides those mentioned above, drum, sheepshead, grunters and sea-trout.

I shall never forget this day's sport, no matter what other rich or varied sports I may enjoy in the future, so great was the variety of fish caught and so exciting the nature of the fishing.

For instance, I was trolling for sea-trout, but when I hooked a fish I never knew what it was until I got it up to the boat. The same state of affairs existed when fishing with cut bait for redfish.

CHAPTER XXII.

ON BOARD THE "SKY LARK."

WHEN I returned from the Pass, Saturday evening, I was delighted to meet, on entering the house, Captain O. C. Squyer, of Minneapolis, Minn., an intimate friend of long years ago, who had come all the way from Jacksonville to meet us and join in the pleasures of a few days' fishing and shooting. Accordingly, we all took passage on board the "Sky Lark," early Sunday morning, and set sail for the Pass again. As soon as we entered it we threw out another artificial minnow, and for three hours, as we sailed leisurely along the Pass, the scenes of yesterday were "acted o'er again."

First, we hooked a beautiful sea-trout, and after half an hour's royal sport playing him, landed him safely in the boat. What a magnificent picture ! He is unquestionably the handsomest fish in the Gulf. In profile he is very like the trout of the northern and eastern streams, but the coloring is entirely different. The color of his back is of a rich, dark marine-blue, the sides slightly lighter, and the belly almost white, while the spots are jet-black. This fish grows to a very large size here, frequently measuring twenty inches in length and weighing eight pounds. The meat is clear white and of a

very delicate flavor. Following this, we took several *Cavalli*
Spanish mackerel, mangrove, snapper and "bony-fish."

On arriving at the mouth of the Pass, we pulled up on
the main beach, where the surf was running high, and threw
for redfish with fair success. The tide started out about noon,
and as the fish refused to take bait after that hour, we laid
by our tackle and spent a few hours very pleasantly "gathering up the shells on the shore." About four o'clock we
returned home. On Monday morning Captain Maurice bade
us good-bye, and returned home. We parted with him reluctantly. He is a kind-hearted, genteel, companionable
little fellow,—a sailor "to the manner-born and thorough-
bred."

Mr. Webb's two sons, William and Jack, returned home
Sunday night, and on Monday morning Jack kindly offered
to pilot Captain Squyer and I to South creek, a distance of
three miles, where we could shoot some alligators. I was
thirsting for the blood of a "'gator," and this proposition
met with my hearty approval. Jack took his brother's Winchester, the Captain a double shot-gun, and I my little 32-
caliber Stevens rifle. We each put a substantial lunch into
our game-bag, and were soon on the war-path.

A mile from the house we came to the first of a series of
ponds, in the open pine-woods through which we were to
pass. In each of these we found plenty of the large water-
birds so numerous in this state. We took an occasional shot
at them when one offered a very tempting mark, and bagged
a large number during the day.

As we entered a small bay-head about two miles from
home, Jack, who was in the lead, stopped suddenly and said,
"There's a deer!" I stepped to his side and looked in the
direction indicated. There, sure enough, about a hundred
yards ahead of us, was a fine young doe feeding in the scrub

palmetto. Jack whispered to me, "Shoot and I'll take the second shot," at the same time bringing his Winchester to his shoulder. There was but a small portion of the animal's body visible through the leaves. I drew a bead on that portion and let go. She doubled up and started to run. At the second jump Jack fired and she increased her speed. We let the dog loose, and catching sight of the animal he pressed her closely. After running perhaps a hundred yards she raised her tail and bounded away as if unhurt.

Many deer hunters claim that a wounded deer always runs with its tail down, and would at this point have decided that we had both missed. But for my own part I knew this could not be so. I khew my aim was sure and that my little "hunter's pet" never failed to do its work perfectly when held correctly. Jack was equally certain of his aim, and, besides, the deer had shown plainly at first that it was badly hurt. So we followed the direction the deer and dog had taken and after running perhaps half a mile found our deer lying prostrate with old Rover standing proudly over it. We found upon examination that my ball had passed through the animal's loins and that Jack's had broken one hind leg at the knee and fractured the other just below. When we found her this fractured leg was also broken, but we were unable to decide whether she had broken it in running or whether the dog had wrenched and broken it after he caught her. At any rate we were sure the ball could not have broken the bone outright, for she could not have run ten feet with both hind legs broken so high up.

To dress the deer, cut the feet out and tie the skin of the legs together was but the work of a few minutes. Then we debated briefly whether we should return home at once or continue on our course to the creek; but as it was only a mile distant and as the deer was not a large one we decided on the latter plan. Jack swung the deer on to his back and we took turns carrying it until we reached home.

We arrived at the head of South creek where it drains a large pond, and where we could easily step across it, about noon and sat down to eat our lunch. After performing that pleasant duty we shouldered our venison and guns and started down the creek.

It increases in size rapidly, and but a short distance down we came to some deep holes where we saw large numbers of gar-fish sporting in the sunlight. We shot a few of them merely for pastime.

We also saw several very large rovallia, a fish that abounds in the fresh waters of this state. It is said to be very gamy and to possess excellent qualities as a food fish, but as I have neither fished for nor eaten them, I cannot speak from personal knowledge.

About a mile below where we first came upon the creek, and two miles from where it empties into the bay, we reached tide water, and Jack told us to look out now for 'gators. Sure enough, we had gone but a few steps further, when we saw two of the monster old saurians lying out on the bank sunning themselves. They took the alarm, however, while we were yet a long way off, and plunged into the water. As we neared the place we saw several others swimming in different directions in the same hole. They all disappeared as soon as they saw us, so we laid down our luggage, and sat down in the shade of a tree to await results. In a few minutes one of them stuck his head out of the water, not more than thirty yards away, whereupon Captain S. gave him a charge of buck-shot in the vicinity of the eye and ear. He lashed the water into a foam in his gyrations, and sank out of sight, probably mortally wounded. Presently another one put his eyes out of the water to look at us. He was near the opposite shore, perhaps fifty yards from where we sat. I let go at him, and although I scored a palpable hit, did not kill him.

A 'gator always tells you, unerringly, whether you have killed or only wounded him. If wounded, he plunges and thrashes around at a lively rate for a few seconds, and sinks out of sight; but if killed dead he performs about the same series of evolutions, turns on his back and dies, remaining on top of the water. This is the time to go for him if you wish to capture him, for he only lays on top of the water fifteen to thirty minutes, when the air escapes from the lungs, and he sinks. It is very difficult indeed to kill them on dry land nowadays, for they are shot at so much that they are exceedingly wild. But whenever you flush one from the bank, and he goes into the water, sit down and rest, and you may depend upon it you will have to wait but a few minutes before he will put his large black eyes out of the water and look around to see if you are still there. Then you have a fine target for your rifle. His large, bright, black eye is a decided improvement on any Creedmoor bull's-eye.

The smoke had scarcely cleared away after my last shot, when a third 'gator looked up near us, and instantly caught a right fielder in his left eye, that turned him over. We then supposed we had made it so warm for them that no others would show themselves for a while, so we started down the stream. The Captain and I had gone a little ahead, when Jack, who had not yet started, called to us, and said: "Here's another 'gator." I went back, and there, sure enough, was an old fellow swimming along down the creek as unconcernedly as though he had never heard the report of a gun in his life. I waited until he came within about fifty feet of me, and then gave him one in the leeward optic. He turned two or three somersaults, and stopped on his back with

one fore foot sticking out of the water. We left him there as
a warning to his kind not to tempt the deadly accuracy of a
Stevens rifle.

As we were now thoroughly sated with this class of sport,
we returned home.

Ever since our arrival here we have been anxious to catch
a shark, and after supper that evening we prepared Mr. Webb's
shark tackle, which he kindly loaned us, procured several
mullet (weighing about two pounds each) for bait, and proceeded to our evening's sport. The tackle consists of a half-
inch rope about fifty feet long, a common dog-chain, double,
for a leader, and a hook of quarter-inch steel wire bent on a
two and a-half inch circle. We cut one of the mullet in two,
hooked both pieces on and cast out, first making the line fast
to the wharf. We left a coil of the line on the wharf, and
sat down near it to chat, and wait for a bite.

Presently the coil began to move off. I sprang to the
line, caught it and pulled, but my pulling made no difference
whatever with Mr. Shark. He went on until the line tightened
up on the wharf. This brought him to the surface of the
water. He made a terrific plunge and got off. I took up
the line, put on a new bait and cast again. In a few minutes
we had another pull with the same result. During the evening
we had seven bites from shark and a thousand or more from
sand-flies, but failed in every instance to fasten our fish,
owing probably to the mouth of the shark being so hard and
bony that it is difficult to make the hook penetrate it.

About ten o'clock at night we gave up the sport, went
home and retired, having first baited our hook carefully and
thrown it out in hopes of fastening one during the night.
Early the next morning I went to the wharf and found the line
standing out taut. I took hold of it eagerly and was
delighted to find that I had drawn a prize; that one of the

monsters of the deep was securely fastened on the hook. By hard pulling I got him in near enough to the wharf to see that he was indeed a monster. I could not land him alone so I hastened back to the house and called Captain S. to come and assist me. He was soon ready for the task and we returned to the wharf. By hard pulling we succeeded in bringing our prize ashore. It proved to be a jew-fish, measuring five feet eight inches in length, three feet nine inches in circumference, and weighing 153 pounds. In his struggles he had broken one strand of the chain and one strand of the rope, leaving but one of the chain and two of the rope between him and liberty. This fish is very much like the northern black bass in form and color, and might with propriety be termed an overgrown specimen of that family. We were much better pleased with our catch than if we had taken a shark, for this fish, while much more rare than the shark, is valued highly as an article of food. It is prepared in the same manner as the codfish, and the flavor is very much like that of the cod. I cut off the two pectoral fins, preserved them, and shall add them to my collection of Florida specimens. They each measure fourteen inches in length and nine in width.

After seeing the jew-fish dressed and put away, I took my rifle and again went to South creek, but saw no large game of any kind. I killed several white egrets and ibises, and again amused myself for an hour or two shooting gars, of which I saw a great number in the upper portion of the creek. I returned home about three o'clock in the afternoon, and Mr. Will Webb informed me that he had prepared a "pan" and had made all necessary preparations for a "fire-hunt" that night, and cordially invited me to accompany him. I gladly accepted, for although I had heard much of this novel method of deer hunting, had never before had an opportunity of participating in it. We split up a quantity of fat pine, or "lightard," as the "crackers" call it, put it into a coffee-sack and loaded Will's double-barrel shot-gun with buck-shot. By this time supper was ready. We ate as quickly as possible, for it was now dusk.

We built a fire with our light-wood in the pan, which was attached to a pole about six feet long. Will shouldered this and his gun, while I shouldered the bag of light-wood and took charge of the dog. In this order we moved out.

As we passed through the gate at the outer edge of the farm and entered the heavy pine-woods the scene became weird and impressive in the extreme. The fat-pine fire in our pan flamed up, throwing a brilliant and glaring light among the tall pines to a distance of a hundred yards or more. The shadows of the trees reached away into the midnight darkness, moving as we moved and standing still when we stood still. When we stopped to listen, as we frequently did, the heavy silence was oppressive. It was, however, occasionally broken by the hooting or awkward flapping through the trees of some great owl who had been bewildered by the sudden appearance of our light. Occasionally as we passed a slough, a night-heron would fly squawking over our heads, apparently anxious to divine the nature and cause of this mysterious illumination. Dozens of jacksnipes arose at our feet as we passed through the marshes and uttering their familiar "scape, scape," flitted away into the darkness. Then again as we came near a bay-head or thicket we occasionally heard the well-known "whistle" of a deer—some wily old buck, perhaps, who had been " fire-hunted " before, who was, therefore, unwilling to stand until our light came near enough to assume its wonted mesmeric influence over him, and who bounded away before we came near enough to "shine his eyes."

Finally we reached North creek. We followed up its

bank some distance and then turned toward the house again.
Will kept turning steadily from right to left and from left to
right, throwing the light over as large an area as possible and
scanning the ground closely. Finally he stopped and said to
me in a whisper, " There are a pair of eyes." He told me
to step in front of him. I did so, and he adjusted the light
so that I could see plainly what appeared to be two balls of
fire, only a short distance from us. I stepped behind again,
and we discussed them for a few minutes. Will said they
were not a deer's eyes, that a deer always gazes intently and
steadily at the light without moving, while these looked at it
a moment, looked away, then looked at the light again.
Furthermore he said these were too close to the ground to be
a deer's eyes ; that a deer holds its head high in the air when
puzzled and frightened by the light.

When these and other points had been canvassed thoroughly we walked toward the object and found it to be a yearling
calf. A less skillful and experienced fire-hunter than Will
would have blazed away at this pair of eyes at first sight, and
probably have had to pay from five to ten dollars for his sport.
We moved on, and as we entered a patch of shrub palmetto
where the ground had recently been burned over and new
grass had sprung up, old Rover sniffed the air anxiously,
whined, and in other ways gave unmistakable evidence that
he scented game. Will said, " Look out for eyes now, this
is a favorite feeding-ground for deer." We examined the
sand, which was bare in places, and saw plenty of fresh signs.
We moved cautiously on a few rods farther, when Will stopped
suddenly and looked earnestly to the left. I followed the
direction of his gaze and saw a pair of flaming eyeballs not
more than thirty yards from where we stood. Not a word
was spoken by either of us. We both knew intuitively
what they belonged to. Old Rover trembled all over like an

aspen-leaf, but uttered no sound. Will brought his gun forward, glanced along the barrels and pulled. The report rang out on the silent bosom of the night like a peal of thunder from a cloudless sky. As it echoed away through the tall pines we heard a faint rattle among the palmetto bushes, and all was still as death again.

We walked hurriedly to the spot where a moment before we had seen the startling vision, and there lay a noble buck breathing his last. Six of the nine buckshot had taken effect, four in the head and two in the left shoulder. We severed his windpipe, lashed his feet together and carried him home.

Such was my first night's experience in fire-hunting, and I sincerely hope this will not be my last. I had always considered it a species of pot-hunting, and had never thought I should enjoy it until since I came to Florida, and heard so much of its merits as a genuine sport. I should not even now wish to hunt deer in this way often, for I still think the fire-hunter takes an undue advantage of the game; but to the lover of nature (and what true sportsman is not?) a fire-hunt must always possess a peculiar and indescribable charm, especially in Florida. No sportsman who visits this state should under any circumstances leave it without a taste of this most novel sport.

CHAPTER XXIII.

DEER-STALKING AND FIRE-FISHING.

THE MULE ELEMENT STRONG IN ME — "WALKING BY FAITH, NOT BY
SIGHT" — IN SEARCH OF ALLIGATORS — A FIGHT BETWEEN AN EAGLE
AND A FISH-HAWK — A TWO-YEAR-OLD DOE STARTS FROM THE
THICKET — I FIRE, ROVER STARTS ON THE CHASE — I CARRY HOME
MY PRIZE — FIRE-FISHING — SHEEPSHEAD — NEEDLE-FISH MUL-
LET — A HUNDRED POUNDS OF FISH IN THREE HOURS — WE CATCH
AN INQUISITIVE SHARK.

EARLY on Wednesday morning I started to return to
North creek, the scene of our previous night's fire-hunt, in
hope of getting another shot at deer, which we had found
were plentiful in that locality. Mr. Webb told me to keep
well to the right, after leaving the trail at the rear of the
farm, and that if I did not I would strike a large tract of
scrub live-oak thickets; that I could not get through them,
and would have to go a long way out of my course to get
around them. I had heard a great deal about these impenetrable scrub-oak thickets, and was anxious to see one. Besides,
I am liberally endowed with that peculiar natural quality
which in the mule is termed stubbornness, and was anxious to
find a thicket that I could not get through. So I kept well
to the left, and sure enough after I had gone a half or three-
quarters of a mile from the farm I felt my legs becoming
seriously entangled in what at first seemed to be a vine of
some kind running on and near the ground, but on examination I at once concluded it was the much-talked-of and much-
dreaded scrub live-oak. It has something the appearance of
a grape-vine in places. It runs every way from the root, and

intertwines itself among the scrub palmetto and other vegetation in the most intricate and provoking manner possible.
It is crooked, gnarly, full of knots, thorns, and altogether
forms one of the most disagreeable jungles I ever undertook
to explore.

Proceeding farther into the thicket it became denser, and
of a larger growth, reaching a height of six to ten feet. I got
down on my hands and knees and tried to crawl under it, but
it was thicker on the ground than a foot or two above, so I
got up again. My flesh crawled, however, as I thought of
the chances I incurred of stepping on a rattlesnake, or wak-
ing up a panther in this paradise of theirs. ' I could not see
three feet from me in any direction except straight up, and I
verily walked "by faith and not by sight."

Old Rover, my only companion, who generally kept a few
yards ahead of me, now came voluntarily to heel, perfectly
willing I should break the way for him. By hard work I
think I made fully a quarter of a mile an hour for the next
two hours, and this with the sun beaming down at a "ninety
in the shade" rate.

Finally, about eleven o'clock A.M., I found myself standing upon the bank of the creek, or perhaps it might more
properly be termed a river here, for it is sixty yards wide,
with an average depth of three to four feet. I stopped and
debated, *solus*, what I should do next — how I could best get
out of this jungle. There was scrub oak to the right of me,
scrub oak to the left of me, scrub oak in the rear of me,
and the river in front of me. This oak grows so close to
the water's edge as to leave no room there for a passage way
— the branches overhanging the water several feet.

As my original plan was to go up the creek a mile or two
after I reached it, I decided to carry it out, and dropping
back some ten or twenty yards from the bank of the stream,

again commenced my tedious march.   I moved as cautiously as possible and occasionally crawled up to the water's edge and peered cautiously up and down the stream in search of alligators.   Presently I saw two lying on a low grassy bank away up the creek, sunning themselves and looking like great black logs.   I drew back again and proceeded as quietly as possible to a bend in the creek that would bring me within range of them.   They heard me before I reached the point, however, and plunged into the water.   I stepped behind a neighboring pine-tree and waited a few minutes for them to come up.   I did not have to wait long.   One of them arose to the surface a hundred yards below me.   I did not molest him, for I thought I could do better.   In a few minutes the other put his eyes out of the water near the opposite bank, not more than fifty yards away.   I looked through my globe sight, saw his great black eye glisten in the sunlight, and pulled.   He doubled up, and his back came out of the water until he formed a great half-circle.   Then he went down, and next his head and tail came out approaching each other until they almost met.   Then he disappeared again, and at once reappeared, doubled and twisted into an almost indistinguishable mass.   When he unfolded himself this time he remained on top of the water, lying on his back, and then I knew that he was dead.

He was a very large one, some ten or eleven feet long.   I was anxious to get him out and preserve some of his teeth, but, as I had no boat or other means of reaching him, was unable to do so.   Another half-hour of hard, tedious crawling took me out of the scrub-oak thicket into the open pine-woods and I sat down on a log near the bank of the creek to rest.   Here I saw a scene enacted the like of which I had never witnessed before, though I had read and heard of it since the days of my early childhood.   A large fish-hawk, that had been soaring up and down the stream, saw a good-sized fish lying near the surface of the water, and, folding his wings close to his body, darted down upon it with the velocity of an arrow, caught it and carried it up into the top of a low pine-tree, where he prepared to make a meal off it. A great bald eagle, who had been sitting secreted in the top of one of · the tallest pines in the neighborhood, awaiting this opportunity, pitched from his lofty perch, reefed his pinions, shot through the air like a bolt of lightning and struck the fish-hawk with such force as to send it whirling through the branches of the tree. The fish fell to the ground. The eagle followed, picked it up and carried it away. The fish-hawk, after having recovered from the effects of the shock it had received, flew into a neighboring tree and sat there for a long time, silent and sullen, brooding over the burning insult he had received, but which, owing to his inferior size and strength, he was powerless to resent. I left the poor bird there and went my way, unwilling to add to his wrongs by sending a ball after him. ·

As I turned to go toward home I entered the tract of land that had recently been burned over, where the night before Will had killed the buck while we were fire-hunting. I examined the ground and saw plenty of fresh signs. I called Rover in and kept him close. As I ascended a slight ridge he caught wind of game and looked anxiously to the left. I moved cautiously in that direction a few steps, when a fine two-year-old doe, who had been lying under a bunch of scrub oak about thirty yards ahead, arose and bounded away to the right. After making a few jumps she stopped to look and listen, as if not quite certain where the noise that had startled her came from. Here was my golden opportunity. I stood behind a scrub palmetto that almost entirely concealed me from her searching gaze. She was not over fifty yards away and stood broadside toward me. I took my rifle quickly to my eye, drew a firm and steady aim on her shoulder and fired. She made a few halting, undecisive leaps and then settled down to a steadier, though evidently painful, run. By this time I had slipped in another cartridge, and as she crossed a slight opening in the palmettos, probably a hundred and thirty yards off, I pulled in about thee feet ahead of her and let go a second time. Rover had started for her at the first shot, and as she was badly hurt and losing strength all the time he gained rapidly upon her. I stood and watched the race. I saw the deer pass along the margin of a pond three or four hundred yards distant, and as she attempted to jump a log she staggered and fell. The dog was upon her in a second, and I started in hot haste to secure my prize.

She was still alive when I arrived, but I hastily dispatched her with my knife. I found on examination that my first shot had penetrated her shoulder, passed through and out on the opposite side, just in front of the other shoulder. My second shot had missed entirely. She was probably not running as fast as I estimated and I had held too far ahead. I dressed the deer and carried her home.

On arriving at the house, Mr. Griffith, a son-in-law of our host, who lives only a mile below, was there with his boat, and kindly informed me that he had prepared a fishing-jack, and made all other necessary preparations to take us all out fire-fishing that night.

This is another species of sport I had never yet tested, and was delighted with the prospect of an evening's experience in it.

As soon as we had eaten supper, it being then dark enough for our light to show well upon the water, we started out. Our party consisted of Mrs. Guptill, my wife, Mr. Griffith, Will Webb, Captain Squyer and myself,—six in all. We disposed ourselves about the boat, so as to trim it to the best advantage.

We had two spears, or graining-irons, as the natives call them, and a harpoon. Will gave Captain S. one of the spears, me the other, and took charge of the harpoon himself. Mr. Griffith took the first stand at the stern and pulled us over shoals and around the margins of small islands and oyster-bars where the best sport was to be had.

Our fat pine fire in the jack, which occupied the bow, cast a brilliant light on the water, enabling us to see the smallest fish in three or four feet of water as plainly as though it were midday. This glaring light coming suddenly upon the fish seems to blind them, and many of them lie perfectly still watching it, while others run wildly hither and thither completely bewildered. They frequently run their muzzles squarely against the sides of the boat.

By this means the fish are rendered comparatively easy prey to the spear, if in the hands of a person who understands throwing it. Our first run was over a sand-flat in about two feet of water, where lay scattering oyster-shells. Here we were enabled for the first time to study another of the eccentricities of nature, of which we had often heard and read, but never before seen demonstrated,— it is the habit of the sheepshead to lie down at night and sleep, like any other Christian. They lay flat on their back (or rather sharply on their back, for they are a flat fish with a sharp back), propped up against an oyster shell and using another for a pillow. Will killed several of them before I saw any, and I asked him where he was getting so many sheepshead. He said he was picking them up out of their beds. Then pointing ahead, on my side of the boat he said;

"There's one lying against that oyster shell, take him."

"What," said I, "that little white object? A sheeps-head is dark on his back."

"Yes, but that's his belly you are looking at. He's lying on his back."

By this time we were over him. I struck; and sure enough stuck a prong of the spear into his belly. We killed a large number of them in this way during the evening, and when we had secured as many as we cared for, quit killing them, but occasionally we turned them over gently with the spear, woke them up, saw them rub their eyes with their pectoral fins (metaphorically speaking) until fully awake, when they would

"Dart away
As if to say,
You don't catch us napping."

Other varieties of fish, such as mullet, red-fish, trout, man-grove snapper, and others swim very rapidly when frightened by the light, and in throwing at them one must make a time allowance the same as when shooting birds on the wing. Besides a "depth" allowance must be made. That is, if the fish be some distance away from the boat, and you throw at him at an angle of, say forty-five degrees, you must aim from six to eighteen inches under him, owing to the depth at which he lies below the surface of the water. Taking these facts, together with the motion of the boat, into considera-tion, fire-fishing is no boy's play after all, but a genuine and exciting sport, requiring almost as much practice, skill and judgment to become proficient in it as does shooting on the wing.

We ran into several schools of mullet and it was amusing to see the rapid speed they made in getting away from the light. Hundreds of needle fish, a beautiful little denizen of the salt water, sported on the surface, followed the light and seemed to really enjoy its influence. We captured several of them, and I preserved the head of one, which I have added to my collection as a relic of the occasion.

We killed over a hundred pounds of fish during the two or three hours we were out, among which were the sea-trout, drum, grunter, mullet, mangrove snapper, red-fish, etc. Mr. Griffith killed one drum that weighed over eight pounds. A regular old bass drum, as it were.

As we passed over a sand bar about nine o'clock a great white shark came alongside to inspect our cargo and see what our headlight was made of. Captain Squyer had the harpoon in hand at the time, and when the old monster came within easy reach, plunged it through his body just back of the head. Mr. Shark's curiosity was satisfied at once, and he headed for deep water with all the speed he could command. There were thirty feet of line attached to the harpoon and made fast to the bow of the boat, and as he took it out, Will, who was then at the helm, threw the bow straight toward the fleeing carcharion, and as the line tightened up away we went across the bay at the rate of about fifteen knots an hour. He towed us back and forth, up and down, at this exciting rate for fifteen or twenty minutes before his strength failed him in the least. The ladies shrieked with fright occasionally as he made a sudden turn that well nigh capsized the boat, but we went through the hazardous ordeal safely. Finally he weakened, and Will poled us up near enough to give him one of the smaller spears. This, by a lucky shot, broke his back, and nothing now remained but to tow him ashore. When we reached land all hands went ashore, united their strength and hauled him up. He measured eight feet four inches in length, and weiged 227 pounds.

With this capture we closed the evening's entertainment, and went home.

There are many sportsmen who condemn fire-fishing as a species of butchery, and in fact I have always hitherto regarded it in that light myself, but since this experience I must admit that I rather like it. I should not want to indulge in it often even now, but for an occasional evening, with pleasant companions, as we had on this occasion, and in waters teeming with fish, as do those of the Gulf coast of Florida, I must accord to it the blue ribbon for vigorous, exciting manly sport.

Jack and I held a consultation before retiring that night, and decided to start early the next morning for a camp hunt of four or five days on the Myakka river, ten miles distant, where turkeys, deer and other large game are always plentiful.

CHAPTER XXIV.

FOUR DAYS ON THE MYAKKA RIVER.

THE CAMPING GROUND OF COUGHPENNSLOUGH — THE " PALMEETER CAB-
BAGE "— THE SPORTSMAN'S PARADISE — I BECOME PIOUS — SATAN TO
THE FRONT— A MOSSY BED — TA-WHOO-OO-OO-AH —" GOBBLE, GOBBLE,
GOBBLE "— THE WOODS ALIVE WITH SQUIRRELS — THE BOUNDING
BUCK — A FLOCK OF TURKEYS — ROSEATE SPOONBILLS — THE SAD
WORDS " GOOD-BYE."

ACCORDING to previous arrangement Jack harnessed the
horse and hitched him to the cart. We loaded in our tent,
blankets, provisions, ammunition, etc.; he took the lines,
and we were off for a four days' camp hunt on the Myakka
river. For several years past I have heard the praises of this
mystic region sung by sportsmen who have visited it and
experienced its charms, and the glowing accounts I received
of it from Mr. Webb and his family only served to heighten
my anxiety to see it with my own eyes. We left home at
half-past ten in the morning. Our route lay through a tract
of open pine woods, the monotony of which was relieved by
ponds scattered along the entire distance, at each of which
we got a shot or two at the large water birds, which always
hover around them.

At half-past one o'clock we arrived at the scene of one of
Billy Bowlegs' old camping grounds during his war with the
United States troops. He gave it the poetical name of
Coughpennslough; and it is said that one of his favorite
warriors lies buried not far from here, who was court-mar-
tialed according to the Indian custom and shot on account of

some offensive remark made in the chief's presence concerning the name given to this camp.

We took dinner on this historical ground. Our box of provisions being in the bottom of the cart and covered some two feet deep with our bedding, tent and other camp luggage, we decided not to undertake the task of digging it out, but to fall back on the resources of the country for our snack. So we took out the ax and cut down a palmetto-tree, then we cut off about two feet of the top of the tree, split it open and took out the central portion — the bud — a core three to four inches in diameter and eighteen to twenty inches long. Upon this, seasoned *cum grano salis*, we made a frugal lunch, and one which any epicure might have envied us.

This "palmeeter cabbage," as the crackers call it, is really delicious in flavor and highly nutritious. It is white and brittle like celery, but much richer in taste. The people here boil it for the table, when it assumes more of the character and flavor of asparagus. In many families it forms a staple article of food, and I am of the opinion that were it introduced in the North it would at once be considered a great delicacy there. It is certainly far superior to celery as a relish or asparagus as a side-dish.

There is not the least danger of any one starving to death in a Florida wood so long as he have an ax or hatchet with which to cut palmetto buds.

Jack and I stored away a good-sized bud, and after eating two or three oranges each by way of dessert, boarded the "Myakka Express" again and rolled on toward the happy hunting ground. When we got within two and a-half miles of the river we stopped and cut a liberal supply of light-wood to take with us, as no pine grows nearer the stream than this, and there is no pleasure in camping in this country without a liberal supply of this staple commodity.

In fact, many Floridians say they had rather try to keep house without sweet potatoes than without "lightard." Jack tells a story of an old cracker who sold his farm and prepared to move out of a certain township. One of his neighbors came to remonstrate with him, and asked him what he wanted to leave the neighborhood for; if this were not as good a country to live in as any other. "Yes," said the old man, "this is a good enough country, only there's no lightard here."

We loaded our "lightard" into the cart and drove on. After going half a mile we emerged upon a beautiful broad prairie some two miles wide. Upon the further side of this we saw a strip of heavy timber through which runs the river. We pushed on across the prairie and at three o'clock entered a grove of tall, stately live-oaks on the bank of the long-looked-for and anxiously-sought Myakka river, and pitched our tent. And what a lovely site for a camp! It is on a high bank where the river makes a horse-shoe bend, and we are in the toe of the shoe, so to speak. The massive live-oaks stand close together, the limbs of each one intertwining affectionately with those of its neighbor, and the long, gray, Spanish moss hanging to within a few feet of the ground. This moss, together with the leaves of the trees, formed a covering above us so thick as to entirely exclude the rays of the sun by day and to protect us from the dew at night. The river is but a few feet from us in front or on either side, and in the rear are open glades that furnish excellent grazing for our horse.

Jack staked him out and we took our guns and went up the river for a few hours' shooting before dark. This is indeed the happy hunting ground — the sportsman's paradise.

As we walked quietly around a bend in the river, just out of sight of our camp, and came upon an open glade or

meadow, of perhaps an acre, a sight met our eyes that might
have inspired the soul of a poet to sing his sweetest songs, or
have awakened in the mind of the prosiest human being
visions of Paradise.   There sat great flocks of large, richly-
colored birds, the backs of which were nearly white, the
wings and breast a rich and varied pink, changing in some of
the males to almost a scarlet.   These are the roseate spoon-
bill.

In another part of the glade is a large flock of the stately
wood ibis, with a body of pure white, and the wings a
glossy, radiant purple and black.   In still another part, a
flock of snowy white egrets, and here and there a blue or
gray heron, or other tropical bird.   Alarmed by our approach they all arose, but as if aware that their matchless
beauty was a perfect safeguard against the destroying hand of
man, they soared around over our heads for several minutes
before flying away.   As they thus hovered over us we stood
and contemplated the scene in silent awe and admiration.
Our guns were at a parade rest.   We had no desire to stain a
single one of their elegant plumes with their rich blood.   Our
souls were filled with thoughts of heaven and the bright angels
who hover o'er its golden gates.

Finally, Jack yielded to a desire to secure one of the birds
for mounting, and selecting one of the finest specimens, as
they sailed over us, fired.   The bird fell into the river,
and an alligator, a lank, hungry, ugly looking old cuss, who
had been watching for such a chance to secure a meal, went
for it and took it under the water in a twinkling.

Then our visions of paradise fled, and we almost imagined
we were in the other place, face to face with old Satan himself.

We strolled up the river a mile, to the foot of Lower
Myakka Lake which is about a mile and a half wide at the

widest part and two miles long. In the winter season it is a favorite duck ground, as are many of the smaller ponds along the river, and the tropical water birds breed here in great numbers.

We saw several large flocks of teal, but did not care to shoot them. Jack took a shot at one flock, however, and secured three for supper.

It was growing late, and we returned to camp without finding any better game. We proceeded at once to prepare supper, put up the tent, make beds, etc. We dressed our ducks, cut palmetto-stems, split one end, sharpened the points and impaled the birds on them. We then sharpened the other end and stuck it in the ground, so as to hold the duck over the fire. They were soon roasted to a turn. It was now dark. Jack started to the river to get water for our coffee, and as he passed the end of a large hollow log that lay a few feet from the fire, he heard a slight noise in it. We cut a stick and passed it in, when we found there was "something alive in it," as Dundreary says of his hat. We put a bunch of dry moss in the opening and set fire to it. In a few minutes a 'possum came tumbling out through the fire, and old Rover, who stood there waiting for him, made short work of him.

After supper we pulled down a large quantity of moss and made a bed in the tent, that a king might have envied. I have been told that this moss was full of red-bugs, and that any one who attempted to sleep on it would find himself drilled full of holes by them before morning; but we slept on it here four nights, and did not get a single bite.

We sat around the fire an hour chatting, enjoying the balmy night air and making our plans for the morrow, after which we laid down,

> "And all night slept
> In Elysium."

About five o'clock in the morning, we were awakened by a great owl who perched on a limb directly over us, and called out in his shrill, piercing voice, Ta-whoo-oo-oo-ah !

Jack reached for his gun, crawled out, and by the light of the moon, which shone brightly at the time, shot him. Later in the day, Jack skinned the bird, and will send the skin to a Boston taxidermist. His stately form will probably ere long adorn the window of some apothecary's shop, and I would that a photograph of the scene of his taking off might be hung beside it. It would add greatly to the interest of the occasion.

There were the heavy branches of the great live-oaks draped in long gray moss, with the pale light of the moon flittering through them ; the blue smoke from our camp-fire curling gently up through the trees ; Jack in his long white nightdress, fluttering ominously in the wind, stalking through the woods with his gun across his arm like a specter ruffian, bent on some foul deed of midnight murder. Finally there was a flash, a string of livid fire reaching away up into the tree-tops, a sudden peal of thunder, a flapping through the branches, a "thud" on the ground and all was silent again. But to describe it is unsatisfactory ; such a picture must be seen to be appreciated. When this was over we got into our harness, put a few biscuits, a few oranges and some salt into our game bags, and as soon as the first messenger of day was visible in the east, we started down the river. By the time we had gone a mile it was light. As we entered the edge of a small hammock, we heard a turkey fly into a palmetto-tree. We walked cautiously toward the tree and as we stopped to listen another stepped out into an opening not more than fifty yards away. I raised my rifle and fired, but from some unaccountable cause, missed. The bird was out of sight before Jack could get a shot. Then we ran in opposite direc-

tions in hopes of surprising the flock and getting another
shot.   Presently I heard both barrels of Jack's gun and went
toward him.   I found him loading, with a fine gobbler lying
dead at his feet.   He had buckshot in one barrel and number six in the other.   He had bagged this bird with the buck-
shot, but the one he put the number six into, although badly
hurt, had gone away.   We went on down the river some
three miles farther, but failed to get another shot.   The
woods are literally alive with squirrels here, but no one shoots
them; they are considered too small game to kill in this
country.   Consequently they are as tame as the English sparrows in our streets.   They frequently sit and bark saucily at
us while we pass within ten feet of them.   It is no uncommon thing to see five or six on a single tree.   About ten
o'clock we got hungry and I picked off three of the little
fellows.   Jack made a fire while I dressed them, and we had
them on toasting sticks almost before they had quit kicking.
They were soon nicely browned, and on these, with the biscuit we had brought with us, we made a sumptuous breakfast.
We then returned to camp, and when we arrived there, found
the fire we had lighted in the hollow log the previous night,
to smoke the 'possum out, still burning.

It had burned the top of the log off, leaving a large
trough-shaped cavity which was a mass of live coals, and
which served as a capital oven in which to roast our turkey.

We dressed the turkey, put a stick through him, drove a
fork on either side of the log, and laid the stick in the forks,
so that the fowl rested over the hottest part of the fire.   As
one side baked done, we turned him over.   There was no
smoke, and our oven was a perfect success.   Soon after we
put the turkey on, we heard two shots about a mile west of
our camp.   We knew at once it was Will, who had promised
15

to come out to-day and join us, so we answered with a double salute from Jack's gun.

Just as dinner was ready, Will came in sight, carrying a fine old gobbler. We were delighted to see him in this wilderness, for we had not seen a human being, nor even a track of one, since leaving home. After dining heartily on roast turkey, sweet potatoes, and fresh biscuits, with oranges for dessert, we took to the woods again, each going in a different direction.

Jack crossed the river and went east. Will went down, and I up the river. I had not gone more than a mile when I heard a rattling noise in the sea-ash thicket, and looking under the branches saw a fine large buck come bounding directly toward me. He had been frightened by something, probably the report of Jack's gun on the other side of the river. He had not yet seen me. I stood perfectly still until he came within about fifty yards of me, and taking a steady aim at his breast, fired. He turned suddenly to the right, made one jump, and fell dead. The ball had gone a little higher than I aimed, and entered his neck near the base of the windpipe. It had cut the windpipe and shattered the neck bone. I dressed the animal, and found he was rather heavy to carry, so returned to camp, got the horse, and got back to camp with my venison just as Will returned from the opposite direction with another good large gobbler.

In half an hour more Jack returned with a turkey and four ducks; with this score we closed the day's sport, and spent the evening after supper dressing our game. While we were at supper a large 'gator raised his head in the middle of the river opposite our tent. I sent a message from "old reliable," and in an instant more he was lashing the water into a foam, minus an eye.

At daylight the following morning we were again on foot,

in hope of finding more turkeys, for we had found several large flocks already, from which we had as yet taken but a few. We scattered, and an occasional shot from each told the others that our search was not in vain. About ten o'clock we all turned up at camp once more, and pooled our issues. We had three turkeys in all, and Jack had fourteen coots that he had killed at a single shot. We then roasted one of the best turkeys and a loin of venison, in our hollow log oven— which was still in fine condition—for dinner. As I dressed the turkey I noticed that there was a large cavity in it after removing the entrails, which I thought might as well be utilized, so I put a teal duck into it, and placed the turkey over the fire without mentioning it to either of the boys. When we sat down to dinner, Jack took hold of the turkey to carve it, and saw a leg of the duck protruding.. He pulled the little fellow out, held it up, and drily remarked: " Well, I've traveled this road a year or more, but never saw a gobbler with such a young one in before." The "young one" was well done, however, and we relished it quite as much as any dish on the bill of fare.

After dinner I went south about three miles. On the way I killed a large wood ibis, and hung it up in a tree so that I could get it on my return. I took off my vest and buttoned it around him to keep the buzzards, wild cats, etc., from eating him. Farther down the stream I saw a flock of six or eight turkeys, but could not get a shot at them. About sundown I turned and started toward camp, listening intently in hope of hearing turkeys coming in to roost, but was not favored with any of that welcome music. I kept a sharp lookout, however, in all the tall trees, knowing that it was possible for them to fly in within a few yards of me without my hearing them.

Finally I saw one in the top of a large live-oak. I fired,

and cut out a bunch of feathers, but the bird went away. I felt very sore over this loss, and hurried on toward camp.

In a few minutes I saw another in a still taller tree. It was now so dark I could not see the sights of my rifle at all, so I turned down the rear sight, glanced along the barrel, saw the large, dark body of my bird against the sky, pulled, and was rewarded by seeing him tumble through the thick branches to the ground. I was under the tree by the time he reached the ground, and picking him up hurried on. In a few minutes I saw another, this time a large gobbler, perched high in the top of a tall tree. When I fired he started to fly toward me, but by the time he got over me his strength failed, and he fell within two feet of where I stood. I slipped in another cartridge, took my bird, and started again.

By this time the stars were shining, but I continued to scan the tops of the trees closely. Presently I saw another dark object against the sky, and knew from the shape that it was a turkey. It was, perhaps, thirty-five yards from me. I took the best aim I could, pulled and scored my third bird, this time a fat young hen.

What a magnificent hand! Two kings and a queen! For the wild turkey *is* truly the king of birds. My blood bounded through my veins as I contemplated my game. Three straight birds, two in deep twilight and the third by starlight. Not a bad score for a rifle, eh?

It was now so dark that my only means of finding my way to camp was by following the bank of the river. It was light enough close to the water to walk comfortably, but back in the thicket it was so dark that an Indian could not see to get through it.

I succeeded in finding my wood ibis, and when I added it to my already large bag, had a full load. It is about the same size as the turkey. The four birds weighed over fifty pounds. I tied their heads together and swung them over my shoulder, two in front and two behind.

The river is so crooked that following it closely made me about three or four times the distance to walk that I should have had could I have gone straight through the woods, and I did not reach camp until after eight o'clock. Will and Jack were there dressing game and preparing supper. Will had brought in another turkey, and Jack a deer and twenty-one teal ducks. He killed the ducks at two shots — thirteen to his first barrel and eight to his second. Teal are very plentiful here and very tame. The mallards and other large ducks have not come in yet.

We were out at daylight again the following morning and decided to make but a brief hunt that day and start for home at noon. A mile below camp I got a running shot at a deer and missed. Soon after I came upon a flock of turkeys, feeding under some live-oaks. I knocked one over and as they ran tried another but failed to get him. I then started for camp, and as I had no hope of seeing any more large game concluded to take in a few squirrels.

As I walked rapidly toward camp I picked off those nearest to my path, and when I got in and counted up my bag had sixteen. I also killed one of the brightest and handsomest roseate spoonbills I could find. Not having time to skin it properly for mounting I cut off the wings and head and shall preserve them. I did the same with my wood ibis, killed the day before. Soon after I reached camp Jack came in with still another turkey. Will drew a blank this time. He failed to get a shot at anything. After breakfast we broke camp and commenced preparations for the homeward march. I saw a small alligator lying on the bank a few rods from us, and being anxious to take home a skin of one, picked up my rifle. At the sight of it he went into the water. I waited a few

minutes and he came up to take a look at me. I sent a ball
through his head and pulled him out. In a few minutes he
recovered from the shock and commenced thrashing the
ground at a lively rate. I cut his throat open and severed the
windpipe, but he would not lie still and tried very hard to
breathe. I opened his body and took out the lungs, heart
and all the entrails, and even then it was a full hour before
it would lie still enough for me to skin it. If a cat has nine
lives, this animal must have at least nineteen.

I could give further details of this case more wonderful by
far than those I have mentioned, but I forbear, lest they should
prove offensive to some sensitive reader.

Suffice it to say that the contortions and violent struggles
continued for at least three hours after what I have described
took place. I have heard some most marvelous accounts of
this animal's tenacity of life — its *post mortem* powers, so to
speak.

Will Webb told me that he killed a large one near their
house some years ago. He shot it through the head several
times with a rifle, and then took an ax and pounded its head
into a pulp. He took out several of its largest teeth to
preserve as specimens; then cut it open and took out a
quantity of the fat which is extensively used in this country
for gun oil. They then left the carcass lying, but what was
their surprise on going back the next day to bury it, to find
that it had actually crawled away! They could see its trail,
plainly, where it had gone into the water. Such stories sound
incredible, but the facts can be corroborated by correspon-
dence or conversation with anyone who is familiar with the
nature and habits of the 'gator.

We loaded our game and camp equipage into the cart and
about one o'clock P.M. reluctantly bade adieu to the enchanting Myakka, with all its charming associations; its great live-

oak forests; its dense sea-ash thickets; its everglades; its flaming-hued water birds; its deer, turkeys, and the thousand and one other attractions that render it so dear to a sportsman and a lover of nature.

Though I may in future years visit every famous hunting ground on the continent; though all such trips may be eminently successful, I can never hope to experience more genuine pleasure in so short a period of time than I did in this four days on the Myakka river. I shall ever cherish it in my memory as one of the brightest, most romantic and exciting episodes of my whole life.

We arrived at Mr. Webb's just as the sun was going down among the white caps on the Gulf, and on the morrow began preparations for our return North. We packed our trunks, taking great care to put our collection of specimens in in such a manner that they would carry safely. Mr. Webb loaded about thirty boxes of oranges, our baggage and two days provisions into the little "Sea Bird." By this time night had arrived, and it being our last night here we concluded to go fire-fishing once more.

As soon as it was dark, Jack, Mr. Griffith and myself took the spears, lit our fire in the fishing-jack and pushed off. We had excellent sport and killed a large number of fine fish. Among the number was one angel-fish, a variety we had not caught before. We also killed a good-sized sting-ray, and I preserved his tail. It is only an inch in diameter at the base and twenty-three inches long. We returned to the house about nine o'clock, having taken over sixty pounds of fish.

The next morning, December 11th, we stepped on board the "Sea Bird." Mr. and Mrs. Griffith, Jack, my wife and I, and sailed for Manatee, where we were to take the steamer for Cedar Key.

We got into the Mangroves at low tide, about noon,

and had considerable difficulty in getting through them. Jack had to wade ashore and get a skiff, with which we transferred our freight and passengers over the worst portions until the boat was light enough to pass the shoals. We got through about five o'clock, and from there we had a smooth voyage. We sailed all night, Jack and Mr. Griffith taking turns at the helm. About ten o'clock we spread our blankets on the deck, laid down, and slept soundly with the canopy of heaven as our only covering. The ladies made no complaint at this rough fare, but on the contrary really enjoyed the novelty and romance of it. At six o'clock in the morning we landed. made coffee, and ate a hearty breakfast of cold turkey, biscuits, etc., with some delicious bananas fresh from Mr. Griffith's grove, for desert.

We landed at Manatee at two P.M., just as the steamer "Valley City" hove in sight. Here we were compelled to say the sad words "good-bye" to our friends, Mr. and Mrs. G., and Jack. We boarded the steamer and were soon under way for Cedar Key, where we arrived early the next morning. At night we went out on a small schooner to take the Havana steamer which lay at anchor at the mouth of the harbor, eight miles out, for New Orleans. But soon after we left the wharf a storm came on, and it grew so dark and the water so rough that the pilot said he could not follow the channel, and was obliged to cast anchor.

So we were compelled to lay here all night, cooped up in the hold of this little vessel, with no room to lie down and scarcely room to sit down. It rained in torrents nearly all night, and blew in upon us every time the hatch was opened, which seemed to be about every ten minutes: When daylight came, we found that the tide had gone out and left us aground "high and dry." We waited patiently until about eleven o'clock A.M., when it kindly came in again and took

us off the bar. The storm having abated, we were now enabled to go on our way rejoicing, and reached the steamer
about noon. Having been cooped up on the little schooner
eighteen hours without food, drink, or a place to lay our
heads, we were truly grateful when we entered the commodious and handsome cabin of the good steamer " Chase," and
when a few moments later we were called to a sumptuous and
palatable dinner, Captain Baker's order to us to help ourselves was obeyed as promptly and vigorously as was any command he ever gave his obedient and well-disciplined crew.
We had rough weather all the way across the Gulf, and were
glad when we entered the mouth of the Mississippi river and
the vessel ceased her uneasy rolling and tossing. We passed
the Eads jetties just after daylight on the third morning after
leaving Cedar Key, and had a pleasant and interesting trip
up the river, arriving at New Orleans late at night.

CHAPTER XXV.

WORDS OF ADVICE TO TOURISTS TO FLORIDA.

EXPENSES OF A TRIP — MUST CALL AT ST. AUGUSTINE — BRING YOUR GUN
AND RIFLE — PROVIDE PLENTY OF AMMUNITION — DON'T FORGET
SHARK TACKLE — TAKE A SMALL TENT — A LIGHT RUBBER COAT — AND
A HEAVY BLANKET — THE ONLY FOOT-GEAR NEEDED IS A PAIR OF
COWHIDE SHOES — TAKE ALSO SOME SIMPLE MEDICINES — QUI-
NINE — CALOMEL — THE EXPENSES OF THE JOURNEY SMALL.

THERE are, perhaps, a few sportsmen in the country who
have not at some time felt a wish to visit Florida, and perhaps a majority have thought of a trip to the "land of flowers" as among the possibilities of the "dim distant future."
Others have gone farther, and planned the trip into definite
shape, even to fixing the time of starting.

In the minds of such the first questions arising are, What
is the best route to Florida? What portions of the state are
the most prolific in game and fish? In which localities can
I find the best accommodations at the lowest prices? What
class of guns, ammunition, and fishing tackle will I most
need for the game and fish peculiar to the country?

What will be the necessary expense of a two or three
months' trip to Florida and what season of the year is most
suitable for such a trip? These and similar questions have
been asked me repeatedly since my return from Florida, and
it is my purpose in this chapter to answer them to the best of
my ability, and to give such other facts as in my judgment
may be useful to persons going there. First, then, as to the
route. Competing lines of railroad offer several different
routes, each possessing certain advantages, but perhaps the

shortest and most direct, and that by which the trip may be made in the shortest space of time, is by way of Louisville, Nashville, and Montgomery, Ala. By this route, tickets to Cedar Key and return may be purchased over either of two or three roads running south from Chicago, good for six months, for about $65. This route takes the tourist to Baldwin, only twenty miles from Jacksonville. Here a stop-over check should be procured, good for fifteen days, in order to visit Jacksonville, St. Augustine, and to make a trip by steamer up the St. John's and Oclawaha rivers.

No trip to Florida could be complete if it did not include a view of the magnificent scenery of these two streams, and of the antique city of St. Augustine. The additional expense of this trip, to the sum above stated, would be about $27, including meals on the river steamers, making the round trip from Chicago to Cedar Key and return cost $93. The distance thus traveled will be about 2,800 miles by rail, and about 950 miles by water — 475 on the St. John's and 450 on the Oclawaha.

If a party of three or more go together, excursion rates may be procured that will materially reduce the rates of fare as above stated.

As to the portions of the state where fish and game are most abundant, opinions of those who have spent much time in traveling over the state differ. Some claim that the Indian river country is the best; others that the Oclawaha and St. John's rivers flow through the finest game country, but, all things considered, I am of the opinion that for both fishing and shooting the lower portion of the Gulf coast is unsurpassed by any other part of the state. Besides, it is more easily accessible than other favorable resorts, and the accommodations that sportsmen may find there are better than those usually found, on the Indian river especially. Steamships run twice a week from Cedar Key to Manatee, and after reaching that point the sportsman cannot fail to find fish and game abundant at every turn.

Then, as he proceeds south along Sarásota Bay, Charlotte Harbor, Oyster Bay, San Carlos Harbor, Cape Romano and Ten Thousand Isles, the field grows richer all the time. At Manatee a small schooner can be chartered to take a single person or party of five or ten to Mr. Webb's, a distance of forty-five miles, for $10. Or, if notified by mail a few days in advance, Captain Will Webb will meet the steamer at Manatee with his new schooner, the "Vision," and take passengers to his father's house free of charge. Here first-class accommodations can be secured at five dollars a week, including use of small boats for fishing, jack-lights and spears for fire-fishing, etc. Will charters his schooner to parties at five dollars a day, including his services and those of two other men, and two small boats for running up small streams into the interior of the country. No better or pleasanter outfit than this for a coasting expedition could be imagined.

The schooner is new, is thirty-six feet long, thirteen feet beam, has a capacity of nine tons, and draws but two and a-half feet of water. It has sleeping accommodations for ten persons, is strongly built and substantially, so as to be thoroughly sea-worthy in any weather, and yet is of such light draft as to be able to ascend the larger streams and run into small bays and inlets where many vessels of less capacity could not go. By taking along a small supply of provisions, a party of five can live comfortably on this vessel for four to five dollars a week each.

Captain Will and his brother Jack, who always accompanies him on these expeditions, are both competent guides and know every foot of the ground, so that no additional expense need be incurred in this direction. In a cruise of three to four weeks the entire coast can be thoroughly explored, hunted and fished, from Webb's to the Florida reefs, at the extreme south end of the peninsula, including short trips up the Myakka, Caloosahatchie, Fahkahnatehee and other rivers. At Cape Romano, Fort Myers, Punta Rassa, Fort Poinsett and many other points along the coast, deer are abundant, and bears, panthers, wild cats and wolves are frequently met with. The fishing is superb all along the coast, and the naturalist may collect many rare and interesting icthyological, ornithological and conchological specimens not to be found elsewhere in the United States.

A shot-gun and rifle will both be needed, though a cylinder-bore shot-gun, and supply of buck-shot cartridges in addition to the supply of small-shot may answer all purposes. The greater need of the rifle is for the larger game which frequently offers long range shots where a shot-gun is entirely useless, and if the sportsman be a clever rifle shot, he should always provide himself with both.

A large supply of ammunition should be provided for each, for there is such a great variety and such countless numbers of birds and animals constantly presenting themselves, that although many of them be not game, still the temptation to shoot them is so strong that few resist it. For instance, there are cranes, pelicans, cormorants, water turkeys, alligators, etc., offering shots at all ranges, and affording such fine opportunities for practice that any one is justifiable in improving these opportunities when not in localities where game is to be found. I estimate, from experience and observation, that an enthusiastic sportsman will shoot away 300 shells in each week that he may spend in Florida, and if he be provided with rifle and shot-gun both, perhaps an equal division of this number between the two would not be far from the proper figure.

A liberal supply and good assortment of fishing tackle should be taken, and this of the best quality. The native Floridian uses only a heavy hand-line and large, strong hook for his fishing, his motive being fish not sport; and he will laugh at the sportsman who goes there from the North supplied with fine tackle. He will tell you that you will lose your fine line, and perhaps your rod and reel, before you fish an hour; that a twenty-pound red-fish, drum or grouper, or a hundred-pound jew-fish or shark will probably walk away with them before you have fairly commenced fishing. But he is welcome to his opinion and his heavy hand-line. I prefer my good, strong bamboo bass rod, my Meek & Milam reel, my fine-braided linen or sea-grass line, patent sinker and Limerick hook. There is a pleasure in fishing with fine tackle, even if you don't get a bite, and if you do get one there is so much more sport in handling your fish with your fine tackle than with your "main strength" tackle, that any true disciple of Izaak had rather catch one fish with the former than half a dozen with the latter.

I grant that you will frequently lose a hook when a shark, jew-fish, taupon, or other sea-monster takes hold of it, as they frequently do, but on the contrary you will take many a fine, sensitive, gamy fish that would be frightened away by your neighbor's clothes-line and awkward-looking slug of lead.

Shark tackle is all well enough when you go fishing for sharks, but when fishing for game fish use fine tackle. Take with you then a good, strong but light and flexible bass or salmon rod, a supply of Bradford & Anthony's hard braid water-proof linen lines, a number 5 or 6 Milam reel, a supply of Limerick hooks, assorted sizes, from number 3-o to number 9-o, a lot of artificial minnows and spoons for trolling, a landing net, a gaff-hook, and you will be properly equipped

in that line. A minnow seine would also be desirable, as live
minnows are the best bait attainable for many of the best salt-
water fish, and few people there have any better arrangement
for catching minnows than with a "pin hook," which is decidedly slow.

A supply of first-class shark tackle should by all means
be taken along, for much exciting sport may be had hooking
these and other monsters of the deep. About fifty feet of
strong, half-inch rope, two feet of chain, such as is used for
halter chain for horses, to go next the hook for a leader, if
you please, and half a dozen large-sized shark hooks complete
the list.

These latter may not be found in Chicago but can be ordered from the East. It is not advisable to depend upon getting anything needed for the trip after reaching Jacksonville or
Cedar Key, for neither the goods nor the assortments kept
there will be found at all satisfactory. A couple of spears,
one large and heavy, suitable for shark, etc., and one smaller
for other fish will also be found a good investment. Most
residents and guides have these, but not in sufficient numbers
to supply parties where several wish to use them at the same
time.

Each person or each party of two should take a small, light
tent, capable of accommodating two for camping expeditions,
and this should be provided with light muslin ends, thin
enough to admit the air freely, but thick enough to exclude
sand-flies and mosquitos. The ordinary musquito bar is
useless in Florida, for the sand-flies, which are far more
troublesome than the musquitoes, pass through it readily.
Each person should take a good heavy blanket, and will find
use for it almost any time in the year if camping. The clothing should be strong, but light, so as not to be oppressive
during the hot days that the visitor will experience, even in

midwinter. A light rubber coat will be found an indispensable necessity as a protection against the frequent rains and heavy dews when out at night. A rubber pillow will also add greatly to the comfort of the trip. Rubber boots are not needed. You can wade in the salt water all day and all night if need be, and experience no bad effects from it; besides, the weather is so hot as to render rubber boots decidedly uncomfortable. The only foot gear needed is a pair of cheap, heavy cow-hide shoes. They should be cheap, for the salt water will rot them out in a few weeks. Every one who goes to Florida has wet feet every day, and still, colds, sore throats, and the like are unknown there. The " Crackers," who live on and near the coast, are in the water almost every day of their lives gathering oysters, fishing, lifting their boats over the shoals, etc., and yet they are uniformly healthy. Indeed, it is said that it is no uncommon thing to see barnicles growing on their legs, so much of their time is spent in the water.

It would be well to take along a few simple medicines, such as quinine, calomel, etc., to be used as occasion may require. The radical change in climate usually affects the health more or less. Any physician will tell you what would be most suitable in this line.

Aside from the items mentioned above, but little baggage will be needed, and but little should be taken. Good clothes are not needed and will look out of place after you reach the thinly-settled districts. No books need be taken, for you will have neither time nor taste for reading, and they will only add to the bulk and weight of your luggage, unnecessarily. There are so many wonders and objects of interest in this marvelous region that you could not spare time to read an hour each week if you had a whole library at your disposal.

As to the necessary expense of the trip, one hundred dollars will pay the railroad and steamboat fare for the round trip, including the run up the St. John's and Oclawaha rivers and to St. Augustine. This includes steamboat fare from Cedar Key to Manatee and return. Ten dollars per week will cover all necessary expenses while on the lower coast, and a much less sum—perhaps five dollars a week—will cover them if a party of three or more go together, so that for a trip of two months, including the time of going and coming, the necessary expense for one person alone can be limited to about one hundred and seventy-five dollars, and considerably less where several go together.

16

CHAPTER XXVI.

RECOLLECTIONS OF BOYHOOD.

BACK TO THE OLD HOME — THE BARRETT BOYS — THE OLD SCHOOL-
HOUSE — HAIL, GENTLE ROBIN — THE OLD FENCE CORNER — THE
CHURCHYARD — THE SNOW-BALL CONFLICTS.

> " I'll wander back, yes, back again,
> Where childhood's home may be,
> For memory in sweet refrain
> Still sings its praise to me."

MAN may roam wheresoever he will, and his absence be
prolonged to whatever extent it may, yet the memory of the
old homestead will always be cherished. The reflex of the
scenes of childhood are indelibly stamped upon the human
mind, and can never be effaced. In the midst of busy scenes,
of exciting surroundings, when the mind is weighed down
with the cares of business, how often does memory steal away
from the harsh, practical present into the dreamy, poetical
past, and recall the days of childhood, of boyhood, of youth.
How whole years of that blissful period of life will pass in
rapid review through the imagination, and how fervently do
we sigh as we awaken from the delightful reverie :

> " Backward, turn backward, O Time, in thy flight,
> And make me a boy again, just for to-night."

And yet when we realize that it cannot be so, that " the
past is joined to the eternal past," we brush the tear from the
furrowed cheek, and return to the realities of the hour.

For nearly a quarter of a century since I left the old home,
I have roamed through the world and battled with its stern
realities. During that time I have seen, perhaps, as much of

life as is usually given to men to see in the same period.
Fortune has smiled and frowned upon me by turns, but even
under the influence of her brightest smiles I have never forgotten the humble home, the old log cot, wherein were spent
as many happy days as were ever allotted to any human being
in a like number of years, no matter with what luxuries he
may have been surrounded. From the splendors of capitals,
of fashionable salons; from amid brilliant circles of gay
friends; from the banquet table, my thoughts have oft turned
toward the old, old homestead, and with the poet I have sung:

"Be it ever so humble, there's no place like home."

I have often sighed for a look at the old home, the hills,
the rocks, the trees, the little brook, and the many objects
whose images are so indelibly stamped upon my memory, but
never until now have my longings been gratified.

After an absence of more than twenty years, I find myself
standing on the platform at the railroad depot which is nearest
to my old home. The train has moved away, and I turn to a
stranger who stands near, and inquire for certain of my old
friends and neighbors. To my great delight I learn that
many of them still live in the neighborhood, and I start at
once in search of them. I choose to go across fields and
through woods, in order to examine well remembered objects
and localities, and see if they still have the familiar look they
had when last I saw them.

I am told that about a mile from the station three of my
old schoolmates, the "Barrett boys," are living on adjoining
farms, and thitherward I wend my way. First I find little
Harry, the happy, genial lad of bygone days, and always one
of the favorites of the school, with both the teacher and the
pupils. Now he has grown to manhood, is a well-to-do
farmer, married, and has several children growing up around
him. But he is the same bright, cheerful, agreeable Harry

as of old. He told me of nearly all our old playmates; where they were, how they had succeeded or failed in life, etc. Our interview was intensely interesting to me, but could not be prolonged, for my time was limited. Next I sought Al and George, and after like pleasant chats with them, I continued my rambles.

I directed my steps next toward the old schoolhouse, and in doing so passed over a piece of road that I had traveled hundreds of times before. It leads from my father's old farm to where a favorite uncle then lived, a distance of two miles. At that time it wound through a dense wood nearly the entire distance. Now this is nearly all cut away, and rich fields of grain are growing on the ground that was then shadowed by giant oaks.

Here is the "big mound," but how much smaller it looks now than formerly. Then we thought it a mountain, and to climb to the top of it was considered a great feat. Indeed, it is a high hill, and from its top one may see into two or three adjoining counties; but since I left here I have seen and ascended mountains so high, that, by their side, this looks like a mole-hill.

I was frequently sent on errands to my uncle's, and passed over the ground upon which I now stand alone. I can see myself now,

"In my mind's eye, Horatio,"

a little barefooted lad, with skin tanned to almost a coffee brown by the summer's sun; clad in a "hickory" shirt, a pair of blue deming pants, rolled up to the knee and held by one suspender; a home-made straw hat, generally minus either a rim or crown, for I used it to carry stones in to throw at birds, to catch ball, or for any other purpose I happened to want it for.

I remember on one occasion I was walking leisurely along,

in a brown study about how I should slay the deer, bears, buffaloes, and other large animals when I got "big." I was so absorbed in my reverie that I did not notice a hog that had his snout under the dry leaves, and was eating acorns just here, under this large oak. He did not see me until I was within a few feet of him, when he happened to raise his head. He was wild, and with a loud "woo," broke away through the dry leaves at a rapid pace, making a great racket. I didn't wait to see what it was, but thinking it surely a bear, or some other wild animal, just in the act of springing upon me, I turned and fled, screaming for help at every jump, and ran until I was out of breath before I looked around to see how close it was to me. Then, when I found it was not following me, I stopped and listened. I wondered what it was, and finally, after thinking the matter over a while, and calling to mind what kind of an animal I had often heard make such a noise as that, I concluded that I had made a fool of myself, and went on about my business.

On another occasion as I was passing near the same place, I alarmed a flock of wild turkeys, and they flew into the trees. I had my pockets full of rocks as usual, and commenced throwing at them. After several misses, I happened to hit one on the neck and killed it. It was about two-thirds grown, and I carried it home in great glee. I have my doubts now about their having been "wild," sure enough, for there was a . farm-house not far away where they may have belonged, but I was honest in my belief then that they were really wild, and so my conscience has never upbraided me for killing it. But wild turkeys don't generally sit and let a boy throw stones at them very long; neither do tame turkeys usually take to trees when frightened, so it is still a question as to whether they were wild or not.

How strangely familiar this old road looks! Here is a

large tract of the old forest that still stands in all its virgin grandeur. Here stand the great spreading oaks, the tall graceful maples, the sweet-scented lindens. Here still grow the dear old May-apples, whose thickly-spreading umbrellas cover large tracts of the ground. Here bloom the fragrant wild flowers just as of yore. All these have for these many years escaped the destroying power of the woodman's axe and the husbandman's plow. Here, in boyish glee, have I chased the pretty butterfly; here I have gathered these wild-flowers, and here listened to the music of birds whose well-known voices greet my ears as I write these lines.

Hail, gentle robin, brown thrush, grosbeak, bullfinch, oriole, taniger, bluebird — all friends of my boyhood days! I greet you with all the warmth and fervor of a long unbroken friendship. Though separated from you many long years, I have never forgotten, never ceased to love you. Nay, gentle songsters, start not at sound of my voice or sight of my face, I would not for the world harm one of your beautiful feathers.

Every bend and every straight reach in this old road I remember as though I had passsed over it but yesterday. Here is a level piece on top of the hill where in summer I seldom passed without seeing a partridge, or pheasant, as we called them, "wallowing" in the dust. Sometimes there would be several of them, and if in the latter part of the summer or fall the mother and her brood were often seen. They would strut along the road in front of me, showing but little alarm, for they were seldom hunted in those days. Now they are not to be seen, and the neighbors tell me they have all been killed off long ago; that they are extinct so far as this locality is concerned.

Here at the foot of the hill is a neighboring farm that my father rented one year. I remember that in the fall, when we were pasturing some young horses and cattle in one of the fields, I found a nest of yellow-jackets near the fence at one side of the field. I would throw clubs at the nest until I got the occupants well stirred up, and then go and drive some of the colts or cattle over the nest. The yellow-jackets would of course get their work in lively, and then it was fun to see those animals run. I had a little dog that I didn't like very well, an ugly, mangy cur. I used to stir up the yellow-jackets, and then carry this dog and throw him over the fence into the nest. He would make a bee-line for a spring about a hundred yards away, jump into the water and lie there until his persecutors had left him. But the poor animals soon learned to shun this particular fence corner, and after a day or two I couldn't get any of them near it.

I was what the neighbors called a bad boy—not, I must contend, from any vicious motives, but from mere reckless-ness, thoughtlessness and love of fun.

In my rambles through the woods and over the farm, I al-ways carried a bow and arrow, before I got large enough to be trusted with a gun. I acquired considerable skill in the use of the former, and used to make it warm for the squirrels, chipmunks, woodpeckers, etc. I was as fond of fishing then as now, and in order to procure my tackle used to dig gin-seng in these woods and sell it. It usually brought thirty cents a pound green, or sixty cents dry. I have dug and sold many a pound of it. After I commenced shooting, I used to buy my powder and shot in this way.

Emerging at last from the woods, I reach the site of our old schoolhouse. Alas! how changed is the scene now! The schoolhouse—that dear old log-cabin, wherein I have spent so many happy days—is gone! Not a vestige of it re-mains—not even the foundation-stones. I seek a history of its taking off, and from an old neighbor I learn that the logs of which it was built decayed and fell away, until it was no

longer safe to occupy it. It was about to fall down, and so
the school-directors ordered it torn down. The foundation-
stones were hauled away and used in the new schoolhouse,
which was built a mile below. The fence, which inclosed
my father's field near the schoolhouse, has been extended so
as to take in the schoolhouse lot, and it has been broken up
and farmed for several years past. The old oak-trees that
shaded our playground have been cut down, and the stumps
are decayed and gone. I cannot even locate definitely the
boundaries of our old ball-ground, nor can I find any of the
old landmarks that are so dear to my memory. Verily the
hand of time has fallen heavily on this sacred spot. I un-
cover my head as I gaze upon the wreck of the past, and
through my blinding tears the familar faces of teachers and
playmates rise up before me.

Where are they now?

Some of them, as I have said, still live in the neighborhood; but others, alas! are scattered to the four corners of
the earth.

"And some are in the churchyard laid!"

And what a flood of tender memories comes with those
faces! Here I conned almost my first lessons in books. Here I
received many wholesome lessons, many good impressions that
have never been effaced from my memory. Here were scenes
of childish glee and childish sorrow; childish conquests and
childish disappointments. How my boyish heart used to
bound with delight, as, by spelling a hard word correctly, I
was allowed to walk proudly to the head of my class, "turning down" a dozen of my classmates who had missed the
same word before it came to me. And, then, how I have
bitten my lip in sorrow and shame, as I missed an easy word,
and a rival has taken my place at the head.

We had night spelling-schools in those days—not those

society spelling-bees that were the rage three or four years ago in the towns—but genuine old-fashioned contests in orthography.

To the east and west of the schoolhouse are steep hills. Here in winter time we used to coast on sleds and Norwegian snow-shoes. We would go spinning down these hills, through the thick woods, at a speed that makes my head swim now to think of it. It is strange that some of us were not killed. I remember once two of the boys, Harry Barrett and Mark Ridenour, were sent to the spring at the foot of one of those hills for water. They each took a tin pail, both mounted one sled, and let go. Away they flew with the speed of the wind. When half way down, Mark lost his hold, and fell off, rolling some distance in the hard-crusted snow. The sled struck a tree and threw Harry past a large stump, so close to it that one side of his face was scratched, and his shoulder badly bruised. Had his head struck the stump fairly it would undoubtedly have killed him. His water-pail was smashed flat in the melée.

I was riding down one of these hills on my snow-shoes one day, and when I had reached a speed of about nine miles in three minutes, one of my shoes struck a grub, and went out from under me. I don't know how many somersaults I turned, nor how much of the distance I slid on my back, on all-fours, or otherwise, but I didn't stop until I reached the foot of the hill. I was badly cut and scratched by the heavy crust on the snow, and by contact with the brush, etc., but fortunately had received no more serious injuries.

We played " town-ball " and " bull-pen " in those days. Town-ball resembles our modern base-ball in some respects, but was much more severe, as in order to put a man out we must hit him with the ball, instead of crossing him out or hitting the base as in base-ball. We used a hard ball, and occasionally one of us would get knocked down when it happened to come in hot and hit us on the head. I have frequently worn black spots on various parts of my body for two or three weeks that I got in this way. But fear of getting hit developed great elasticity in our joints, and we became very "artful dodgers."

We frequently had some terrific snowball combats when the snow became wet and heavy. When we commenced snowballing we meant business, and frequently got badly hurt in this way, too. I remember a remarkable shot I made with a snowball on one occasion. We had chosen sides, taken our ground, and deployed as skirmishers. After the fight had grown warm, I made a ball very hard, and threw it at one of the other boys. He was just making a large one, and was packing it very hard. He had it about completed when mine arrived, struck his squarely, as he was pressing it between his hands, and knocked it all into "pi."

Such were some of our boyish sports. We never stopped to think of the danger we incurred, but only went in for fun, and we usually had it.

From the schoolhouse site, I stroll across the old field adjoining, and which in fact now includes it. Even here I stop and ponder. I have plowed and hoed the corn, raked and bound the golden wheat and oats here, when there were perhaps fifty large stumps on each acre of the ground. Now there is not one. They, like many other of the old landmarks, have succumbed to the inevitable — they have decayed and disappeared, and the field now looks like a natural prairie. But here, at the lower end of the field, are at last some objects that are just as they were when I last saw them. They are those great ledges of solid limestone, that crop out of the hillsides and tower perpendicularly to heights of twenty, thirty, and even fifty feet. No, they have not changed. True, they look not so large nor so high now as they appeared to my boyish vision, but that is because I have seen more of the world than I had then, not because they have grown less. They have withstood the storms of time, and will for ages yet to come without any material change.

CHAPTER XXVII.

THE DAYS OF LONG AGO.

MY DOG AND I — RING AND THE HOGS — WOODCHUCK HUNTING — OLD
RING! "THOUGH LOST TO SIGHT TO MEMORY DEAR" — ALL IS
CHANGED — OLD MEMORIES CROWD UPON ME — THE OLD LANDMARKS
GONE! — THE OLD SPRING — THERE IS A TIME FOR TEARS.

THESE rocks and hills used to be a great resort for the
ground hog (*Arctomys monax*), or "woodchuck," as we then
called it. I have killed large numbers of them here. I had
a dog that was as fond of hunting as I was. He would
"tree" them, and I always went to him when I heard him
bark, regardless of distance, state of the weather, or any other
obstacle. They generally took shelter in the crevices and
fissures of these rocks, or in hollow trees or logs. My favorite
method of capturing them was to take a piece of strong cord,
and form a loop on the end of a pole. Then running this
pole into the hole where the animal was, I would punch him
with it until he got mad, and began to bite at it. When I
got a "bite" I would pull just as in fishing, and very soon
would succeed in catching the loop of string around his front
upper teeth, when I had only to haul away until I landed him
at my feet, where my dog always stood ready to clinch him.
Ring was a small, light-built dog, about one-fourth bull, and
the balance — just dog. He didn't weigh over twenty pounds,
but was a wonderful specimen of pluck. So is an old male
ground-hog. We used to have some wonderful fights. We
frequently caught ground-hogs as heavy as Ring was, and I
I have often seen a fight last half-an-hour before the ground
hog would succumb to the chewing and shaking that the little

mongrel gave him.   Sometimes the ground-hog would get the
dog by the lip, the cheek, the ear, or jaw, and hang there
until nearly every bone in his body was chewed up before he
would let go.   Sometimes the dog would be on top and
sometimes the ground-hog, and when the fight was over the
ground for a space a rod square would be strewn with blood
and hair.   It was rough on both the animals, but fun for the
boys, besides, I knew it would be the " making of the pup,"
so I always let them fight it out to the death.   The boys used
to gather in from the whole neighborhood on Sunda   to go
out and have a woodchuck hunt.

Here, as I look around, I can find several of the fissures in
the rocks from which I have pulled my victims, and I fancy
I can almost see traces on the ground yet of some of these
fights. Just here by this ravine used to lie a large hollow log,
from which I have dragged several of them at different times;
but it has rotted down, and it is only by the closest scrutiny
that I can find traces of the bed of old decayed wood, where
it once rested.

And poor old Ring !   Dear, faithful old companion of
my boyhood — where art thou now ?   Oh, thou hast passed
away long years ago, and I trust, to the happy hunting
ground.   Couldst thou see the bitter tears that course down
my cheeks as I write these lines, thou wouldst know that thou
art still

> "Though lost to sight,
> To memory dear."

And now I come at last to the old house, the old homestead,

> " The little old log cabin by the lane."

But alas ! how changed it and all its surroundings !   True,
the house itself still stands, but it looks not as it did when
last I saw it.   The logs are far gone with decay, and it, too,

must soon yield to the ravages of time. The old barn is gone, the granary is gone, the shop is gone, the spring-house is no more, and I learn on inquiry they all rotted down long ago. But the spring, that clear, bubbling fountain, is still there. It looks just as it did, I lift a cup of its pure liquid to my lips, and it is as cooling, as refreshing, as welcome to my taste as of yore. Never did the oldest Maraschino, or the rarest Cognac taste half so good as does this sparkling fluid.

I approach the house, and am met at the door by a strange lady. I announce myself. She receives me politely; says she has heard my name, has heard her grandmother speak of my mother, but she herself was but a child when we left the country, and never saw any of us. The interior of the house shows as great a change as the exterior. True, it is neat and clean—the mistress is a tidy housekeeper—but the windows and doors have been changed, and, worst of all, the old fire-place, the dearest relic of all, is no more. It has been bricked up, and near its place stands a modern heating-stove.

What a train of memories cluster around that dear old fire-place! Here, during the long winter evenings, we gathered around it, and by its cheerful light and genial warmth, conned our lessons for the morrow, or perused an interesting book, or the weekly newspaper. Here I first read Irving's "Life of Washington," the "History of the American Revolution," the "Life of Daniel Boone," and many other works that made deep and lasting impressions on my mind, and whose teachings I shall never forget. Here, when some of the neighbors came in to spend the evening, we used to sit and crack nuts, and listen to great hunting yarns and Indian stories, which my father and some of our neighbors were fond of spinning. I have sat and listened to these harrowing tales until my hair would stand on end, and then it invariably happened that my mother would want a pail ot water from the spring, or an arm-load of wood. I was always ordered to bring it, and, of course, being ashamed to confess that I was "afraid," would go without a word of objection. Although the spring and wood-pile were not more than three rods from the door, I always imagined, especially if the night was very dark, that one of the bears, panthers, wolves or painted savages, of which I had been hearing so much, was at my heels ready to spring upon me ; and you may rest assured that I didn't loiter much by the wayside. I only made about three steps in going to and returning from the spring. My mother used to compliment me on making the trip so quickly, but she never knew why I did it.

I look about the grounds. Here is where the old granary stood. I remember the woodpeckers used to come here in large numbers during the winter season to help themselves to the corn. I used to bait a fish-hook with a grain of corn, hang it near the granary, and catch a woodpecker as we do a fish. I should consider this cruel sport now, but didn't know any better in those days, until my mother caught me at it, told me it was wrong, and forbade me to do it any more. I afterward learned to shoot them with the old family rifle, which measured "six feet in the barrel." I shot it several years before I was tall enough to load it, and always had to get an older brother or my father to load it for me.

Here, in the yard, just above the house — I can locate the spot within a foot — is where I once dug a "den" for a young pet "woodchuck," and turned a box over him to keep him safe. But he dug out the first night, and I never saw him again, unless Ring and I killed him after he grew up, and then I didn't recognize him.

And here on the hillside, about two hundred yards from the house, in a thicket of brush, is where I once killed eleven quails at one shot, with a neighbor's old single-barreled shot gun. It was in the winter. I tracked them some distance on the snow, and just at dusk found them huddled in a bunch under an old log that laid up some distance from the ground. They were bunched so closely that I could have covered them with my hat, and a good aim at about twenty yards left but a small chance for the poor little fellows. Only two of them escaped. I should blush to do so mean a thing now, but it was different then. I knew no better. I had not then been educated in the ethics of the field, and thought I had made a wonderful shot. I boasted of it for weeks and months afterward. I presume that many of my brother sportsmen of to-day have made such shots when they were boys. Probably they would not like to confess it now, but I don't know that I feel ashamed of it. I mention it to show the advancement that we have made through the influence of the wholesome teaching that we get from such sources as the *American Field.* There are hundreds of young clodhoppers to-day, such as I was then, that do such potting every chance they get, and don't know there is any harm in it. But I have digressed from my subject.

Here, on the opposite side of the hill is where the old sugar camp used to be ; but all those old maples from which used to flow such generous quantities of the rich saccharine fluid, have long ago been cut down, and the land whereon they stood is now a green field. I look in vain for a trace of the old furnace, and the cabin that stood in front of it, but not a vestige of either remain. But I see a plowman not far away; I will ask him. Yes, he points out a small pile of stones near the middle of the field, which he says marks the place where the furnace stood.

"We tore it down when we cleared this piece," he said.

I approached the spot he indicated, and found a few

stones that once formed part of the old furnace. I stood
over them and ruminated. I had spent many happy hours
on that spot. We used to gather in several barrels of sap
during the day, boil it down, and frequently as the evening
approached on which we were to "sugar off," we invited the
boys and girls of the neighborhood to come in and join us in
a candy-pulling. Those were jolly parties that assembled on
such occasions, and we used to make the old woods ring
with our mirth and song. Oh, what a delicious *bon bon* is a
dish of warm maple wax, pure and fresh from the woods! I
can taste it now, in imagination. Reader, if you have never
tried it in this way, if you have never stood around the large,
cheerful furnace and lifted the bubbling mass from the kettle
onto your plate of snow or ice, if your knowledge of maple
sugar is confined to to the adulterated stuff you buy of the
grocer, and that which is dished up at church festivals, you
can have no conception of the sweet recollections that crowd
through my brain, as I stand over this sacred pile.

"How dear to my heart are the *sweets* of my childhood,
    When fond recollection presents them to view."

I remember once we had collected several barrels of sap
during the day, and I told my father and older brothers that
I would come back that night after supper and boil it down.
They said it was not necessary, that we could easily boil it
down the next morning before we should need the barrels;
but I insisted, so they told me to do as I liked. After supper
I took a newspaper and went to the camp. I put in a booming fire, filled up the kettles, and sat down in the cabin to
read by the light of the fire. Almost the first lines I read
were an account of a man in an adjoining county having
killed a large catamount that measured seven feet from tip to
tip. I dropped the paper and began to peer out into the

17

darkness. I fancied I could see a pair of large fiery eyes glaring upon me, and hear the dry leaves rustle, as a monster catamount, probably the mate to the one that had just been killed, crawled stealthily toward me. I thought of all the harrowing stories I had heard and read, of terrible encounters with these monsters; how people had been eaten up by them, and only a boot or a hat had been left to tell their fate. I sprang to the furnace, pulled all the fire out, threw the burning brands into a hole near by, and lit out for home at a rate that would make Maud S. envious. Every few seconds I looked back over my shoulder to see if the catamount was coming, and imagined that I was only saving my life by running faster than he could. When I arrived at the house I stopped outside the door until I had recovered my breath and cooled off. When I went in the folks inquired why I had come home so early; why I didn't stay and boil down the sap, as I had set out to do.

"Well," I said, "it was kind of lonesome out there all alone, and I concluded to leave it till morning." My good mother said she thought that was a wise conclusion, and this is the first time I ever confessed the true cause of my going home so early that night.

I return to the house, and again slake my thirst at the cool spring. Just below the spring stood the old milk-house, through which flowed the cool water from the spring. What delicious cool milk, and hard, yellow butter used to stand in this cool retreat. I remember once I caught a neighbor's dog in the milk-house. He had pulled the pin out of the door-post, and opened the door with his paw. I discovered him just as he entered, before he had time to do any damage; but he had gone there with mischievous intent. Besides, I had a grudge against him, for once when I had gone to his master's house he had bitten me. Now I had him where I wanted him, and I resolved to get even with him before I let him out. I stepped to the clump of water-hazels that stood a few feet away, and cut two large, heavy branches, about five or six feet long. I trimmed them up, returned to the milk-house, and went to work on that dog, and whipped him until my vengeance was thoroughly appeased. I then released him and sent him home, a wiser and a better dog.

On the hillside, a short distance from the house, i find the remains of an old oak stump, in which I once bored a hole and put a large charge of powder. It was on the morning of the Fourth of July, and when I "touched it off" at daylight the report woke all the neighbors within a radius of three miles.

In the piece of woods just south of the house I once pushed down a tall stump or trunk of a decayed tree, in which was a flying-squirrel's nest. The mother flew to a tree near by as the stump fell, and so escaped, but the young ones, although nearly full-grown, were not strong enough to fly. I caught up one of them, but no sooner had I done so than it caught my thumb just near the root of the nail, and inserted its sharp, cutting front teeth to the bone, above and below. I had to choke him off with the other hand, and after that I gave flying-squirrels a wide berth. On another occasion, however, I caught a live ground-squirrel, and he bit a finger nearly off before I succeeded in choking him to death.

On a farm adjoining ours there stood an old deserted log cabin. I was roaming around it one day to see what I could find, when, looking through a large crack in the floor, I saw a ground-hog busily engaged in burrowing in the ground. I went out to the fence, got a large sliver off a rail and stabbed him with it so vigorously that I succeeded in killing him before he could get out of my reach.

I continued my rambles through the neighborhood, visiting

old friends, schoolmates and acquaintances, until two days passed rapidly away. Then I returned to the station to take the train for home — my present home. But as I pass by the old farm, I pause once more to take a last fond look at those scenes so dear to me. Ah! when shall I see them again? Perhaps never. Then farewell, dear, dear old home, farewell! Thou art no longer my home; I am a stranger here now, an intruder. There is no welcome for me. Tears dim my eyes as I gaze o'er the green fields, and in my heart, old home, thy memory shall ever be kept as green as are thy hills and valleys now.

CHAPTER XXVIII.

TROUTING ON THE NAMECAGON.

MR. T. S. POWERS A TYPICAL SPORTSMAN—THE VILLAGE OF CABLE—
OUT IN THE STREAM—MULTITUDES OF TROUT—MOSQUITO CREEK.

> He greedily sucks in the twining bait,
> And tugs and nibbles the fallacious meat.
> Now, happy fisherman, now twitch the line!
> How the rod bends! Behold the prize is thine!

I was a passenger on a north-bound train on the North Wisconsin railroad one day near the last of May, and as the train stopped at a small station away up in the great pine woods, I saw half-a-dozen sportsmen, equipped with fishing tackle and camping outfit, enter the smoking-car. I scanned their sun-browned countenances to see if I might recognize any of them, for I feel an instinctive affinity for any man whom I see with a fishing-rod or gun in his hand. I was rewarded and delighted to see in the front rank of the party the genial face of that typical sportsman and prince of good fellows, Mr. T. S. Powers, of Tomah, Wis. He introduced me to his friends, Messrs. M. A. Thayer and his son Charlie, D. D. Cheeney, Henry Foster and Mr. Guell, all of Sparta; R. P. Hitchcock, of Tomah, and Leroy Wheaton, of Hutchinson. All hands gave me a pressing invitation to join them, and as I was on the same errand as they were, I was only too glad to do so.

Our destination was the Namecagon river, one of the tributaries of the St. Croix. The railroad crosses the Namecagon three times, and as we looked at its clear swift waters and foaming rapids from the car windows, we felt assured of

glorious sport on the morrow. We arrived at the village of
Cable, in Bayfield county, Wis., at eight o'clock. After
supper we gathered in the sitting-room of the hotel and were
entertained for an hour by " Doctor " Weir, one of the
bright lights of the town, with some interesting fish stories.

He informed us that we were sure to have magnificent
sport. He said the Namecagon was literally full of trout,
and that many of them were of immense size. He said we
were not likely to catch one of less than half a pound weight
and that two and three pounders were common ; that several
parties had been out lately and each man had caught on an
average a hundred pounds of trout per day ; that if these
trout were too large, and if we preferred smaller ones, there
were plenty of small brooks in the vicinity, tributaries of the
river, where we could catch an average of three hundred per
day to the man that would only weigh from a quarter to
half a pound each.

He said the lakes in the neighborhood were also alive
with fish of various kinds. That at Long lake, two miles
north, we would catch bass weighing from four to eight
pounds as a steady thing ; that a day's string would average
six pounds ; that we would catch pickerel weighing twenty to
thirty pounds each ; of course we would, for other people
were doing so every day. One of the boys ventured to
remark that he thought the Doctor was giving us taffy. But
the Doctor affirmed on his professional honor that every word
was true as gospel.

" Why," said he, " we have eaten fresh fish here until we
are all tired of them ; occasionally one of the boarders con-
cludes that he would like a mess of fish. He goes out to the
lake, and in an hour returns with a coffee sack full of black
bass, but on his arrival finds that about fifteen or sixteen of
the other boarders have been out fishing just for fun and each

one has brought in a coffee sack full. Then they all feel discouraged and the fish are dumped into the alley."

"Why," continued our orator, "one day last winter a man drove down to one of our small lakes to water his horse. He cut a hole in the ice, but the bullheads came up so fast that his horses couldn't drink, so he took a wooden pail and went to bailing them out. He worked away until he dipped out four barrels, and still they were just as thick in the hole as when he commenced, so he got discouraged and drove away. Oh, you needn't wink. It's a fact, for I went down and saw the pile of bullheads on the ice myself. Occasionally the mill boarding-house, down on Clear lake, wants a mess of fish for breakfast. Well, they just send a man down to the lake with a team. He takes out the tail-gate and backs his wagon into the lake till the box is full of bass, then puts in the tail-gate again and drives up to the house. It's a fact. They're so thick in the lake they can't get out of the way, and you dip them up whenever you dip up water."

At this stage of the game somebody moved to adjourn, and we all went to bed. The next morning John O'Brien loaded our traps into his wagon, took us out to the Namecagon river, two miles from town, and we made our camp on a high bank overlooking a bend in the river. It was near noon when the majority of the party got the camp established and ready for business. Mr. Thayer and his son, Mr. Cheeney and myself, went up the river about two miles above camp, Mr. Foster and Mr. Hitchcock about a mile above, and Mr. Powers went below.

The stream at this point is from thirty to fifty yards wide and from one to three feet deep in general, though there are many deep holes in it. I speak of it as in the spring stage of water. In midsummer it is considerably lower. It is very swift, and there are rapids that will tax all your strength and nerve to wade them down stream at this stage. To wade them up stream is impossible. And in wading down, if you loose your footing you will go to the foot of the rapids ere you can possibly regain it.

We who were disposed to wade went at once into the middle of the stream, the others fished from the bank. The former is much the pleasanter method of fishing this stream. We waded out until clear of all brush, and here we could whip and cast to our hearts' content. After fishing one riffle, eddy or rapid until we felt that we had all we could get out of it, we would pass on to the next.

Occasionally you see a large rock in the middle of the stream around which the raging torrent foams and surges. Just below it is a deep hole, where you feel sure there is a large, wary old trout lying in weight for his prey. You feel that it will not do to approach too near him, for he will take fright and bid you a hasty good-bye. So you stop, perhaps fifty feet above him, drop your fly on the water, reel out and let the current take it down until it passes through the foaming crest, past the breaker, and just as it enters the eddy there is a sudden commotion in the angry flood, a flash of light, a show of crimson and gold, a tug at the line, a sudden stroke of the rod, and he is fast! He dives under the rock, but quick as thought you swing him out away from that danger. Then he makes a rush for a clump of driftwood near the bank. As you give him the butt of the rod, and check his mad career, he makes a beautiful break, and shows you his rich colors glistening in the bright sunlight.

Your heart throbs with delight as you see his size and feel his weight upon the line. But you keep perfectly cool; checking him at every turn, and reeling in whenever he gives you a foot of line, until after a hard fight he succumbs to his fate, and you gently lift him into your basket. He is one of those fine, dark specimens that are only found in the larger streams and lakes, and his rounded sides show that he has been well fed.

You pass on down to where you see a large body of drift-wood, near the right bank, and from the quiet repose which the water bears there you know it is deep under that drift. You stop fifty to a hundred feet above it, and repeat the tactics described above. As regularly as the fly reaches within a few feet of the drift you get a rise, until you take out perhaps half-a-dozen fine fellows, when the others, if there are others there, begin to "smell a mice," and you pass on.

Thus the time passed with us, and thus the sport was varied, until we had covered over two miles and arrived at camp at five o'clock in the evening, hungry enough to eat the largest trout in the river. On counting up our strings we found that they ran from fourteen to twenty-five to each man, aggregating one hundred and sixty. The smallest one in the lot weighed a quarter of a pound and the largest a pound, the aggregate weight being over fifty pounds.

That night a heavy rain came on and raised the stream nearly a foot, so that our sport was not so good on the following day, though we succeeded in taking ninety-three. The rain continued at intervals during the day, and as the river was likely to remain swollen for several days, we decided to remove over to Long lake and take a turn at the bass. The Namecagon river is certainly one of the finest trout streams in the Northwest. We saw and heard enough to convince us that there are no small trout in it. The large ones drive the small ones out into the small streams. In our two days' fishing we did not catch a single fingerling—nothing that would weigh less than a quarter of a pound, and we heard similar reports from several other parties who were fishing at the

same time we were, and had fished it before. Then it bears
a great many very large ones. We caught several weighing
from twelve ounces to a pound, and some of the other parties
caught trout while we were there weighing over a pound.

The stream heads in Namecagon lake, eight miles east of
the village of Cable. This lake no doubt bears some very
large trout, though I failed to learn that any have ever been
taken out of it. The stream can be fished either from the
banks, by boat, or by wading, from this lake down to the
mouth of Musquito creek, a distance of perhaps fifty miles,
and they told us that the fishing is as good the entire distance
as it was where we fished. As already stated, it is broad,
shallow and swift — being from thirty to fifty yards wide —
and there is no brush to bother any one who wades or fishes
from a boat. To launch a boat or canoe in the lake and then
fish down to Mosquito creek, or to one of the several railroad
crossings where you could board the train, would make a
delightful voyage and furnish fine sport.

These trout take almost any kind of a fly or bait eagerly.
Live minnows would be the most killing .bait for. the larger
trout. I had excellent sport with an artificial minnow. We
also caught several fine ones with live frogs.

To reach this stream you should take the St. Paul train on
the Northwestern road to Hudson, and from there go north
on the North Wisconsin division of the Chicago, St. Paul,
Minneapolis & Omaha railroad to Cable. Teams, boats and
guides can be had at that point at reasonable rates.

CHAPTER XXIX.

PIKE AND BASS FISHING ON LONG LAKE.

AN AFTERNOON'S CATCH, 180 POUNDS OF FISH! — LEROY AND THE POL-
LYWOGS TOP THE NARROWS — HUNTING A LOON — "YOU'VE GOT A
WHALE, SURE" — AN ENORMOUS PICKEREL — THREE DAYS' CATCH,
620 POUNDS — HOME AGAIN.

WE landed at the foot of Long lake about noon, made
camp, and prepared for business. We launched the boat we
took with us, and procured two others that we found on the
lake. The majority of the party disposed themselves in the
boats for trolling, the others still-fished from logs and fallen
trees along the shore. I employed John Moulton, a young
man who lives on the bank of the lake, to row for me, and
Mr. Powers and myself started for the Narrows, a point
where the best fishing is said to be.

But we didn't have to wait to reach the Narrows to find
good sport. We had gone but a few strokes from camp when
the trouble began. Our oarsman kept near the shore, and
from almost every submerged log or tree top, of which there
are a great many all along the shores, there came a bass that
went for one or the other of our spoons, and there was but
little time during the afternoon that one of us was not engaged in reeling in a fish. The bass were of the small
mouthed variety, *Micropterus salmoides*. They are very
vigorous in this high northern latitude, and furnish magnificent sport. As we passed an island about three miles from
camp, Mr. Powers hooked a pike that weighed ten and three-
quarters pounds, and as we returned later in the evening, he
took another from the same hole, weighing eleven and one-

quarter pounds. We returned to camp at six o'clock, having had all the sport we wanted for one day. Our friends in the other two boats, and those who were fishing from the shore, all brought in fine strings of bass. The afternoon's catch weighed in the aggregate 180 pounds.

The second day being Sunday, we concluded to make a holiday of it, and go fishing, for a change. Mr. Thayer, his son Charlie and Leroy Wheaton in one boat, and Moulton and myself in the other, pulled up the east shore of the lake about a mile, to where a small lake is connected with the main one by a narrow channel. Here we landed, and went into the small lake for the purpose of procuring bait. We dipped up a good lot of minnows, and got a few frogs and clams.

To see Leroy catch pollywogs, and to hear the droll remarks he made about them, was more fun than fishing, and I spent an hour watching and listening. He is an original character, and furnished fun for the whole camp all the time we were out. He is one of the most useful men in camp, or on any hunting or fishing expedition, that I have ever met. He is large and muscular, good natured, willing, and anxious to please and accommodate every one with whom he comes in contact. He will pull on a pair of oars all day, and come into camp at night as full of fun and frolic as when he started out in the morning. He is one of the most skillful deer hunters in the state, and the crack of his Winchester sounds the funeral knell of almost every deer that exposes itself to his deadly aim. A gentleman who hunts a great deal with him tells me that he has, on two different occasions, seen him jump two deer together in the thick woods, and kill both of them before they could get out of reach. In many respects he is a second edition of old Leatherstocking.

The small lake where we got our bait was also alive with

bass. Mr. Thayer and Charlie waded in a few steps from the shore, and with the pollywogs that Leroy furnished them, caught bass almost as fast as they could handle them. But after watching the sport for a while, Moulton and I pulled out on the main lake again. We tied up in several favorable looking places, and tried still fishing, but did not have as good success as in trolling. We could catch small rock bass, and perch by the dozen, but we were loaded for larger game than these, and didn't care to waste time with them, so we returned to our spoon victuals.

We went up to the Narrows, about four miles from camp, and then returned, having taken as many bass as we cared for, and had all the sport we wanted. Several of them were very fine ones—weighing three to three and a-half pounds each, and one weighing four pounds. The other members of the party had equally fine sport, and some of them showed larger strings than I did. Mr. Powers "took the cake" for this day's work by scoring another pike that weighed exactly twenty pounds, and measured forty-three and a-half inches in length. We skinned this fish, and Mr. Powers has since had him mounted. The total catch for the day weighed two hundred and ten pounds.

The next morning when we awoke it was raining heavily. The clouds were thick, low, and almost black, and the rain came down in a steady, settled manner, which indicated that it had set in for all day. It afforded a gloomy outlook for the day's sport. The majority of the party avowed their determination to stay in camp, but two or three of the more enthusiastic said they were not afraid of a little water, applied externally, and they would go out. They said they only objected to water when it became necessary to take it internally.

While we were rigging our tackle, and breakfast was in

course of preparation, a loon made its appearance on the lake a short distance from camp. I asked Leroy if he would go with me and give the loon a chase. With his usual vim he answered " You bet." The other boys laughed at us, said we were "loony," that we could never kill him in the world, etc.; but I had hunted loons before, and knew that they were mistaken.

I took my little Stevens pocket rifle (which I always carry with me when fishing), Leroy took the oars, and we pulled out toward the loon. When we got within about fifty yards of him, he dove. We pulled in the direction he took, and when he rose I fired at him. He went down again, and when he reappeared I shot at him again; the bullets in each case cutting very close to his neck. The third time he came up he was not more than forty yards from us. I drew another bead on him, and by a lucky shot killed him—the bullet passing through his neck about an inch below the occipital joint. We returned to camp with our prize, and received the hearty congratulations of our friends on our success. The bird was one of the finest specimens I have ever seen, the plumage being unusually full and beautiful. I brought the skin home, and have had it mounted.

Breakfast over, we donned our rubber suits and pulled out up the lake. The rain still fell in torrents, accompanied by a cold wind. Our friends told us the fish would not bite in such weather; and when we had rowed three miles without getting a strike, we began to think their predictions would prove true, and that we should have to return to camp with— "fisherman's luck."

But we kept our courage up, by hoping that it would clear up later in the day, and that we should yet have some good sport. Finally, as we passed the island, our two boats not more than twenty yards apart, my oarsman said :

"Mr. Powers has got a fish."

"So have I," I said, for at that moment I felt a terrific surge at my line, and as I commenced to reel in, my fish started for the middle of the lake. I knew at once that I had a very large fish, and I told John to throw the boat out away from the shore, in order to keep him clear of snags. A few strokes of the oars set us out of all danger, and then the fun commenced. At first he fought deep. I kept a taut line on him, and whenever he slackened on it, I reeled in. He would come a few feet toward the boat, then turn, and with the speed almost of lightning take out a hundred or two hundred feet of line; and though I kept the heavy drag on and thumbed the reel besides, it seemed mere play for him to run with it. Finally he made a partial break, showing only his broad, forked tail. Mr. Powers asked me what I had.

I told him I thought it was a bass, but if so it was a very large one. Just then, the captive made a fearful lunge into the air, clearing the water by fully four feet, and making a desperate effort to shake the hook out of his mouth. He showed his monster form to our eager eyes but a moment, and then went down again.

"Yes," said Powers, "You've got a bass, in your mind. You've got a *whale* there, and you want to be very careful that you don't lose him."

All this time the great monster kept up the fight, running, leaping, diving straight down, down, down, until he would take out sixty or seventy feet of line and perhaps lie directly under the boat. Then he would start for the shore again, as if bound to snag the line; but the drag, my thumb, and the butt of the rod, would make him break again and change his course.

Talk about gamy fish!

Why, reader, if you could imagine what it would be to

lasso an old she-tiger in one of her native jungles, you can form some idea of what it is to hook one of these fish. But no pen can describe the scene. You must catch one of them yourself before you can know what magnificent sport it is. Suffice it to say, that after a hard fight of three-quarters of an hour, I so far exhausted him as to bring him alongside the boat, when Mr. Powers, who had meantime boarded my boat, lifted him in with the gaff-hook. He proved to be one of the same species as the others, the great northern pike, *esox lucioides* (Agassiz), usually, but incorrectly, termed pick-erel. He measured forty-six inches in length, seven and a half in depth, and four and three-quarters in breadth. I sat there and admired him for some minutes before I was ready to move. I felt all the prouder of my prize for the reason that I had killed him on light tackle; my outfit being a twelve ounce bamboo bass rod, a number six Milam reel, a number four braided linen line, and a number five spoon.

Here was glory enough for one day. I had taken the largest fish that has ever yet been taken from this lake, so far as known to the settlers in the vicinity, the largest caught previous to our visit having weighed eighteen and three-quarter pounds, and Powers' best one, twenty pounds, and as the rain continued to fall in an almost unbroken sheet, we turned our bow toward camp. Mr. Powers landed another pike while I was playing mine that weighed eighteen pounds. The two struck within a few seconds of each other, for the instant I saw him commence to haul in on his line I felt the first surge at mine. The boats were opposite each other, and, as stated before, only a few yards apart.

Powers, Thayer and Leroy staid out until three o'clock in the afternoon and returned with ten of these large pike, making fifteen in all that we had caught in the two days, the smallest of which weighed ten pounds. They also brought in a fine string of bass, making the day's catch weigh in all 230 pounds, and the grand total for the three days 620 pounds.

These pike differ as widely from our common pike, both in appearance and habits, as do the muscalonge. In shape and gaminess they closely resemble the latter, though the markings are entirely different. The great Northern pike is one of the most gamy of all our fresh-water fishes. He fights like a wild cat from the time he is hooked until he is landed, or escapes, while the common pike·makes a spurt or two when first hooked, and then allows you to drag him in as you would a chunk of wood.

This Long lake is a very paradise for the disciples of Walton. It is about seven miles long, and from a quarter to a mile wide; has high, bold, stony, and in many places bluffy banks, and the water is so pure and clear that you may see a small pebble at a depth of twenty feet or more. All around the shores are old logs and trees that have fallen into the water and sunk, making capital feeding and hiding grounds for large fish. It has never been fished but a very little. Up to last summer, Ashland, thirty-five miles distant, was the nearest point to it, and from that point there was no road, and no means of reaching it, except on foot.

Last fall the North Wisconsin railroad was completed to within two miles of the lake, and during the fall and the present spring and summer hundreds of pounds of fish have been taken out of it. Still there seems to be no perceptible diminution of the supply. You can still catch fish there so rapidly that you will soon tire of the sport and want to rest.

There are good accommodations at the lake. Plenty of ice is put up each winter, so that you can save your fish and bring them home. There are several boats on the lake that can be had at reasonable rates. To reach the lake, go to Hudson, Wisconsin, and take the north-bound train on the

18

North Wisconsin railroad, to Cable. From there (a distance of two miles) you can get a team to take you out.

I have spun this narrative to a much greater length than I intended. We packed our two largest pike in ice, and I brought them to Chicago. Dr. Velie, secretary of the Academy of Sciences, one of the most skillful taxidermists in the West, has mounted my twenty-three pounder in fine style.

Mr. Powers has also had his twenty pounder mounted. We brought several of the large pike with us, and about a hundred pounds of bass. The others that we caught we either ate, returned to the water while alive, or gave to people at the camps, so that none were wasted.

CHAPTER XXX.

THE LAKE SUPERIOR REGION.

FROM MARQUETTE TO DULUTH — A MILD WINTER — A CROWD IN "MACKI-
NAW FLANNEL"— THE LUMBER INTERESTS — FISHERIES — BROOK
TROUT — DUCKS AND GEESE IN SEASON — LITTLE HUNTING — TROUT
LAKE — A CHARMING LOCATION FOR SPORTSMEN.

> " There is a pleasure in these pathless woods,
>   There is a rapture on the lonely shore,
> There is society where none intrudes,
>   By the deep sea, and music in its roar.
> love not man the less, but nature more,
>   From these our interviews, in which I steal
> From all I may be or have been before,
>   To mingle with the universe and feel
> What I can ne'er express, yet cannot all conceal."

THERE is indeed a grandeur, a sublimity, an impressive solitude imparted by the unbroken forests which line the shores of Lake Superior, as they lay wrapt in their heavy mantle of snow, which it would be vain for me to attempt to describe. The scene, although in such wide contrast from that which the same country presents in summer, is none the less attractive and beautiful.

I have recently spent many hours alone, wandering far into the depths of these grand forests, that now slumber amid the silence of a still rigid winter, a silence unbroken save by the moaning of the wind through the tops of the tall pine-trees, lost in admiration of the scene before me. To most people the woods present but a lonely and dreary aspect in winter, but to me the scene is sublime. I love the very solitude and loneliness which the season occasions, and enjoy it

275

quite as much as the more picturesque and musical features presented in the summer season.

Throughout this entire range of country skirting the south shore of Lake Superior, from Marquette to Duluth and extending from the lake a hundred miles to the southward, the ground is now, on the first day of April, covered with snow to a depth of from two to three feet. The lakes and streams are covered with ice twenty to thirty inches thick. Lake Superior itself is frozen all along the shore and for many miles out toward its center. The lighthouse-keeper at Outer Island, which lies twenty miles out in the lake from Bayfield, reports that no open water is visible from the tower even with the aid of a powerful telescope, and it is stated that a short distance west of Bayfield the lake is frozen entirely across.

Teams are passing between the various towns along the lakeshore on the ice, and I have myself just returned from a delightful sleigh-ride to Bayfield, a distance of eighteen miles from Ashland, the entire trip having been made on the ice, and over water measuring from twenty to one hundred feet in depth. Considering the time of year and the extremely mild winter that has prevailed south of here, the novelty of the sensation, as we sped through the keen frosty air, which was rendered musical by the cheerful sound of sleigh-bells, may be more easily imagined than described. Even now the mercury runs down to zero or very near it every night. In mid-day it ranges from twenty to forty degrees above.

The lumbermen are still busily engaged cutting and banking logs, ready to run down on the "June rise." Thousands of men and teams have been employed all winter cutting and banking logs along the streams and railroads, and hundreds of thousands of dollars will be put in circulation when these vast forces are paid off for their winter's work. These lumbermen, or more strictly "loggers," are an interesting species of the *genus homo*. They live principally on pork, beans, corn-beef and coffee, the pork forming the leading article in the bill of fare, by a large majority. This class of food produces so much animal heat in their bodies that they can stand cold equal to an Esquimaux, and even in this semi-arctic winter they wear very light clothing. They seldom wear coats or vests, even when not at work. Their pants and shirts are made of the thick heavy "Mackinaw" flannel, and if, owing to an unusually cold snap or to their not being at work, they feel cold, they simply put on another shirt. This flannel is made up in very flashy colors, the most popular being blue, crimson and scarlet, though some of the men wear grey. A crowd of them together present a most fantastic picture. One man wears a red shirt, blue pants, black cap and moccasins; another wears a blue shirt, red pants and a red cap; still another wears a suit of all red and his "pard" one of all blue, and large cow-hide boots. Many of them wear red and blue flannel or knit caps, and occasionally some one will heighten the picture by wearing a broad-brim black or drab sombrero and a red scarf or handkerchief tied around his waist. There are also many Indians and half-breeds in this country, with whom this taste for gaudy colors is inherent, and they even out-do their white brethren in their display of colors.

As we roll up to a station, many of which consist of but a few log-cabins, in the midst of this wilderness, and this gaily attired throng turns out to see the train come in, the traveler need draw but slightly on his imagination to fancy himself passing over the Alps and his train suddenly surrounded and attacked by the Alpine banditti.

One of these loggers, who had evidently made up his mind to "settle" here, had been away to the settlements, had married and was returning with his bride to his forest home, on the same train on which I was a passenger.

He was a "sandy" complexioned man, with red, bushy hair, red mustache, and had not shaved for about two weeks. He wore a pair of red flannel pants tucked in his boots, a gray flannel shirt and (for this occasion only) a short, heavy black coat. The bride was a rather comely but extremely awkward-looking girl of probably twenty summers (and about the same numbers of winters), attired in a "home-made" grey dress, red and white plaid shawl, green knit scarf and a black bonnet trimmed with a large black ostrich plume.

The groom patronized the train boy liberally, and he and the bride munched pop-corn, peanuts, oranges, figs and candy all through the journey. They looked and acted as if very happy.

Fire has destroyed large tracts of pine and hard wood in this portion of the state. Whole townships are frequently laid desolate in a single day. After the pine-tree is killed by fire it soon decays and falls. It is truly a sad sight to see thousands of acres of valuable timber thus offered as a sacrifice to the consuming element, and yet there seem to be no means of preventing it. Notwithstanding the frequent ravishes of fire and the millions of trees that are annually cut off by the lumbermen, there is still but a very slight diminution of the supply, so vast is the extent of this pine region that one may travel twenty, thirty, or even fifty miles in many places, through unbroken forests, without seeing a cabin, a footprint, or any other sign of a white man. It is estimated by good judges that it will take fifty years to exhaust the supply of pine in this state, at the present rate of consumption.

Next in importance to the lumber interests in this portion of the Lake Superior country are the fisheries. Hundreds of men in this place and Bayfield, as well as at other points along the shore, live by the rich products of this fertile body of water. It is estimated that nearly three hundred tons of lake-trout and whitefish have been shipped from these two points within the past four months. The greater portion of these are caught in nets, set through the ice, though a great many men are constantly employed in catching with hook and line.

Holes are cut through the ice where the water is thirty to sixty feet deep, and a hook, baited with cut bait or pork-rind, is dropped down within a few feet of the bottom, and is then kept moving up and down. When the fisherman feels a strike, he gives the line a sharp jerk, and when he finds that he has fastened his fish, he runs with the line until the fish is brought through the hole and landed on the ice. This is rendered easy by cutting the hole much larger at the bottom than at the top. A day's catch varies from twenty up to one hundred pounds, though occasionally a man has been known to take as high as four or five hundred pounds in a day. Only trout are usually caught with hook and line, the whitefish being all taken in nets. The fish bring four cents per pound on the ice. The men protect themselves from the severity of the weather by erecting wind-breakers near their stands. This is done by planting stakes in the ice, and spreading blankets, or pieces of canvas over them. In summer time the hand-fishing is done from boats, with equally as good success as in winter.

This is a very popular resort for fishermen and sportsmen during the summer. Nearly all the streams emptying into Lake Superior teem with brook-trout, and the small inland lakes, which are very numerous, contain great numbers of black-bass, pike, pickerel and muskalonge. Some marvelous accounts are given of the great catches of brook-trout, that have been made in this section, and were they not substantiated by men of undoubted veracity, we could scarcely credit them. A gentleman, his wife and daughter, who spent several weeks here last summer, frequently caught as many as

three hundred trout in a single day, in Fish creek, which empties into Chequamegon bay, only three miles from here. An old
gentleman from Pittsburg, who has visited this locality several
times, has caught two hundred in less than a day on several
occasions. Hon. Samuel S. Fifield (the present Lieutenant
Governor of the State), editor of the *Ashland Press*, states
that he made a trip up White river two years ago, in company
with two other gentlemen, and that in two days' fishing they
scored over six hundred trout. A great many brook-trout
are taken in the lake and bays along the rocky shores, and it
is here that the largest ones are usually found. They are
frequently taken as large as three or four pounds in weight.
Those in the streams in this vicinity are also large, the
average weight being from half-a-pound to a pound. An old
fisherman who has lived here for over twenty-five years informs me that, notwithstanding the great number of fish
annually taken from these waters, he can see no preceptible
decrease in the supply; that each year's catch is as large as
that of any previous year, the only difference being that
not so many of the very large fish are now taken as in former
years; still the great slaughter that is being practiced by
many who come here from abroad, such as in the instances
mentioned above, must and will eventually deplete the
waters, and the practice of taking such large numbers merely
for the momentary pleasure it affords, or for the sake of
publishing the scores at home, cannot be too severely condemned. A law should be enacted making it a misdemeanor,
punishable by a heavy fine, to catch more than a reasonable
number of fish in any one day.

Game is also abundant in this south-shore country. Deer
especially are very numerous. Strange as it may seem there
is but little hunting done here, either by the Indians or white
settlers, though there are a few of the former who live by the

chase and they supply the home market and ship large quantities of game abroad.   Most of the Indians hang around the towns and live by fishing, making maple sugar and working at such work as they çan get to do.   The majority of them have more or less white blood in their veins, and they, as a rule, care less for the pleasures of the chase than the full-bloods.   I am informed that of those few who are skillful hunters, a single man frequently kills four or five deer in a day.   Mr. J. B. Bono, proprietor of the Fountain House, at Bayfield, told me that last September three Indians killed fourteen deer in one day within twenty miles of Bayfield. Fur animals, such as the otter, beaver, mink, marten, wild cat and lynx, are also numerous.

There are thousands of ducks and geese here in season. Mr. Bono tells me that he employed an Indian to go out and kill a lot for his hotel last fall.   They took a boat and went into some marshes at the mouth of Sand river, a few miles west of Bayfield, and in three hours' shooting killed 190 ducks.

Visiting sportsmen have frequently made equally large bags of both ducks and geese.   Ashland and Bayfield are both popular and pleasant summer resorts, and during the past two summers have been crowded to overflowing with pleasure seekers.   Aside from the fishing and shooting which the region affords, it is a delightful place in which to spend the summer.   Both towns are supplied with large, pleasant and well-kept hotels.   The climate, even during July and August, is pleasant, the nights especially being decidedly cool and invigorating.   A good heavy blanket is needed every night in summer.   The Chequamegon House, at Ashland, is an elegant building and is handsomely furnished.   There are always plenty of boats and guides to be had at reasonable prices, and sailing and rowing on the bay afford a most delightful pastime.

The village of Phillips, seventy-six miles south of here, on the Wisconsin Central railway, is also a most charming summer resort. It is situated on the bank of Elk lake, a beautiful little sheet of water, affording delightful rowing, sailing and bathing facilities and the surrounding country also abounds in fish and game.

A great deal of game is killed in this vicinity by those who take the trouble to hunt it. Mr. Fewell shipped over 3,000 pounds of venison from this place a year ago last winter. Only a very little has been killed during the past winter. More trapping has been done, however, than in previous winters. He has shipped this past winter large quantities of furs, mostly beaver and otter. I met here Mr. C. R. Patterson, an old Indian trader, who has a post on the headwaters of the Flambeau river, about a hundred miles northeast of Phillips. He described a lake that lies a few miles from his post, called Trout Lake, which he says abounds in a variety of trout closely resembling the brook-trout, but which differs from them slightly in some respects, and grow much larger. They often attain a weight of thirty pounds. They also differ widely from the lake trout. They are readily taken with either the fly or live minnow. Several Chicago sportsmen have visited the lake, and can bear testimony to the superior quality, large size and great numbers of the trout it contains. The lake is eight miles long, six miles wide, and contains several islands, each of which covers ten acres or more, and affords beautiful camping-grounds. Mr. P. says all the varieties of game that inhabit this country are abundant in this locality.

Taken all in all, this northern portion of Wisconsin is probably the best fish and game country now to be found in the Northwest. It is reached by way of the Chicago, Milwaukee & St. Paul and the Wisconsin Central railroads, the latter road reaching clear through to the great lake. This company furnishes excellent facilities to sportsmen, transporting dogs, boats and camp equipage free, and stopping trains at any point between stations, where they may wish to get on or off. Sportsmen visiting this region will find in Mr. Fewell, of Phillips, and Hon. Sam Fifield, of Ashland, pleasant and valuable acquaintances, and should not fail to consult both as to the best localities in which to find particular sport of which they may be in search.

CHAPTER XXXI.

AUTUMN RAMBLINGS IN NORTHERN MICHIGAN.

AMONG THE WOLVERINES — OFF TO THE TWIN LAKES — MY "HUNTER'S PET" — THROUGH THE PINE FOREST — ONE SHOT AND ONE MISS — A PACK OF WOLVES — HIDING-PLACES OF THE BEAR — A SHOT AT A DEER — ON BOARD THE "NORTHERN BELLE."

ON the night of September 2d, 1878, a party of five of us, weary of the cares and duties of the office, and longing for a few weeks' rest and recreation, boarded the train on the L., C. and L. railroad, at Louisville, Ky., which was at that time my home, and retired for a night's slumber in a clean and comfortable bed in a Pullman sleeping-car. We soon forgot all our cares, and awoke at the call of the conductor at four o'clock A.M. to find ourselves in Cincinnati, where we partook of a hearty breakfast, and at a quarter-past seven A.M. left that city over the Cincinnati, Hamilton & Dayton railroad for Richmond, Ind. At this point we transferred, in the union depot at ten minutes to eleven A.M., to the cosy and comfortable coach of the Grand Rapids & Indiana railroad, which carried us through to our destination without any other changes. The conductor and other officials of this road resorted to every means at their command to make our journey and that of every passenger under their charge as comfortable as possible. I have made several trips over this road, and in each case have been very favorably impressed with the uniform courtesy and kindness displayed by all its employés toward their patrons.

At half-past six A.M. of the 4th instant we arrived at Elmira, a small station twenty-five miles south of Petoskey, and 579 miles from Louisville, where we alighted from the train. We had made the run in thirty hours, which, after deducing the three hours' lay-over in Cincinnati, makes a creditable showing for the roads as to speed.

We loaded our tent, provisions, guns, fishing tackle and other baggage into a wagon which we had engaged for the purpose, and started for Twin Lakes, in Montmorency county, forty miles east. By noon we had made half the distance, and stopped to lunch near a small frame house, which our driver informed us was the last human habitation we would see on the route. His statement proved correct. The remainder of the ro 'e lay through a most wild and desolate region of country, co.ered with a rich growth of giant Norway pine, interspersed occasionally with vast and almost impenetrable swamps of hemlock, tamarack and white cedar. We passed over one tract of perhaps a thousand acres, where years ago fire had, during a dry season, passed through and killed all the timber. Subsequently other fires had followed and burned up every vestige of dead timber, reducing the country to the condition of a natural prairie. This is now grown up with scattering dwarf-pines, or as the settlers call them, "jack-pines." These openings or plains furnish fine grazing lands for deer, and at the proper season are the favorite hunting-grounds for the Indians and white hunters, as the game can be seen much farther than in the woods.

About nine o'clock at night we reached Twin Lakes, upon the bank of one of which we pitched our camp, built a rousing fire, made a pot of strong coffee, of which we drank liberally, and lay down to enjoy the rest we so much needed after our long journey. On the following day, some of our party amused themselves by taking a few fine bass and pickerel from the lakes, others by shooting a few ducks, and the balance by strolling through the woods, enjoying the fresh, invigorating atmosphere, etc. Our teamster, Steve Bradford, remained with us until the following morning, and during this day took several good fish. On Monday morning he left us to return home. An old hunter and trapper who had previously encamped in the vicinity of our camp, and who had been away several days on a hunting expedition, returned to his camp at this juncture, empty-handed. To our eager inquiries regarding the prospect of killing a few deer within the next few weeks, he replied that there was scarcely a possibility of our doing so, as at this particular season the does were weaning their fawns and were lying hidden away from them all through the day; that the fawns being naturally the most timid creatures in the world, would not venture out to feed during the day alone; that the bucks were also lying hidden away drying their horns, and that each ventured out to feed only at night, and then only for a short time—barely long enough to eat a quantity of food sufficient to last them through the following day. He said that had we chosen a time a few weeks earlier or later, we would have found them ranging freely during the day, feeding and exercising, and would have had no trouble in securing frequent and easy shots; but at this particular time it would be almost impossible to find a deer under any circumstances.

We were sadly disappointed at hearing such unfavorable news, but resolved to make the best of it, and put forth strenuous efforts to secure at least venison enough to supply our camp during our stay. The old hunter readily consented to act as our guide, and to do his best toward finding a deer. According, early on Monday morning he reported at our tent, armed with a Henry repeating rifle, ready to take the war-path. I took my Stevens breech-loading rifle, of the "Hunter's Pet" pattern, a light but very effective weapon. Doctor Shortt, another member of our party, took a breech-loading shot-gun, loaded with buckshot, and together we three filed out through the pine forest and soon entered upon one of the jack-pine plains, as the settlers call them. We had not proceeded more than a mile over this plain when we started a magnificent buck from his hiding-place. We were walking single-file at the time, our guide in front and we following. As the dear sprang up our guide brought his rifle to his shoulder and pulled, but his cartridge failed to go. He being directly in front of me some twenty paces, and the deer running directly from us, prevented me from getting a fair shot without endangering our guide's life. Still, as the buck bounded slightly out of his line and plunged into a thicket, I made a snap-shot and missed. As the Doctor was still in the rear of both of us, it was impossible for him to shoot at all. So at the end of this, our first inning, our score stood one shot and one miss.

However, we could scarcely regret our ill luck, for we were so enraptured by the beauty and grace of this magnificent animal as he arose from his hiding-place and bounded lightly and gracefully away, like a phantom in the midnight air, or a shadow on the wall, that, notwithstanding our greed for game, we should surely have suffered severe remorse of conscience had we succeeded in sacrificing his rich life. After this episode, we hunted faithfully all day without getting another shot.

About three o'clock in the afternoon we separated, so as to cover more ground. About the same time a heavy rain-storm set in, which continued through the day and night. The Doctor and the guide soon returned to camp by different routes, but I continued in a northwesterly course to a large tract of heavy, hardwood timber, where our guide had informed me we would be more likely to find game at this season than in the open pine woods or on the plains. I had no better success here, however, than in the pine lands, and, finding darkness drawing nigh, I decided not to return to camp that night. I accordingly took a trail that led to a shanty where lived a German settler or "homesteader," as they are called here. I reached this house just as it began to grow dark, and was informed that I was then twelve miles from camp in a direct line, and had traveled during the day about fifteen or sixteen miles. I was kindly cared for by this generous, warm-hearted German and his wife, both of whom I soon learned were well educated in their native tongue, and also in French and Spanish. The man is by profession a civil engineer and draughtsman, and formerly held a good position in the employ of a railroad company in Germany. His wife had been a teacher in the schools of Berlin, and later a governess in the family of a wealthy nobleman. They now live in a log shanty about twelve feet square, with a roof composed of slabs or puncheons, split from pine logs, and without a floor of any kind.

The roof leaks like a sieve, and on this occasion they were tramping around in the mud while attending to their household duties. There was not even the conventional large fireplace and bright log fire to cheer the scene, but only a dull fire in a small stove. However, their warm hearts made amends for all that their home lacked in the way of comforts and conveniences. I was treated to a frugal supper of roast bear-meat, potatoes, bread and tea, and the rain ceasing soon after, I retired to rest and slept soundly till daylight.

This family has a fine piano standing on the ground in one corner of the room, upon which are piled some two or three hundred volumes of choice books in different languages, but principally in German. On their homestead is a small lake, covering about ten acres, which is the head of Thunder Bay river. The lake is about thirty feet deep in the center, clear as crystal, has no inlet save springs in the bottom of it, and has an outlet about fifteen feet wide, and from one to two feet deep, with a strong current. The lake is full of fine fish.

I started early in the morning for camp, where I arrived about noon and found the boys delighted to see me. They had passed an anxious night and forenoon, thinking some harm had befallen me — that I had wounded a bear and had been attacked and killed by him, or something of the kind. They were glad to learn, however, that I had merely been on an exploring expedition to the head-waters of Thunder Bay river.

On my return to camp on Wednesday I learned that the other members of the party had, during my absence, taken a pickerel thirty inches long and weighing eight pounds, several four-pound black-bass and numerous smaller specimens of both species. While two of them were out in a boat fishing, a large black bear came to the edge of the water about two hundred yards away, stood up on his hind legs and quietly contemplated the strange intruders before him. One of the party brought his Burgess repeating rifle to bear upon Bruin, and fired several shots before getting the exact range. He finally got it, however, and plunged a ball through the animal's haunches which caused him to seek shelter in a neighboring swamp in a hurry. The party landed and followed him as far as they could find his trail, but as they soon struck dry ground they could then see it no longer, and were compelled to abandon the chase and return to camp, greatly disappointed at their failure to capture so rich a prize.

Early the next morning, accompanied by my guide, I again took to the woods, determined, if not to capture venison, at least to explore the surrounding country until I was fully satisfied as to its character and resources. About four miles from camp we entered a vast tract of hardwood timber, of a

19

most luxuriant growth, many trees measuring four to six feet in diameter. This tract abounds in wild fruits of various kinds. We found during the day blackberries, raspberries, huckleberries, sugar-pears, ground-hemlock berries, winter-green berries and red cherries, upon each of which we feasted to our hearts' content. About noon we started another fine buck, at which I got a running shot, but through such thick brush that I failed to bring him down. The guide's gun again failed to go when he pulled, at which he grew exceedingly "hot," and threatened all manner of violence to the weapon if it should ever behave so badly again. At two o'clock we arrived at a lumber camp on Hunt creek, one of the tributaries of Thunder Bay river, where we had expected to take dinner; but unfortunately we found the camp deserted and the cupboard in the same deplorable condition as Mrs. Hubbard found hers when she went to it to get her poor dog a bone. However, we did not fare quite so badly as the historical canine, for we had brought a light lunch with us to provide against such contingencies. After eating it and resting an hour we started for another camp fifteen miles farther down the creek, where we intended to spend the night. We hunted through the woods in the direction of the camp until near sundown, when we struck a wagon-track which the guide said would take us to camp, and which we would easily reach before dark, but he had been misinformed in regard to it, and having never been over the ground before, soon concluded that there was a probability of our having to sleep on the ground that night. We pushed on, however, as long as we could possibly see the track and then followed it several miles farther by feeling for it with our feet. With great difficulty we kept in it in this way until it grew so dim that we could do so no longer, and at nine o'clock we were compelled to abandon all hope of finding the camp that night. We

accordingly halted, built a fire of dry pine logs, and, without
a mouthful of food of any kind, lay down on the bare ground
for a night's sleep.   We had walked during the day thirty-
five miles and were tired enough to sleep without the luxury
of a tent and good, warm bedding.   Several times during the
night we awoke to find our fire burned down low and ourselves
numb with cold, but we piled on more fuel, toasted ourselves
before the bright blaze and returned to our slumbers.   Just
before daylight a pack of wolves came within a quarter of a
mile of our fire and gave us a matinee of their wild, weird
music.   The performance was opened by a male voice, of a
tenor quality, which was soon joined by a female in a rich
contralto, then by an alto, then by a soprano, and so on until
at least a dozen had chimed in and sung their parts.   The
chorus probably occupied fifteen minutes and then gradually
died away.

As soon as it became light enough for us to see readily,
we shouldered our rifles, and, leaving the trail which we then
ascertained did not lead in the direction of the lumber-camp
at all, we took a due easterly course, and had not walked
more than three miles before our ears were gladdened by the
sound of human voices, which we found came from a point
about a mile to our right.   Turning and walking briskly in
that direction, we soon reached the camp.   The cook, a
large good-hearted Irishman, sat us down to a sumptuous
breakfast of baked beans, boiled corned-beef, bacon, potatoes, biscuit and tea, and ordered us to help ourselves.
Never did the most dutiful soldier obey an order with more
alacrity than we obeyed that; and never did a vanquished foe
disappear more rapidly before the onslaught of an advancing
column than did that provender under the ceaseless fire of
our voracious appetites.   It was the first regular meal we had
eaten in twenty-eight hours, and in that time we had walked

nearly forty miles. After fully satisfying our appetites, we filled our game bags with bread and meat for a noonday lunch, and again set out in the direction of our own camp. During the forenoon we crossed one of the almost impenetrable swamps with which this country abounds. This one is thickly grown with spruce, tamarack and white cedar. Underneath this growth the formation seems to be a light quicksand, which stands full of water. We stood on the roots of the undergrowth, which forms a network, or screen, over the quicksand, and, jumping up and down, the ground and bushes would shake for two or three rods in every direction. These swamps seem to be the favorite hiding-places of the bear, for they are literally cut up with bear-tracks and wallows, and in some places well-beaten paths are seen where the bears pass from one part of the swamp to another. My guide informed me that if we would sit down here, by one of these paths, and wait a few hours, we would be almost sure of a shot, but our plan would not admit of this loss of time ; so we pressed on and arrived at camp late in the afternoon, tired enough to thoroughly enjoy the comforts it afforded us.

Other expeditions in different directions from camp were made during our stay, but they so closely resembled those already described that further particulars of them would not be interesting. However, we failed to find any more deer, though we were constantly coming upon tracks and other signs where they had been feeding during the night.

On Saturday evening, our time having arrived to return to the railroad, our team came to take us back. We were glad to see the familiar face of our honest driver, especially as it was one of the few human faces we had seen since our departure from civilization. Our camp was on what is called the "Tote road," upon which one team passes each week, "toting" supplies from the nearest railroad station to the lumber camp, a distance of nearly forty miles. The appearance of this wagon is as much of an event to the few people in this wilderness as is the entrance of a circus into our town to the colored people.

Early on Sunday morning we broke camp, loaded our baggage again into the wagon, and started to retrace our steps toward the confines of civilization. We reached our driver's house, a cozy, comfortable farm-house, six miles from the railroad station, at five o'clock P.M., and remained over night. Here one of the most exciting episodes of the trip occurred. As we neared the house we had heard the baying of a hound in the woods, and our driver had remarked that we might reasonably expect a shot at a deer before dark. Sure enough, while we were preparing for supper à deer came bounding across the opening, and plunging into a small lake on the farm, started to swim across. We. at once gathered such weapons as we could readily get hold of and started for the lake. Two of us went toward the point where he would come out of the water, and Sam Hutchings ran round to the side where he had entered the lake. As we headed him off he turned and started back, and when within about thirty yards of Sam, who had hastily caught up his Smith & Wesson revolver, and who, by the way, is a somewhat famous pistol shot, he sent a ball through his head and ended his career. He proved to be a nearly full-grown fawn, and we made several meals from the choicest parts during the remainder of our trip.

After partaking of an early breakfast with the farmer, we bade good-bye to his family, and he drove us over to the station in time for the train to Petoskey, where we arrived in due time. At eight o'clock A.M. we took the train for Lakeview, at the head of Crooked lake, six miles distant, and an hour later were on board the little steamer "Northern Belle," at

that point embarked for Cheboygan, forty-four miles distant.
The Captain informed us that we would probably see plenty of
ducks, loons, etc., on the trip, so we brought out the
"hunter's-pet" rifle and enjoyed some very fine sport, shooting from the bow of the vessel.

Several ducks were taught the folly of exposing themselves
to the unerring aim of some of our crack shots. A small
diver was killed by an unusually long shot, several on board
pronouncing the distance at least two hundred yards. A wood-
duck was cut down on the wing as he crossed the channel
about forty yards away. Several others were killed as they
sat in the water, and all while the boat was in motion,
making, altogether, a rather remarkable score for a morning's
shooting with the rifle. This trip through Crooked, Burt and
Mullett Lakes and Crooked, Indian and Cheboygan rivers is
one of the most novel and delightful that could possibly be
imagined. The water is clear as crystal, the air pure and
invigorating, the scenery picturesque and beautiful in the
extreme. Crooked river is, indeed, appropriately named. In
many places the turns are so abrupt, that it is with the utmost
skill and care that these little steamers can get through.
Mullett and Burt lakes are becoming quite popular as summer
resorts, and numerous hotels have been and are being erected
on their shores for the accommodation of the hundreds of
pleasure-seekers who now visit them every summer. Bass and
pickerel abound in these and neighboring waters, and the
Cheboygan river, at points a few miles above Mullett lake,
affords the finest grayling fishing in the state.

We arrived at Cheboygan late in the afternoon, and at
once boarded the steamer "Mary" for Mackinaw Island,
which we reached at seven o'clock.

CHAPTER XXXII.

THE ISLAND OF MACKINAC.

THE STRAITS OF MACKINAC — THE PERFECT TRANSPARENCY OF THE
WATER — PURITY OF THE ATMOSPHERE — ANTIDOTE FOR HAY FEVER
— FORT MACKINAC — THE ASTOR HOUSE — THE ENCHANTING ISLE —
SOUVENIRS — THE CAPTAIN'S DREAM — PELICAN LAKE — AN AQUA
INCOGNITA — THE HOME OF THE MIGHTY MUSCALONGE.

OUR visit to the beautiful island of Mackinac was of the
most delightful character and one long to be remembered. It
is one of the most delightful spots on earth. Situated at the
confluence of lakes Michigan and Huron and at the western
entrance to the Straits of Mackinac, it is surrounded by water
than which none clearer, purer or more beautiful is to be
found on the globe. It is so perfectly transparent that every
pebble of the size of a pea may be easily distinguished at a
depth of thirty feet or more. We saw fish from the piers at
the boat-landing not more tnan two inches long in water
twenty to thirty feet deep, and could actually distinguish
their fins at those depths. The atmosphere is as clear and
pure as the water, and at this point, as well as at Petoskey,
Cheboygan, and in fact all through this region, is a perfect
antidote for hay fever. Hundreds of sufferers from this disease
seek and find relief at these points every summer. The island
is two and a-half miles in width and about four miles long.
Its greatest altitude above the level of the lake is 330 feet.
It contains many features of natural and historical interest,
prominent among which is old Fort Holmes, where one of
the important engagements of the war of 1812 took place,

and where the gallant General Holmes fell while defending it. The ruins of the old stockade are well preserved. Other points attracting the notice and admiration of the visitor are Scott's Cave, Sugar-loaf Rock, Arch Rock, Fairy Arch of the Giant's Causeway, Point Lookout, Devil's Kitchen, Lovers' Leap, Skull Cave and Chimney Rock. Many of these scenes are sublimely beautiful, but space will not admit of descriptions here. The island is covered with a thick growth of cedar, balsam, fir, soft maple and some of the smaller varieties of hardwood. Hard gravel roads in various directions form delightful drives and enable visitors to reach with facility every notable point.

Fort Mackinac, with its frowning artillery and its sentinel pacing his beat, reminds one of the necessity of securely guarding this, one of the nation's natural strongholds, even in time of peace. The fortifications are whitewashed, and the barracks and officers' residences are painted white. These, with the surrounding evergreens, present a most picturesque view.

The greater portion of the island has been, by an act of Congress, set apart as a national park, and a magnificent one it will be when properly improved.

The Astor House, one of the principal hotels of the village, was at one time the headquarters of the Hudson's Bay Fur Company, of which John Jacob Astor was the head. Many of the account books, records and papers, some of them in Astor's own handwriting, are still kept here and are a source of great interest to visitors.

Our stay at the island was prolonged several days beyond what we had intended, by reason of a heavy gale which blew steadily from the west, rendering the lake so rough that the steamer could not make the trip from Petoskey. We had no occasion to regret it, however, for the fresh, invigorating atmosphere and the rich and attractive scenery made the time pass most pleasantly.

On the fourth day after our arrival, the wind having fallen somewhat, the bright little steamer " Mary" arrived, and at three o'clock P.M. we bade good-bye to the enchanting isle, the " Gem of the Straits," and steamed out into Lake Michigan. The water was still very rough, and several of the passengers were soon seen hugging the guard-rails, looking pale as death, and sadly sighing, " Oh, my !" The run to Petoskey, a distance of sixty miles, was made in five hours. Arriving there, we put up for the night, and at six o'clock the following morning we boarded the south-bound train on the Grand Rapids & Indianapolis railroad, "homeward bound."

While the trip had not been so fruitful of results, in a sporting sense, as we had anticipated, owing to our having chosen an unfavorable time, yet it has been fraught with other and more important results. We have seen and explored a vast tract of uninhabited wilderness, which, to the lover of nature, is as fascinating as any in the United States. We have seen a number of the noted summer resorts of the North ; we have enjoyed the most refreshing and invigorating atmosphere to be found anywhere ; have indulged in the most vigorous physical exercises, such as walking, boating, etc., and have returned home with greatly improved health and with such ravenous appetites that our hotel and boarding-house proprietors have already threatened us with an advance in the price of board.

We have had strange experiences ; have witnessed many amusing incidents and encountered some strange characters, whose portraits will never be effaced from our memories. The warmest and most lasting friendships have grown up between members of the party, where before only a passing acquaintance existed.

We have retained lasting souvenirs of the event in the shape of some excellent photographs of our group, camp, the lake in which we caught many fine fish, etc., for all of which we are under obligations to the Doctor, who carried the photographic apparatus and took the negatives. As an amateur photographer, as well as in many other respects, he is a brick. Among the many enjoyable incidents of the trip, we shall always remember how the Doctor went to sleep in a coach with his head thrown back and his mouth open; how he woke up to find it full of paper, and how all the other passengers enjoyed the joke much better than he did; how the Captain was alarmed when suddenly aroused from his slumbers by something trying to walk over or through the tent, which he imagined was a huge bear, but which proved to be only the old hunter's harmless dog looking for a bone on which to make a lunch; how on the return trip his (the Captain's) appetite grew so ravenous that he invariably ordered everything on the bill of fare at hotels. How the Parson, alias "Humpty Dumpty," showed up when about to take the war-path in search of large game, with the skirts of his rubber bonnet tucked up behind and sticking straight out at the sides like the oars of our skiff.

For years past I have heard strange rumors of the finny monsters that were said to dwell in Pelican lake. Heretofore, it has been a strange *aqua incognita*, said to lie away in the northern wilderness, somewhere in the central portion of Lincoln county, Wisconsin; but this was all any one could tell me of it. Only the Chippewa Indians, a few hardy woodsmen and a very few adventurous sportsmen had seen it, and they brought to the less favored portion of creation such news as they saw fit to give concerning the strange water.

Residents of Wausau and Merrill have told me that they

have frequently seen muscalonge weighing thirty to forty pounds, brought into their towns by the Indians during the winter months, that had been speared through the ice, and which the Indians said they had brought from Pelican lake. The same parties told me that six and eight pound bass were "said to be" common there. With such stories ringing in my ears, I fondly dreamed of visiting the lake some day in the dim, distant, threadbare future. The opportunity came sooner than I anticipated, for the Milwaukee, Lake Shore & Western Railway Company pushed its line northward through the wilderness with such energy and rapidity that early in the present season it reached Pelican lake, built a comfortable depot on its banks, and commenced running regular trains to that point. When I saw this announcement I lost no time in procuring a couple of through tickets, checking my tackle and camping outfit, and, accompanied by my wife, started for the happy fishing-ground.

We reached the lake at one o'clock in the afternoon, procured a boat, shipped our baggage, and, pulling down the west shore half a mile, made our camp on a high bank beneath the shade of several large birch and pine trees. The banks are walled up nearly all around the lake with large red granite boulders, and the bottom is closely paved with the same material, though generally in smaller pieces. The water is of a dark coffee-color, imparted by the many small streams which flow into the lake, and which in their turn drain numerous small swamps in the vicinity. The water seems pure, however, as evidenced by the enormous size to which the fish grow in it. The black-bass bit finely during the three days we were there, those we took ranging in size from two to four pounds. My wife took one on the trolling spoon that weighed, after being out of the water several hours, four pounds and thirteen ounces; I think it doubtless lost the other three ounces after being taken out, and before it was weighed. She caught three others that weighed sixteen and three-quarter pounds, under like conditions.

We also caught a number of pike weighing from two to seven pounds each, but were not fortunate enough to get one of the large muscalonge, though other parties took several while we were there. Conductor James Shehan won the big hook, with one that tipped the beam at twenty-one and a half pounds after being dressed. A party from Antigo caught one on Saturday that weighed twenty-three gross, and the hotel keeper at Eland Junction fed his boarders all the following week on one that weighed twenty-five and a half pounds gross; but the boys watched him when he went to dress it, and saw him throw away the two good-sized boulders that he had forced down its throat before weighing it.

Several others, equally large, had been taken during the two or three weeks preceding our visit, but "there are as good fish in the lake as ever yet were caught," and doubtless enough of these lusty fellows yet remain to furnish grand sport for everybody that may go there for several years to come.

CHAPTER XXXIII.

A NARROW ESCAPE.

ENCHANTING SCENERY — A SUDDEN SHOT — I FALL ASLEEP — AN AWFUL
AWAKENING — HAND-TO-HAND FIGHT WITH A GRIZZLY — "HOLD
THE FORT" — A SWARM OF MOSQUITOES — A TERRIFIC SLAUGHTER.

IN the fall of '72 I was hunting black-tail deer in the
Rocky Mountains with a party of friends from Omaha. We
left camp one morning at sunrise, and after going about two
miles separated, each selecting his own route, with the under-
standing, however, that we were to take our stands as near
the point at which we then stood as the lay of the land
would admit of. The dogs were put out at the same time.

I started up a narrow canyon, both sides of which were
almost perpendicular, and which was not more than thirty
yards wide at its base. The walls were of red sandstone,
nearly two hundred feet high, and presented a rugged, picturesque appearance. I walked leisurely along, my mind
wholly occupied with the beauty and grandeur of the scene,
and totally unmindful of the distance I had traversed, until I
reached the head of the canyon, and here pausing and looking at my watch I saw that it was more than an hour since I
had left my companions, that I was at least two miles from
our starting-point, and probably about that distance from
any other member of the party. Just at this instant I heard
the dogs give mouth and in a moment more heard a shot,
though by reason of the great distance both sounds came to
me but faintly. I selected a comfortable position by a large
rock and sat down to rest and await any further developments.

I hoped, of course, that having now obtained a sightly look-out, I might be favored with a shot. I waited long and anxiously for the hounds to renew their music, but the welcome sound came not. All was silent as the grave. At length my interest in the sport subsided. I meditated. Then I succumbed to the effects of the balmy mountain air and the mild September sun, and gradually fell asleep. I may have slept an hour, perhaps more, when on the rocks at my very feet I heard a clanking as of heavy chains. I started up, and was horror-stricken to see that there, within six feet of me, stood a huge grizzly bear, and that to one of his fore feet hung a powerful steel trap, which, with the clog attached, he had dragged from the vicinity of our camp, where we had set it and several others for wolves. His legs and belly were all besmeared with his own blood; the froth was dripping from his mouth, and his eyes glared like balls of fire as he reared upon his haunches to strike me to the earth. With a convulsive and half-conscious movement I caught up my rifle and, without attempting to aim, fired in the direction of the huge monster. Through the cloud of smoke that ensued I saw a large black spot on his breast where the fire from the discharge had burned the hair away. I dropped my rifle and clutched my knife, but at this instant a terrible blow on my shoulder sent me prostrate and insensible upon the ground. An instant later I felt my left arm crushed as if in a vice, and the flesh torn from it as if by the strength of a giant. By an almost superhuman effort I rose upon my knees, still clutching my knife, and with a thrust, such as only the desperation of a dying man can render possible, disemboweled the terrible creature, opening his abdomen almost its entire length. He staggered, fell, rolled a little way down the hill and expired.

Then, weakened as I was from pain and loss of blood, I swooned away. Another lapse of time, of the length of which I have little knowledge. Presently, however, I regained consciousness. I opened my eyes; I still grasped my knife firmly in my right hand. My rifle lay by my side. I picked it up, opened the breech, and to my astonishment found a loaded cartridge in it. I then felt for my left arm; it was there and as sound as ever it was! I then looked for the bear, but he was nowhere to be seen. The truth then gradually dawned upon me that, like many of the hair-breadth escapes we read of, it was all a dream.

After thoroughly arousing myself I entered the woods; the air was filled with the sound of flapping wings and the clamor of hungry voices, proceeding from an innumerable company of bloodthirsty mosquitoes. They sat upon the rocks whetting their bills. At the signal of their leader they charged me. At the first smell of my oil they staggered a little, but soon recovered and came down on me with renewed force, business end first. In less time than it takes to tell it, they had absorbed all my oil, and their bills, which were as long and strong as those of the jacksnipe, were honeycombing my flesh and drinking my life's blood. From the slight regard they paid to the oil, I doubt if even skunk juice would be at all offensive to their iron-clad olfactories. Oh, that I could fill my blood with some deadly poison, that every one that bites might swell up and burst!

I stood their abuse but a few minutes when I surrendered unconditionally, pronounced the oily prescription a delusion and a snare, and proceeded hurriedly to tie a piece of thick muslin over my face, and to pull on a pair of thick buckskin gloves. How fortunate that I had brought these with me. These were too many for them. It was then their turn to fall back; but still they waited patiently about. They sat upon my head, shoulders, arms, and on the trees around me, singing "Hold the Fort," and waiting for me to come out,

But I staid in until I got out of the woods, and meantime took a find creel of trout.

But these mosquitoes take the cake. They go for you at all hours of the day as well as night. They make hay while the sun shines. I have had my ears chewed in midday while walking in sunlight until they looked like a couple of saddle-rock oysters. I have had the back of my neck lacerated until it looked as if I had born the yoke of Egyptian bondage for twenty years. I have had my nose mutilated until it looked like a sun-burned potato. If you are so fortunate as to sleep under a mosquito bar, they waylay you until morning and assail you as you come out. You put some of them on with your shirt and drawers; you put on some more with your socks; you tie up a good many in your necktie, and button up a lot more in your pants and vest. Of course their usefulness is destroyed, but they are there all the same. Then when you go to wash you rub some of them into your eyes, and some more into your ears. You go into the saloon and find them there also; you drink them in your beer. At the table, morning, noon and night, they attend you. You eat them in your sausage, your corn-bread, and your gooseberry pie.

They stick to you when they once get a hold, like molasses to a baby's face. You can't shoo them off; its no use trying, they won't shoo; in fact, I never try, I make it a point to kill every one that I can get my hands on. I allow no guilty mosquito to escape. I have kept a careful account of the number I have killed since June 1st, and it foots up exactly 392,721,837,942, 4-11-44! Some folks may think this statement exaggerated, but let them spend a month in the big woods as I have, and they will be ready to make an affidavit to the truth of it without fear or compulsion.

Ah, mosquito, mosquito ! " Requiscat in pieces, non est cum eat us ! "

MOSQUITO POETRY.

" He lights upon your head,
A naughty word is said,
    As with a rap,
    A vicious slap,
You bang the spot where he is not.

He stops and rubs his gauzy wings;
He soars aloft, and gently sings,
    He sits and grins,
    And then begins
To select a spot for another shot."

The great rains and consequent high waters in Minnesota' and Wisconsin in the early part of June have produced the largest crop of mosquitoes on record, or on earth, for that matter. The old man with the long memory, the far-seeing oracle, the o. h., has never seen anything like it. The mosquito of 1880 is no larger than his ancestor, but he has several other marked characteristics that will keep his memory green in the hearts of his countrymen when the high winds of the North shall sing sad requiems o'er the graves of his defamers. His most striking peculiarity is, as Mrs. Partington would say, his numerousness.

Nomen illio legio, his name is legion. For days after the "flood" you could look in any of the pools or ponds that you encountered at every turn and you would find the water literally alive with "wrigglers"—the larvæ of the mosquito. In due time they got ripe. The myriads arose in their might, clothed in the glory of their full plumage, and are now making themselves felt as a power in the land. They recognize the truth of our national motto —" In union there is strength." They bite, not as the Chicago delegates voted, but all one way. They enforce the unit rule strictly. They are yet young and ambitious, each one anxious to distinguish himself by spilling more blood in his country's cause than his fellow, they are as industrious as though laying up stores of human gore for winter use. They have an appetite like a boy who has just got home from school, or like a true sportsman who has been shooting ducks all day and hasn't killed any. This little cuss is very familiar on short acquaintance. In fact, he don't wait for an introduction at all. As soon as he meets you he pounces upon you and bores for oil.

His body is made of India-rubber, Goodyear's patent, so that it expands to any size desired, and it is put together in sections like a telescope, so that it will pull out to hold all the blood he can get. He can stand more blood without crying "nuff," than any bruiser in the prize ring.

I concluded the other day to go trout fishing. I went, and I shall never forget that day's fishing. A friend had given me a prescription for a wash that he said would keep them off—the mosquitoes I mean, not the trout. I went to the drug store and got a bottle of the mixture. It was oil of tar, oil of pennyroyal, oil of cedar and castor oil. With this vile decoction I calsomined my countenance until I resembled a cross between a Malay negro and a Digger Indian. "In this coat of mail," said I, "I can defy the blood-thirsty cannibals."

⇀Rustlings in the Rockies↽

Hunting and Fishing Sketches by Mountain and Stream.

By G. O. SHIELDS.
(COQUINA.)

With an Introduction by Dr. N. ROWE, Editor "American Field."

PROFUSELY ILLUSTRATED.

12mo. Cloth, Over 300 Pages.

CONTENTS.

Lovers of all kinds of sport will be charmed with these pages. The Author tells the story of his various hunting experiences in such a genial, modest, pleasant manner that you are very sorry when the book comes to an end. You unconsciously catch the hunting fever, and feel like packing up rod and gun and starting away to the mountains.

For those whom stern fate confines to the boundaries of civilization—who lack the time necessary for interviewing the bear, the buffalo and the antelope in their native homes, there is nothing better or more entertaining than a perusal of Mr. Shields' book.

If you cannot rustle in the Rockies, you can read "Rustlings in the Rockies," which is the next best thing.

For Sale by Booksellers, News Dealers, and on Trains.

BELFORD, CLARKE & CO.,
PUBLISHERS,
CHICAGO.

A LUCKY MISHAP,

By EVA CATHARINE CLAPP,

A Powerful New Novel of Modern Life,

By the Author of "Her Bright Future."

CLOTH, BLACK AND GOLD.

The Author of this book made her debut as a novelist in "Her Bright Future," which was most favorably received. The present work is a novel of modern life, dealing very skillfully with one of the living questions of the day. The characters are graphically portrayed, evincing on the part of the author a deep insight into human nature. The story is full of interest from beginning to end, fresh and breezy as a March morning. The plot is intricate and subtle without being unnatural or wildly sensational. The dialogue is well sustained and piquant. The author is evidently of an ambitious turn of mind, and has ventured boldly but not unwisely into the domain of philosophy.

Above all things, "A Lucky Mishap," is a healthful, inspiring book that may be safely placed in the hands of our young people.

Eva Catharine Clapp is destined to become a favorite author with American readers. She has given large promise of better work to follow, and will no doubt take rank with such popular writers as May Agnes Fleming and Mary Jane Holmes.

For Sale by all Booksellers, Newsdealers and on Trains.

BELFORD, CLARKE & CO.,

PUBLISHERS,

CHICAGO.

PECK'S BAD BOY

AND HIS PA

By GEORGE W. PECK,

Author of "PECK's FUN," "PECK's SUNSHINE," etc., etc.

lustrated with Twenty Full Page Engravings by GEAN SMITH.

Cloth, black and gold. Paper covers.

This last book from the prolific pen of George W. Peck, is beyond all doubt the great humorist's masterpiece. Peck's Bad Boy is a "holy terror!" He is full from top to toe of pure unadulterated cussedness. He hungers and thirsts after mischief. No day passes but he invents and puts in practice some new form of devilfry. One such boy in every community would retard the march of civilization. One such boy in every family would drive the whole world mad. The bad boy's Pa may be a fool, but his hopeful son has succeeded in making his life a martyrdom. Every Saturday morning a hundred thousand peopl have sought the columns of *Peck's Sun*, to learn the latest exploits of the young scamp. The demand for "Peck's Bad Boy" in permanent form has been wholly unprecedented. There can be no doubt that this will be the most popular book of 1883.

For Sale by Booksellers, News Dealers and on Trains.

BELFORD, CLARKE & CO.,

PUBLISHERS,

CHICAGO

PECK'S SUNSHINE,

By GEO. W. PECK.

Illustrated by Hopkins.   12mo. Cloth and Paper Covers.

OF_ICE OF PECK'S SUN,
MILWAUKEE, 1882.

To Innocent and Unsuspecting Tourists:

This is to caution you and , ut you on your guard against the News Dealer on this train. He is a bold, designing person, who has purpose. All ʿf the oranges, and bananas, and vegetable ivory that he .lres ʿown your neck is for the purpose of getting your mind in shape, so   perpetrate on you the crowning act. When he gets your system in a condition such as he desires, he will offer you a book called . eck s Sunshine," and   u w ʿl be so powerless to protect yourself that you will buy it. Then ʿour troubles will commence. There is something about that book that will laim your attention and cause you to laugh out in meeting. You   ill strike s me   g in it that will make you forget what station you want   get off   and you are liable to be carried beyond your destination, and have to walk back. The book is full of trichinæ, and people have read   only to go home and send for a doctor, after it was everlastingly too late. The reading of the book seems to have a bad effect on every body. Fun is a good thing   place, but where it causes brother to rise up against brother, too much care cannot be exercised. I know of one young woman who had always led a different life. She was an exemplary Christian, and never missed a church sociable, ʿ a Sun y school picnic. Her voice was always heard in the choir and the sewing society. A   man, little dreaming of the result, presented her with a copy of Peck's Sunshine." She read it, and her whole being seemed to undergo a chi ge. In le ; than a month she was married to the young man. I mention this as a terrible example. I am anxious to get the book off the market, so 1 can writ   another of a more pious nature The sale of this book has been so la ʿe that I   r much damage has been done, and I ask that you beware of the designing young man who offers to sell you the book, but if you insist on heaping coals of fire on my head, buy it, but be careful and not sit in a draft of air when you read it. That was what gave Henry Ward Beecher the hay fever. I am so anxious to stop the sale of the book that I will give a chromo to all who do not buy it.

THE AUTHOR.

For Sale by Booksellers, News Dealers and on Trains.

BELFORD, CLARKE & CO.,

PUBLISHERS,

CHICAGO.

AND

BOOMERANG

By BILL NYE.

12mo. Cloth and Paper Covers.

"In hoc usufruct nux vomica est."—VIRGIL.

This book deals largely with the singular scenery and peculiar people of the Rocky Mountains. It touches gently upon the Heathen Chinee, the gorgeous sunsets, the glad, free life of the miner, the meek-eyed but deadly mule, the docile and timid red man, the abnormally connubial Mormon, and the mellow days of the long ago, when the song of the six-shooter was heard in the land.

The book is ostensibly truthful, and the language is chaste and picturesque.

It is not a work after the style of Herbert Spencer exactly, and yet there is the same gentle sense of creamy, soothing, languid, mysterious incandescence; the same opaque, unfathomable and breezy suggestion of unreliability, together with the general, logical and rhetorical effect of grosgrain perspicuity and imported delirium tremens which characterize the works of Spencer; still the reader will have no soul-destroying perplexity in distinguishing the features of difference between these two great men.

It is merry, hilarious and rollicksome, and yet there is a vague suggestion of sadness in the mind of the reader when he gets through — perhaps a sense of impending evil, and a feeling of insecurity because the author is still at large and no effort is being made by the authorities to bring him to justice. Yet it will do an untold amount of good, for it will supersede the liver pad and porous plaster as a health promoter, while at the same time it will go squirting and squizzling its eternal truths and sunny little prevarications upon the broad highways of life like an intellectual street sprinkler; and times will improve, and the universal prosperity for centuries to come will be traced back to the day this work was turned loose upon the people.

For Sale by Booksellers, News Dealers and on Trains.

BELFORD, CLARKE & CO.,

PUBLISHERS,

CHICAGO.